AMITYVILLE HORROR 3:
THE FINAL CHAPTER

By John G. Jones and published by
New English Library
THE AMITYVILLE HORROR II
AMITYVILLE HORROR III:
THE FINAL CHAPTER

AMITYVILLE HORROR 3:
THE FINAL CHAPTER

John G. Jones

NEW ENGLISH LIBRARY

For my mother in Australia, whose
positive inspiration and support have
made my life a non-stop journey through a
gigantic fun park.

First published in the USA in 1984 by Berkley Books

Copyright © 1984 by John G. Jones, Kathleen Lutz and George Lutz

First NEL Paperback Edition December 1984

NEL Books are published by New English Library,
Mill Road, Dunton Green, Sevenoaks, Kent.
Editorial office: 47 Bedford Square, London WC1B 3DP

Photoset by Rowland Phototypesetting Ltd,
Bury St Edmunds, Suffolk.
Made and printed in Great Britain by
Richard Clay (The Chaucer Press) Ltd,
Bungay, Suffolk.

British Library Cataloguing in Publication Data
Jones, John G.
    Amityville Horror III.
    I. Title
    823'.914[F]   PS3560.O49/
    ISBN 0-450-05780-1

FOREWORD

IN THE early morning hours of January 13, 1976, the Lutz family – George and Kathy, their children Amy, Matt, and Greg, and even the family dog Harry – fled from their Dutch Colonial home on Ocean Avenue in Amityville, New York.

Terrified, disoriented and half-mad from a month of horror, they were finally getting out. They stumbled, half asleep, to their van and raced away into the cold night – away from the evil that dwelt in the house. Away from the ancient horror.

They have never returned.

Soon, millions of people around the world would learn of the Lutz' twenty-eight-day ordeal. It became an overnight media sensation that wouldn't conveniently fade away. Even now, almost ten years later, the public's fascination persists. The continuing story of the Lutzes has been called, quite rightly, one of the most frightening true stories of modern times.

It began in 1975.

It ends here.

And it ends in way that no one – not even the Lutzes – could have imagined.

News of the Lutz' story traveled fast, appearing in wire stories, in newspapers, on television and in magazines. Eventually it was documented in a runaway bestseller called *The Amityville Horror*. Hollywood wasn't far behind. Soon an equally successful film version starring James Brolin and Margot Kidder was produced, also called *The Amityville Horror*.

The real George and Kathy Lutz became unwilling celebrities themselves, appearing on television and radio, traveling the world to tell their story.

At least . . . *part* of the story. There were still secrets the Lutzes didn't want to reveal – or even face themselves. The simple, horrible truth was almost more than they could bear:

It wasn't over.

The horror that had found them in Amityville was not confined by wood and plaster walls. Though it had coiled within the land itself for centuries, it remained dormant no longer.

The Horror had left the house. It was following them.

What transpired after their 'escape' from Amityville was no less terrifying than the twenty-eight days in the house – and it continued for years. George and Kathy were finally forced to face the ongoing terror themselves, and in 1980, in a rare moment of calm, they decided to tell what had happened.

So *The Amityville Horror II* was commissioned. And though the book ended on a note of triumph and hope, I knew even then that the story was far from complete – that the innocent, evil-plagued family from New York had still more horror ahead of them.

Now, at last, George and Kathy Lutz have agreed to tell the final chapters of their grim story – of the enemies they made, the allies they gathered, and the innocents around them who risked their lives – and sometimes lost – to help defeat the entity. It is a story that reaches a climax in one final, violent confrontation with the Horror from Amityville – a conflict of wills that risks everything the Lutzes believe in, as well as their lives and their immortal souls.

In hindsight, looking at just some of the facts that have come to light since the Lutz' ordeal was first publicized, it is not altogether surprising that something like this occurred. On the contrary, considering the power that the entity displayed in the house on Long Island, it seems unlikely that it would simply give up at the Lutz' first sign of resistance. Some small part of us insists that we should have expected the horror to continue – that we should have known. But then hindsight usually *is* 20/20.

The entity that plagued the Lutzes was exposed in 1974, but its existence and influence on humans was evident for many hundreds of years before the events that became known as 'The Amityville Horror.' The plot of land at Amityville itself has been steeped in mystery for generations.

Indians of the surrounding area considered it a power spot – a place inhabited by evil spirits. Tribal members who were believed to be possessed by these spirits were tied to trees on the site and cut off from contact of any kind. They could not be fed or even acknowledged as members of the tribe, and when death inevitably claimed them, they were buried deep, laid in graves in a very special way. The bodies were stretched face down, their hands crossed beneath their head, touching the brow: They looked forever downwards, to the abode of the 'darkbrother' they were sent to join.

Much later, during the Salem Witch Hunts of the late 1600's, a man named John Ketchum was accused of practicing witchcraft. He escaped death at the hands of his accusers by fleeing from Massachusetts, and finally settled on Long Island – on the plot of land that would one day be occupied by the Amityville House. It is said that Ketchum practiced the Black Arts on the land until his death, and that his body is buried someplace on the property. It is said almost as frequently that John Ketchum's body does not rest easy – if at all.

In the long years that followed, other mysterious and murderous events, from the eerie to the tragic, have occurred on the site. But in 1974, the actions of a single night hurled the Amityville House into the public eye.

The DeFeo family lived on Ocean Avenue then. One of the sons, Ronald DeFeo, would turn twenty-two in

November of that year. But time after time, in the long months before his birthday, he fled the House in terror. There were voices in there, he said later. Voices that . . . *talked* to him. *Ordered* him.

Each time he left, he was drawn back. Each time, it was harder to escape.

Finally the voices became too loud; the pressure too great. Finally, Ronald DeFeo did as he was told.

At 3:15 a.m. on a particularly cold November night in 1974, he took a .35 caliber rifle and killed his entire family. He moved quietly, calmly through the Amityville house, intent on his mission. In minutes, his mother, his father, his sisters and brothers lay shot to death in their beds.

Shortly afterwards, he calmly walked into a nearby bar and told what he had done . . . and why. It is a story that he has not changed to this day.

Some time later, Ronald DeFeo stood just as calmly in a court of law and lucidly explained himself. He was, he said, only an agent of the force that inhabited the house on Ocean Avenue. He was simply doing as he was told. He was only following the orders of a greater power.

In the ensuing trial, many questions were never answered – among them, how Ronald DeFeo managed to discharge his rifle six separate times – thunderous explosions in the middle of the night – without waking anyone. There were no signs of struggle, no attempted escapes. Autopsies detected no drugs in the victims' bloodsteams, and there was no forensic evidence that indicated bonds or physical coercion were employed.

It was almost as if the DeFoes were comatose – *unable* to wake – while Ronald performed his grisly task.

Then there was the matter of the corpses' arrangement. They were all found on their own beds, lying face down with their hands crossed under their heads, just as the 'possessed' Indians were buried generations earlier. But Ronald knew nothing of the Indians, or the land's diabolical history. He was simply doing what he was told, he said. That's all.

Ronald DeFeo entered a plea of mental disease or defect – insanity, in lay terms. He was convicted on six counts of murder, and sentenced to six consecutive twenty-five-year terms of imprisonment. He is still in jail in New York State.

Thirteen months after the DeFeo murders, Kathleen and George Lutz came upon the house in Amityville. They were convinced that they had found the perfect place to make their first home.

'It was like a dream come true,' Kathy remembers today. They had been married only a short time, and they couldn't believe their luck.

Both George and Kathy had read a little about the DeFeo killings, but neither of them felt the past was important. They would bring their own love into the house and make it a warm and wonderful place for their family – a *home*.

The Lutzes moved into that home on Ocean Avenue in Amityville, New York mid-December, 1975. They escaped scarcely a month later with their sanity – and their lives – hanging by a thread.

A catalog of the horrors that waited inside the house can be found in Jay Anson's *The Amityville Horror*. Even today, George and Kathy have difficulty describing the ordeal, but some events stand out in hideous detail. Among them:

– The attack on Father Mancusso, a Catholic priest and old family friend who came to bless the house. In the third floor sewing room, the priest was attacked by an invisible force that knocked him to the ground and shrieked at him to get out. Hours later, in his rooms at the rectory, the invisible assailant renewed its attack, this time much more deadly. The priest lay dangerously ill for days. For weeks afterwards, Father Mancusso found himself driven to his bed by headaches, nausea, and a strange, elusive pain that fell like a hammer whenever he tried to discuss or even

9

think of the House and what waited inside it. His frequent telephone calls to the Lutzes were sabotaged by unearthly, abrupt static, then cut off before he could even let them know it was him. And his attempts to return and warn them in person were met over and over with new attacks, new pain, new horror.

– George Lutz' possession. The vibrant, loving and physically imposing George Lutz seemed, in many ways, most vulnerable to the entity's influence. He found himself overwhelmed by an insidious psychic cold that drove him to the heater and later to the roaring fireplace – a cold so bone-crackingly painful he couldn't sleep, eat, or even think clearly. He would wake at 3:15 every morning – at precisely the same time Ronald DeFeo murdered his family – and find himself driven from his bed, sometimes driven from the house itself. And there were the dreams – the compulsions – the silent, wordless voices.

All that, George said later, he could somehow have withstood – if not for the headaches. They are migraines of impossible intensity, so deep and wide that he found himself physically disabled by them, frequently weak as a child. They seemed strongest when he tried to resist – when he thought of leaving the house, of escaping with his family. They could literally drive him to his knees.

– The attacks of the flies. Clouds of them would be found swarming in the sewing room, or blackening the windows . . . swarms that disappeared as instantly as they came. Unbearable smells oozed out of vents and up from beneath floorboards, dissipating just as abruptly.

– The 'friendship' of Amy Lutz and the malevolent spirit she called 'Jodie'. To Amy, it seemed to be a large, friendly pig – a talking, cartoonish ghostie that was her best and dearest friend. To George and Kathy, it began as an imaginary playmate for their young daughter – and became an all-too-real force in the house, threatening the very life of their little girl. Sometimes it seemed to be a black cloud. At other times, it appeared as a set of bloodless eyes, glowing in the dark. At one point George hurled a heavy object at the thing he saw floating outside Amy's bedroom window. It squealed an unearthly cry and fled. Moments later, below the window of Amy's room, he found drops of blood and a trail of huge hooves cut into a new fall of snow.

Each day the horror grew. Objects would fly across the room and explode without warning into sharp and dangerous fragments. Family members would wake to find their loved ones locked in nightmares, or converted into horrible caricatures of themselves, stalking the darkened hallways like animated corpses. Voices called out, flies attacked, ordure and stench oozed from the very walls and in the recently discovered 'red room' in the basement of the home – the windowless underground compartment painted the color of blood. The dreams took hold of George more strongly every day. Dreams of death . . . and self-destruction.

On January 13, he could take it no longer. George awoke to the sounds of furniture crashing about in his stepsons' bedroom. He tried to help and was locked in impossible paralysis. He finally broke free, only to encounter the bodiless, roiling cloud-thing blocking the stairs to escape. In a desperate gamble that ended only inches from disaster, he and his family fled the house on Ocean Avenue forever.

They took only a few pieces of clothing and the family dog in their rugged black van. They never returned to the house in Amityville.

The Amityville Horror II, my own sequel to the Lutz' original documentary, picks up only moments after Anson's account ends. It reveals in brutally abrupt fashion that their escape from the entity's control was only an illusion, and a short-lived one at that.

On the way out of Amityville for the last time, the van was attacked by an invisible force that crushed the roof, caved in the walls, and pounded like a massive hammer on the windows and windshield. It took control of the steering; it conjured up a violent storm as if to drive them from the road. Only the power of a prayer, uttered by George in fearful desperation, drove it away.

Later that night, in Kathy's mother's home, the terrorized family clung to the hope that they had finally escaped the entity's influence . . . but George woke from troubled sleep, in a makeshift bed on the living room floor, to find his wife floating in mid-air. He dragged her down to the mattress only to have an invisible force lash at her. As he watched, helpless, countless livid, oozing green welts opened on her body. His intervention, his entreaty to God, was all that brought her back, unharmed.

Within days, Amy's friend Jodie – Jodie, the pig-like ghost – came to join them, terrifying both Kathy and her mother. Kathy ordered her daughter to tell Jodie to leave; but Amy didn't want her friend to go, ever.

Amityville II chronicles the Lutz' flight across the continent in a vain attempt to escape the entity. There are moments of calm, yes – even contentment. But settling in San Diego, more than two thousand miles from the home on Ocean Avenue, afforded no more than a brief respite.

After all, Amy's 'friend' rode out to Southern California on the wing of their jet plane. She would tell them much later, she saw Jodie there.

Swarms of flies and foul smells drove them from room to room in a San Diego motel. Their first Californian home seemed fine at first . . . then inexplicable attacks of darkness dropped them into terror all over again. Kathy and George experienced a simultaneous dream of death by drowning – *drowning in flies* – and the headaches, the horrible headaches were back in force.

'It's all starting again,' Kathy said, feeling sanity slip out from beneath her. 'God, *it's starting again*.'

The attacks were physical as well as purely illusory, and spanned the entire world. Rattlesnake attacks came on two different occasions, in territory unknown for such attacks. On a promotional tour to Europe, George and

Kathy were immobilized by the sickeningly familiar suffocating darkness of the Horror, even as their eldest son Greg was being dragged out to sea by an impossible new riptide that seemed to affect only him.

But here – and not for the first or last time – the Lutzes found a new force at work in their lives. It was a force for *good* – a countering power to the Horror, that appeared in their darkest days. One of the snake attacks was deflected by a St. Michael's medal. Greg was wearing a similar medallion on the day of his swimming 'accident', when a mysterious man appeared from nowhere, cut through the preternaturally strong current, and dragged the boy to the beach and safety. Before he disappeared as abruptly and mysteriously as he had arrived, he told Terri Sullivan, their babysitter, only two things.

'My name is Michael,' he told her, smiling. 'And I came to help.'

Meanwhile, the pressures and politics of the real world began to impinge on the Lutzes, despite their ongoing ordeal. In an effort to prove their credibility once and for all, they submitted to a lie detector test – a test so successful and convincing that it changed the life of a veteran polygraph expert forever. They agreed to do additional interviews and promotional touring for the release of Anson's book, though their own compensation was pitifully small. And George, an experienced air-traffic controller, found himself unemployed and unemployable, despite a shortage of trained professionals and years of experience.

Still, in the final analysis, *Amityville II* is a story of hope as much as horror – of triumph as well as terror. For as it comes to a close, the forces for good that have been drawing around the Lutzes bring them into contact with a most remarkable man – and a penultimate confrontation with the Entity that will afford them some precious months of essential rest and recuperation.

While on tour in Great Britain, George and Kathy are almost inadvertently introduced to an Anglican pastor, the Rev. Timothy Johnstone. In addition to a prominent

13

reputation as a theologian and counselor, Rev. Timothy is an expert in the occult – in the rather self-conscious parlance of the day, Rev. Timothy was a fully accredited *exorcist*.

In the last chapter of *Amityville II* Johnstone must do battle with the Horror on a number of levels – first in argument with a strangely reluctant and violent George Lutz, then later in a brutal conflagration within the walls of Johnstone's own church. But in the end the evil power that has plagued the Lutzes for years is driven back, forced into retreat by this blinding force of good – the adamantine sword of Faith itself.

'The Reverend was a good man,' George said, recalling the ordeal in Great Britain at their reunion with the children in San Diego shortly thereafter. 'It's possible he *did*, somehow, break the connection.'

And, as if in answer to their prayer, the Lutzes did find themselves at peace. For eight long months, they were just normal people – a normal Southern California family with dreams and plans like everyone else's. There were nightmares on occasion, and money troubles, and a continuing problem with unwanted celebrity, but they dealt with it. They had handled far worse in their lives together.

Then came the day at the campgrounds near San Diego – the day the darkness came. And once again, they had to face the cruel reality of their situation.

The *thing* from Amityville had found them again. The Horror was back, and stronger than ever.

It is on that day, with that quite nearly fatal episode, that *Amityville Horror III: The Final Chapter* begins.

Rev. Timothy Johnstone once told Kathy and George Lutz that 'Reality is what you perceive. If it is real to you, then it is *real*.' In *Amityville III*, as in the previous volume, I have attempted to convey the perception – the *feelings* – as well as the facts. In that effort, and with George and Kathy's permission, you will find the story that follows presented in a narrative, 'novelized' style. But don't let the auctorial omniscience distract you: we are discussing something deadly serious here – something as factual and unassailable as the rise of the sun each day.

Also with Kathy and George's permission, certain minor characters and events have been consolidated to make the story as accessible as possible, and where appropriate, names and locations have been changed or disguised to protect personal privacy.

I find myself compelled to make some comment about the confusion surrounding *The Amityville Horror* and the extraordinary power that the word itself has come to possess, especially in terms of book and film marketing.

Since the release of the original *Amityville Horror*, the term 'Amityville' seems to have become a modern synonym for 'horror'. In that regard, the otherwise innocent place-name has found its way onto the covers of a wide number of novels and non-fiction works, some good and some not, that have done little but confound the genuinely interested reader.

There are three commendable non-fiction works about the house on Ocean Avenue and its history: *Murders at Amityville* by Hans Holzer is a vivid documentation of the DeFeo murders that took place before the Lutzes purchased the home. *High Hopes* by Sullivan and Aronson is another disturbingly realistic account of the crimes. *The Demonologists* by Gerald Brittle is the story of Ed and Lorraine Warren, two of the world's most renowned psychic investigators, and their encounters with various spiritual manifestations. A full chapter in that book recounts their own troubles with the entity that inhabited Amityville for so long. Their central description of the force bears repeating. It is, they said, '*a preternatural being charged with a diabolical intelligence, sealed in inexorable and eternal rage against both God and Man.*'

All these books bear investigation –but as of this writing,

only three books document the actual experiences of the Lutz family and their ordeal in the house and after: *The Amityville Horror* by Jay Anson; *The Amityville Horror II*, by John G. Jones– and the book you now hold in your hands.

Products from Hollywood movies studios have further clouded the picture, so to speak. In 1979, a motion picture authorized by George and Kathy Lutz was released: *The Amityville Horror*, starring James Brolin and Margot Kidder.

Since that time, two other films whose titles incorporated the word 'Amityville' have been released, with varied success. One is a heavily fictionalized account of the DeFeo murders – so fictionalized that even the name of the family itself is changed. The other is a completely fictional story set in *a* house in that much-beleaguered community, but not *the* house by any means. Neither of these films are sequels to the story of George and Kathy Lutz, nor have they any bearing on what you will find here – though George and Kathy do give some interesting insight into filmmaking, its vagaries, and its affect on otherwise innocent souls.

To date, there has not been a sequel to the original, authorized film version of *The Amityville Horror*. It is the fervent hope of both the Lutzes and myself that this will soon be rectified.

In this welter of books, horror films, and 'exposés' of the house at Amityville and similar experiences elsewhere, it is easy to assume that the Lutz family's story is some sort of bloodily embroidered fiction – a twisted fairy tale.

Nothing could be further from the truth. *The Amityville Horror Trilogy* is a horribly *true* account of a normal, everyday family who, quite suddenly, found themselves trapped in terror.

The nightmare lasted seven years, and threatened to destroy everything they loved, everything they believed in. And they did not emerge from the ordeal as the same people who began it in 1975.

And yet, despite the violence, despite the Horror itself, in the final analysis *The Amityville Horror Trilogy* is a story of *hope*, – living, luminous proof of the strongest force of all – the logical, loving opponent to darkness and pain that, ultimately, can conquer Death itself.

It began in 1975, in *The Amityville Horror*.

The terror continued in *The Amityville Horror II*.

Now it ends – in a most unexpected way – here in *AMITYVILLE HORROR III: The Final Chapter*.

> *John G. Jones*
> *Santa Barbara, California*
> *Spring, 1984*

CHAPTER ONE

'ME!'

  'Me, *me*!'

  'Oh, Daddy, please, *me*!'

Kathy Lutz couldn't keep from laughing as she watched Amy, Matt and Greg, jumping up and down, waving frantically, each begging their father to throw the ball their way. Across the field, George Lutz tossed the soccer ball up and down in his large hands. Dressed in a down vest and scuffed jeans, he looked for all the world like a jolly, loving grizzly bear, Kathy thought happily. It was a very ordinary family scene, but it brought such joy to her: a California park, a Sunday afternoon, a picnic with the husband and children she loved so much. It felt good – *very* good. She hoped and prayed the rest of their lives could be this way.

Kathy smoothed the rough woolen blanket beneath her and trapped coarse bits of the weave between her fingers. She tried not to think about the past, but it welled up inside her, unbidden.

It had been a nightmare. No – worse than that, and far more real. It had been a small eternity of such boundless horror, incomprehensibility layered on impossibility, that it had filled her up with fear and hopelessness. Looking back, she felt as if she had been crippled – blinded, deafened, unable to hear or speak or *feel* anything but horror.

Then she and George had gone to England. They were at wits end, every part of their lives strained to the breaking point. Meeting Reverend Timothy Johnstone had seemed a fortuitous accident. But whether accident, or something else somehow beyond their understanding, their meeting introduced them to a man who could help – actually *help* them.

Kathy glanced down casually at Amy's story book, still open in her lap. She had been reading a fairystory to her daughter only a few minutes earlier and the words of the last line caught her eye.

'. . . *and they lived happily ever after*.' Appropriate, and such a nice way to put it. Much nicer, and less likely to conjure up bizarre images, than words like 'exorcism' or even 'cleansing,' as the Reverend had chosen to call it.

But it all amounted to the same thing. Finally, *finally*, the Lutz family was free. The Amityville Horror was gone for good.

'Daddy! Over *here*!' Greg's twelve-year-old voice already had a deepening, adult quality to it.

'No, Daddy, throw it to *me*!' Matt pulled a face, hoping that might influence his dad.

Kathy Lutz leaned back against the bark of the mulberry tree and tilted her face up to the warm sunlight. She drank it in, smiled into it. She let the warmth fill her, front to back. She was glowing: a simple thing like watching her family at play, gave her as much pleasure as she could ever remember having. She even dared to whisper the word – to think it had finally come true.

'*Free*,' she whispered, so only she could hear.

George tossed the leather soccer ball to Greg, and his eldest son lifted deftly onto the toes of his sneakered feet to capture the high, lazy curve. Amy and Matt squealed in good-natured frustration as the ball rolled back across the close-cropped lawn.

Sunlight skittered in lively patches along the field. George could smell summer in the air: wood smoke, smog, ragweed, heat. A light, warm breeze from the eastern desert tugged at his hair and tickled his beard as he leaned over easily, warm and content, and snagged the ball as it came to him.

It was Amy's turn, and she could barely *stand* it. She looked so prim, so impatient, so *alive*, a beautiful blond pixie dancing in place, reaching in the air, smiling and giggling and *knowing* she was next.

'Here, Daddy!' she called out triumphantly. 'Here!'

George heard it as an echo. '*Here* . . . here . . . he . . .'

It was fading away – receding from him, as if in a dream.

He stopped, unsure if it had really happened.

The golden sunlight began to dim. For an instant, he thought a cloud had passed over the sun, and he glanced up, frowning.

There weren't any clouds. He knew that. He knew . . .

The breeze cut off. The sounds of the park, the summer afternoon, began to drain away.

A finger of cold coiled up his spine. George paused in mid-stride, hands above his head, as the soccer ball suddenly gained impossible weight. It was hard and heavy in his hands. It grew cold – deadly cold.

What is it? What's happening? He tried to deny it . . .

. . . but he knew what it was. He knew without question. *No. No. Please, NO!*

Amy was still visible across the field, waiting impatiently, her arms stretched up over her head. Her face was pink and glowing with happiness and excitement. But she was tiny now. She seemed miles away. As George watched her and Greg and Matt, a few feet to her side, jumping up and down, shouting, begging, jostling each other in friendly competition . . .

. . . His three children faded away. In his last glimpse of them, he saw them disappear completely into the insubstantial blackness of the impossible new darkness – a darkness in the middle of the day. Their laughter faded . . . faded . . . and, was . . .

Gone.

George's arms still hung high in the air, straining under

the lead-heavy ball. He tried to scream, but his lips wouldn't move. His tongue was thick and solid in his throat. He blinked and blinked again, but it didn't help. He couldn't stop the darkness from rising higher and higher.

'*Nn . . . Nnnn . . . NO!*'

When the scream flew out of his swollen throat, it fell flatly into the boiling blackness. There was no echo – no space.

George was alone. Abandoned again. He knew what had caused it. Knew it with a painful, crystalline certainty.

The entity that had harried them in Amityville, New York – that had followed them around the world, and receded only a short few months earlier – had returned.

The Horror had come again.

A familiar evil joined him in the darkness. It spoke to him in silent communion, a feeling that George knew far too well. The sensation seeped into him slowly, profoundly, like a debilitating gas.

It was hungry. He could feel its hunger as if it was his own. It was hungry for *him*.

The soccer ball finally fell from George Lutz' hands, plummeting past him without a sound, dropping out of sight, into the dark. A horribly familiar chill crept along his arms like a living thing.

It wouldn't be so bad, he thought. Not really. To be one with the darkness. To let it take me. To finally feel the kiss of eternity, after all these months of struggle . . .

'*Daddy!*'

George heard the voice, thin and bright as golden thread. But it couldn't be important. It couldn't *matter* to him. Only the thing that embraced him was worth his attention. To *that* he would give himself freely. He would let it consume him at last . . .

'*Daddy!*'

Strange, he thought. There was something about that tiny cry that wouldn't let him go. Something . . . familiar. Something . . .

'Daddy, PLEASE!'

The evil feeling . . . *snapped*. George stumbled forward with a convulsive lurch, as if released from invisible bonds. Suddenly the little girl's screaming was painfully loud in his ears.

'Daddy Daddy please help me Daddy PLEASE HELP ME DADDY *DADDY*!'

What was he standing on? Where *was* he? What was that voice, that girl –

Amy, he realized. *Amy*!

It echoed in his mind, coming from all directions.

'Amy!' he shouted. 'Amy, honey, where are you?'

'*Where are you*?' The words echoed back in his daughter's own voice.

The darkness reached out again.

'No,' he said, wrenching free. George swept his arms out in a wide frantic arc. He forced himself forward, raging at his blindness.

'Daddy, I'm *scared*!'

'I'm coming, honey! It's all right, I'm coming!'

She was near him now. He could feel it. He kept calling to her as he moved, listening to her weeping, swinging back and forth like a blind man gone mad, moving, just *moving* to keep away from the thing at his back.

He struck something hard and rough. It scraped his knuckles raw, and the pain, more unexpected than intense, flashed up his arm like a lightning bolt.

It was a tree. A solid thing, he thought. *Something*, at least, in the darkness.

'Daddy . . .?'

The voice was hesitant now, and only inches away. George paused to lean against the tree trunk – still blind, still lost, but listening, *listening*.

Something small and warm touched him on the wrist. It stroked the skin of his palm and curled up slowly, searching out the crevices between his fingers. It tightened. It held him.

'Daddy,' Amy said. 'Daddy, I *found* you.'

He gasped her name and knelt before her, sweeping her up in his arms as if she were weightless. He held her close, curling around her warmth, feeling her tiny heartbeat against him. So small, so fragile, so frightened.

'Dah . . .' she buried her head in his wide, heaving chest. He felt her tears penetrate the rough weave of his shirt, and then she was quiet – asleep, perhaps unconscious.

George got angry. Outrage boiled up inside him.

'You'll never get her,' he said. Resolve solidified like stone in his heart. 'You'll never get *any* of us.'

He lurched away from the tree, determined now, fired with hatred and hope. 'Matt! Greg!' He bellowed in the darkness, trying to force the evil feeling away with the sound of his voice alone. 'Kathy! Where are you?'

The darkness changed suddenly – quickening, somehow, thickening. A ripple of warmth, then cold, then warmth coursed over him as the blackness congealed. George paused.

It was changing, yes . . . but it wasn't over. He could sense that.

No, it wasn't over. *It was only beginning.*

A bloody red shape, alive with fire, raced from the blankness and flew directly for his eyes. George dodged to one side, more reflex than conscious thought, and the object streaked off to his right, grazing his shoulder as it flew past.

An afterimage scarred his retina, and he examined the shimmering ghost intently.

He could make out wide-swept wings sprouting from a fat little body. There was a blankness, a hole at the front of its body. Like a burning sailplane, or a monster kite, or –

– a bat. A bat formed from living flame.

There was a sharp *rip*, and a second fiery Chiroptera sped out of the dark. George spun away, holding Amy more tightly than ever, and ducked down low. His eyes – it was after his eyes. He darted to one side more quickly than before, and the screeching thing swooped away. It was so close he could feel the harsh scrape of its fire as it singed the hair from his bare arms.

He started to turn. Another one screamed past with a sizzle.

Where to go? *Where to go*? There was no left, no right, no doors or windows.

And the evil feeling was nearby. George could feel it waiting at the edge of the darkness, curling like a living thing at the base of his brain.

Why should I leave? he thought with sudden calm. I'll just take Amy with me. I'll lie down right here, here . . .

Another fire-bat shrieked and swooped from the darkness, driving right for his eyes. The black lassitude shattered like glass as he screamed and barely avoided it, and he knew, he *knew* what he had to do:

GET OUT.

George Lutz started to run – to run somewhere, *anywhere*. The darkness came alive with a thousand winged suns, circling around him, screeching fire, darting and swooping to attack. Waves of heat and light surged over him. He could see the after-glows of the burning bats, scored on the living darkness inside his eyelids.

Just run, he told himself. *Run*.

The surrounding blackness was on fire, and hot as a furnace. George gasped for air, and the heat of his breath almost cauterized his lungs. Amy grew limp and damp in his arms, a wax figure beginning to melt.

Just *run*, he said. The swarm of creatures grew thicker. The heat closed in like a fist.

He felt his hair burn away. He tried not to look at the skin of his arms as it turned red, then white, then black. He gagged when it began to bubble.

Liquid gushed from his mouth – some fluid from deep in his body. Moisture steamed in thin vapor from his armpits, his groin, the corners of his eyes. He actually felt his bones grow hot inside his muscled body, roasting him from the inside as they charred away.

And now the insidious feeling at the back of his brain

was a voice – as hard as brass, cutting, clanging, yet also softly alive with promise.

Relax, it said. *Be with me. Be me. All will be well. The pain will leave. You will be cool, George. Whole. And free. Free. FREE.*

He stopped running. He could go no further. He dropped to his knees and the cartilage crackled and collapsed under the sudden weight. The voice was louder now. He could no longer push it away.

George fell on his side and curled into a foetal position around Amy, now a smouldering egg.

It can't be happening, he mumbled inside his burning brain. Can't be real. It's over, all over. We're finally free.

(And quickly, in the last fleeting seconds before surrender: a dream.

('What is real, George?' Reverend Johnstone asked, as he floated, superimposed over a foggy marshland in England, wet and cool. His feet touched the surface of the water and rain pelted down on him. Water welled up around his shoes. 'If you feel it, it's real. If it's real, you can fight it. Accept it as fact and do battle.'

(The water rose up to consume the holy man. He smiled as it swallowed him, and he floated free.

('Accept it and do battle,' he said as he drifted away. 'Accept it . . .')

'Do battle,' George croaked. Smoke was whispering off his skin.

Amy choked and coughed at the smell of her burning father. 'Dah . . .' she said, hiccuping. 'Dee . . .' She whimpered and fell back into sleep.

George forced himself to move. He curled forward, pushed up, *up*, until he was sitting, crouching over his daughter.

He formed a picture in his mind, an image as bright and hard as steel.

He was standing at the altar of St. John's Church. Rain was muttering against the stained glass window. Reverend Timothy was before him, the candles glowing at his back.

In his hands he held a small brush and a vial of holy water. He dipped the brush in the vial, then bent forward and painted a cross on George's steamy brow.

. It was cool there now. George could feel it, he could *feel* it was cool!

Timothy turned away to face the altar. He braced himself, legs wide and locked. For an instant the vision shimmered, broken up by waves of heat, but George bit down on his tongue until he tasted his own boiling blood. That brought it back, *back*, as Timothy raised his voice in the ancient ritual of exorcism.

'Oh God, Son of God, unconquered Might . . .'

George was speaking with him. His breath was a steaming streak amidst the fire creatures, swooping and sizzling around him.

'Beat down, BEAT DOWN SATAN! Cause any evil force to DEPART!'

A fire-bat burst at his side. George flinched at the sudden explosion of light and the accompanying, terrible stench, but it worked. It *worked*. George barely realized what was happening. His total attention was fixed in speaking the words, along with the minister as he loudly chanted.

'We give praise to Christ.'

Another fire creature exploded with an anguished cry. And another. And another.

'. . . His Power and His Grace.'

Now the cries of the bat-things reached a crescendo and faded, receded. Another sound came forth to replace it. George trembled even in his stupor and clutched Amy tightly to him, as it grew up from beneath the invisible ground. It was a guttural moaning that rose, louder and higher with every heartbeat. A bellow, a wail, a scream, an agonized shriek that filled the darkness, drowning out George, blasting the image of Timothy to shimmering bits as it peaked, pierced, exploded . . .

. . . and was gone.

George and Amy were alone again in the darkness. The attack was over. But George had reached the limit of his endurance and try as he might, he was unable to hold on even a moment longer. Vertigo rushed up to seize him, and suddenly he was spinning, slowly at first, then faster and faster. There was a loss of all connection with the earth and the sky, and light and dark . . .

'George?' It was Kathy, calling from far away.

'George?' He tried to ignore it, to hide, but . . . he couldn't. Now he could hear children, too. Laughing. Running. Playing?

He opened his eyes and saw Kathy above him, comically large in his field of vision. She almost blocked out the sun, the trees and the cloudless summer sky.

It hurt to breathe.

'How are you feeling?' she said, one hand resting lightly on his chest.

'I'm – '

It hurt! His throat was raw and hot. The words were spikes of pain piercing the mouth behind his tongue. George stopped, swallowed, tried again. 'I . . . I've been better. What . . . happened?'

'I was going to ask you the same thing.' Kathy tried on a smile. It barely held together.

A memory of burning, a memory of his dying daughter, rushed to fill George's brain. He pushed himself up, ignoring the crackle of his spine, and called out.

'Amy?' he said. 'Amy?' He looked around frantically . . . and found her, running gaily across the clearing, throwing herself on the soccer ball in a mad race with her brothers. The three of them fell in a heap, giggling and wrestling.

Alive. She was *alive*.

'She's fine,' Kathy said. 'Now.'

George pressed at his eyes with the heels of his hands. He forced himself to take a long, slow breath. 'I don't understand. I thought we . . . she and I . . . aaah . . .'

Kathy took his hands in hers and squeezed them tight.

She looked deeply into his eyes, and when she spoke it was slowly and carefully, with a deep, immovable calm. 'Everything went black. I couldn't see you, or the children, or anything. I could hear Amy calling, but I couldn't move.' Her words were like iced steel, dropping slowly, one at a time. 'I. Couldn't. Move.'

George knew that tone. He had heard it before. It was a stony, emotionless croak that Kathy hid behind when things seemed utterly helpless. When she had first acknowledged what was happening in the house in Amityville; when they both realized the entity was following them; when the children were assaulted and nearly killed. It was a ringing hopelessness – the sound of defeat.

'I heard you both crying out in pain. But I couldn't do anything. I . . .' Kathy looked down for a long time, drawing herself together. When she looked up again, her eyes were filled with tears. 'I found Amy wrapped in your arms. I don't know how long I was . . . trapped. I don't know how it ended. Amy doesn't seem to remember anything either. Neither do the boys. It's as if they took an afternoon nap, and had a dream.'

George pressed his lips together and shook his head. 'It wasn't a dream,' he said. 'It was – '

'I know,' Kathy told him, barely whispering. 'I know.'

George reached for her and wrapped his arms around her trembling shoulders. She couldn't stand it any longer. Sobs tore out of her and she clutched at her husband's broad shoulders for support.

'It's all right, babe. We're all right.'

'Haven't we been through enough? Haven't we . . . ?' She buried her head in his chest and let all the pain come out, as George pulled her more tightly against him.

'We have to hold on, Kath,' he said. He knew then that he wouldn't mention the fire-bats or the burning.

It wasn't the first time George had kept something from his wife – and why bring it out now? Why intensify the fear and pain? After all, it could have been only a dream. Maybe there had been only darkness – some sort of mass blackout. He might have created the images himself from his own dread and fear. The mind was capable of such things, he knew, and it would explain how Amy had come back to herself so quickly.

This fragile new hope strengthened him. Yes. A dream – a nightmare, brought on by the age-old combination of too much food, too much sun, and fearful memories.

Staring down at his wife, he opened his mouth to explain . . . and his eyes traveled past her trembling head and saw his own forearms.

My God, he thought. My *God*.

They were a vicious, ugly red. Long ridges of yellowing welts were beginning to erupt from his wrists to his elbows. Looking at them made the first ripple of pain register in his brain, as the tortured nerve endings clawed out of trauma and numbness.

He was burned. *Burned*. Not by the sun – it was far too serious for that. It was from the inhuman heat of the things at Amityville . . . returned to once again haunt them.

It *did* happen. Just as it *had* happened before.

He staggered to his feet, pulling Kathy up with him. He knew he would have to get to a doctor before the shock wore off and the pain became unbearable. He would want to keep the children from seeing that if he could. And he *could*. He would have to.

They had been hiding for eight full months. It had seemed it might be *over*, and he had prayed it was. That they would never again be harassed by the *thing* from the house. Now, George realized a truth. It was all too clear they had only been fooling themselves. Still, it had been necessary to hide this truth from themselves, if only to rest and regain their strength.

But the psychics in England and Europe and all across America – who time and again tried to tell them this truth they didn't want to hear – had been right all along:

Seven years, they had said. Seven years before the Lutzes would be truly free.

George, maybe more than anyone, understood *another*

29

truth: The entity had hounded, harassed and incessantly attacked, him and his family, since the day they had moved into the house at Ocean Avenue, Amityville, New York. It would not easily relinquish this 'right' . . . whatever the reason.

Freedom may be won . . . but at what cost?

They had many months remaining of their ordeal, but somehow, knowing this gave George Lutz a strange sense of calm . . . of purpose. He and Kathy, Amy, Greg and Matt, would hold on and when the final confrontation came, and he was *sure* it would, they would fight – to the death, if necessary.

They would win back their freedom from the thing in Amityville or die in the attempt.

CHAPTER TWO

'YOU COMING up, hon?'

George lowered himself into the wingback chair in front of the fireplace. 'In a while, babe. Think I'll go through some of the mail first.' There was a thick stack of envelopes waiting on the sidetable.

Kathy said okay and went upstairs, and George listened as she padded down the second floor hall to check on the children, washed her face in the bathroom sink, checked them one last time and finally put herself to bed.

The house at La Costa was quiet now. It was late, well past midnight, and the children had been asleep for hours. But George couldn't bring himself to go to bed – not just yet. After all that had happened that afternoon, the idea of slipping gently into oblivion didn't hold much attraction for him.

He traced the bandages on his forearms with sensitive fingers. Not as bad as it looked, the doctor in the emergency ward had said. He'd be fine in a week. No scars. But the physician had asked a lot of questions. He'd never seen burns quite like those before.

George grinned in spite of himself. No, he thought to the doctor, and if you're lucky you'll never see them again.

The huge windows in front of him afforded a magnificent view of La Costa Country Club, still partially lit despite the late hour. The hills were scattered with light, concentric circles that grew thinner and dimmer as they trailed off into the glittering, velvet black. At this time of night, it was difficult to tell exactly where the gentle hills ended and the night sky, studded with stars, began its own ascent.

Too much like my own life, George thought, scratching absently at his thick beard. Hard to tell where the solid reality leaves off and the sky of dreams begins. And it was getting harder to tell the difference between the two all the time. As if we're going farther into the night, and dawn is a long way off.

Dawn is a *long* way off.

He sighed deeply and moved a stack of letters into his lap, slicing open the first with a silver letter opener they kept by the tray. He smiled again, thinking of Kathy's reaction to the first huge packet of mail they'd received from the publishers, some months earlier.

'For *us*?' she had said, genuinely surprised. 'Why would anyone write to *us*?'

George wasn't sure of the answer himself, but write they did – in care of the publisher in New York, to be forwarded to the Lutzes in California. Some even included extra postage for the additional trouble.

Some were crank letters. Some called them names. George could never understand exactly why those people wrote in the first place. Sometimes he wanted to send back notes to them all that said, 'Please ignore it if it hurts so much,' but he'd never done it. What was the point?'

But the other letters – most of the letters – were of a different sort entirely.

'My husband and I are very sorry for the troubles we have read about,' the first letter said. 'In our own troubles (nothing like yours) we have got great comfort from the following Scriptures . . .' George nodded as he skimmed the list, and smiled again when she signed the letter, 'Yours in Christ's Fellowship . . .' Thank you, he thought. God bless you.

The next one was a carefully typed four-page letter filled with tension and trouble of its own. George couldn't bear to read the whole thing. It told a story too much like their own, and only a line, repeated in the first and last paragraphs, stood out in his mind: 'Would you please forward our names to Father Mancusso or the Hardings? We need their help. *Please.*'

George shuddered and put the letter aside. He knew others would join it before the night was through.

'I don't know why you expect us to swallow crap like this,' said the next. 'You start to accept this stuff and you make it real, and the next thing you know it's exorcists and Inquisitions and we're back in the Dark Ages or something. No thanks!'

'Right,' George said quietly to the letter. 'If you don't believe it, it won't happen. Lovely attitude, friend. Just like ours, not so long ago.'

He had a bitter taste on his tongue when he opened the next letter. It was only five lines, handwritten on lavender paper with a silver cross embossed in the upper right corner. 'We pray for you and your family in this time of adversity. Trust in God and He will deliver you.'

More good than bad, George thought. Sometimes he thought it was that realization, hiding in notes like this, that kept them going. And the power of these faithful strangers and their prayers was something to consider: So many times, figures in light had come to the Lutz' aid. His son, Greg, had been rescued by a strange apparition who called himself 'Michael.' And George himself had been miraculously spared when his St. Michael medallion averted a rattlesnake attack. Was it the power of prayer? George wondered. Had *these* people, who never knew them but cared for them anyway, had *they* had something to do with his family's survival?

He shifted in his chair and sighed. Almost against his will, he laid back his head and tried to ease the tension in his shoulders.

Just rest for a minute, he told himself. It was like another voice, from outside him, urging him to sleep. Rest for a minute . . . then . . .

George's body twitched like a single nerve. Every muscle

snapped with an electric intensity, and he bolted out of his chair with a yelp.

He was suddenly alert – completely awake.

Damn!

His mind clicked through a checklist of his surroundings, itching with tension. Window still closed. Door still locked. Glowing embers undisturbed, all inside the hearth.

Nothing.

Nothing.

Nothing.

He let a long sigh escape him. He forced his muscles to relax, and shut down the alarm bells ringing in his mind.

You've twitched like that before, he told himself. You've even read about it in an old medical journal. It's something that happens regularly, right on the edge of sleep. All the synapses fire at once in a sudden release of energy. Usually after a hard day or a traumatic experience.

And this day qualifies as both, he told himself. Relax. Try to relax.

Once, a long time ago, when circumstances had forced him to drive for almost four days without sleep, George had *snapped* like this a dozen times before he'd finally relaxed. He'd kept waking up, thinking he was falling asleep at the wheel, even when he was tucked safely in his hotel bed. And he'd never even heard of Amityville then.

So relax, relax.

But this was . . . different, he thought fuzzily, just as the sleepiness came again. It had an evil, familiar feel to it. It felt as if the sleep was being pressed on him from outside, like some insidious lullaby, forcing him to let his guard down, to let his mind wander. To sleep . . . sleep . . .

The phone rang – a blast of noise that stabbed him like a spike. George jumped to his feet, biting off a second shout, and grabbed at the receiver.

For a moment the phone was dead silent – eerily so. No clicking, no breathing, no sound at all.

Then it exploded in his hand – a roar of static, shrieking and gabbling so loudly that George had to rip it away from his ear. His head reeled as the sound gushed out. It was unlike any noise he'd ever heard before – deep and huge, roaring and gurgling. It even *smelled* evil.

Don't get spooked, he ordered himself. For a moment he stared in shocked disgust at the receiver. Then he slammed it back in its cradle.

Just . . . technical problems, he insisted. Technical problems. But I've never heard a phone make a sound *anything* like that before.

A huge shiver rippled through his body, violent enough to make him stiffen. George hugged himself and rubbed his unbandaged upper arms. It was getting cold down here, so cold . . .

. . . and suddenly he remembered the bitter cold in the house at Amityville.

He could never seem to get warm. No matter how close he sat to the fire, or how high he turned up the furnace, he just couldn't get *warm*. It was an aching chill that penetrated the bone. His muscles, his cartilage, his joints – everything ached with it, everything *hurt*. Later, psychics told him it was an ominously common condition – 'psychic cold', they'd called it.

All he remembered was its terrible seduction. How it called him to sleep, all the time. To dream about . . .

. . . horrible things.

The phone rang again. George jumped higher than before and snatched the receiver up.

The electronic screaming was a roaring bellow, impossibly loud. It seemed to crawl inside his head and burn there, and this time George imagined he could hear voices gurgling inside it – laughing, cursing, calling his name over and over and *over* . . .

He slammed down the phone and collapsed in the chair.

Don't worry, *don't worry*, it's just some technical problem.

He sat there in the silence until the sleep came to claim him. He relaxed against his will. He nodded . . .

And the phone rang again.

Kathy Lutz woke from a deep sleep and reached out for her husband. He wasn't there.

She had found him missing too many times in the last few years, and always for terrible reasons. She was awake in an instant, perfectly clear-headed. She lay still and listened, expecting the worst.

Everything was quiet. No groaning, no pacing – just a regular home, completely asleep.

But the sheets on George's side of the bed were tight and unwrinkled. They hadn't been slept in. And outside, in the hall, she could see a sliver of light penetrating from downstairs. From the living room.

She sat up slowly and stretched from the tips of her toes to the tips of her outstretched fingers.

I'd better check the kids, she thought, slipping into her robe. She wrapped it tightly around her waist as she stepped into the hall.

Kathy stood in the doorway to the boys' bedroom, listening to the solemn, steady rhythm of their breathing. They were sound asleep, just as Amy had been. Nothing was amiss.

She tiptoed to Greg's bedside and rescued his blankets from the floor, draping them silently around the shoulders of her sleeping son. He was growing so fast now. He seemed bigger every day. And he was starting to agitate seriously for a room of his own – bursting at the seams, almost literally. Growing up.

She brushed a lock of hair from his forehead, and he frowned under her touch, shifting in his sleep, digging deeper into the pillow.

Kathy loved him with her eyes, then turned and did the same with Matt. Finally reassured, she slipped out of the room easing the door shut behind her and headed downstairs to check on George.

From the stairs she could see him perched uncomfortably on the edge of the couch, staring blankly out of the large picture windows. As her bare feet touched the edge of the living room carpet, she saw his face quite clearly in the moonlight.

His eyes were drooping, his muscles were slack, and as she watched his head began to nod. He was drifting off, drifting into sleep –

– he suddenly jerked himself up, forced himself awake. His spine straightened, his head snapped up, and he was staring, watching . . . *waiting*.

He seemed frozen in stone for a long moment . . . then he sighed heavily and his shoulders dropped. He began to droop all over again, and slowly, slowly . . .

'Come to bed, babe,' she said gently.

George jumped and spun on her, and for an instant she could see naked, bottomless fear reflected in his face.

'George?'

He recognized her. He relaxed. Both hands came up to rub his face as he fell back against the edge of the couch.

'Come to bed, George,' she said sternly.

'Maybe in a little while,' he mumbled.

She went to him and pulled his hands from his face. His eyes were shadowed and bloodshot. 'What is it? You look like you're about to drop.'

'Insomnia,' he lied. 'Why don't you go back up to bed? I'm fine. I'll be up in a few minutes.'

She didn't believe him for an instant. 'What *is* it? What's the matter?'

For a moment he looked as if he would deny it again, but the weariness got the better of him. 'I don't know, babe,' he said. He looked away so his expression wouldn't betray him. 'Guess I'm a little wound up.'

Kathy sighed and sat next to him. His arms came around her almost automatically, and held her tight. She settled in with a contented sigh.

It was a nice place to be: wrapped in her husband's protective arms. There had been times, she knew, when she might not have made it without this comfort and strength. For a long moment, she blocked out the world and drank in George's warmth and strength, just as she'd absorbed the sunlight that afternoon. For one golden moment, she knew, she was a normal everyday married lady, cuddling up to her husband. She relished the normalcy of it.

Well, she thought, almost amused, I never expected life with George to be dull.

Since the morning he had walked into the diner where she worked, a special bond had been formed. It was both friendship and love, and something better and stronger than the two taken separately. Without it, they never would have survived all that they'd faced.

At times, she knew, she had weakened under the strain. So had he, for that matter. But they had always faced it together – as a family, as a single mind – and that was what had sustained them. How different it might have been, she thought, if she had followed her initial instincts and not married George.

No marriage. No home in Amityville. No flight in terror into the rain. God, it was a tempting little daydream: no years of fear, no unasked-for notoriety, no money troubles or nightmares.

But . . . *no George*. It almost made her head spin. Even with the craziness, even with the pain, there *had* to be George. She could imagine a world without the horror at Amityville . . . but not without this man.

She snuggled in closer, running her fingers along the backs of his firm hands, wincing at the pain hiding beneath the bandages on his forearms, coming to rest against his broad chest.

I'd love to stay here forever, she thought. Forget the world, forget everything. Just sit here and drift and –

George grunted convulsively and leapt to his feet, knocking her roughly away with the back of one hand.

Kathy cried out in spite of herself, shocked and hurt.

He didn't hear her. He was beyond hearing. He was standing in the center of the room, his hands clamped on the sides of his head. The heels were digging furrows into his temples, grinding and grinding, trying to wipe something away.

'What is it? George, *what is it*?'

'The *ringing*!' he shouted, suddenly swaying as if buffeted by invisible blows. 'That damn *ringing*!'

He lurched forward, bellowing his rage, and snatched up the telephone from its side table next to the wingback chair. With one tremendous *jerk* he ripped the instrument from the wall. The cord *twanged* metallically, then with a whipcrack, released and snapped like twine.

He lifted it over his head, growling.

'George! DON'T!'

He couldn't hear her. With a vicious, brutal heave he threw the phone across the room. It crashed into the stone wall next to the fireplace with tremendous force and shattered. Bits of brown plastic casing ricocheted like shrapnel, ringing off the lamps, chattering across the coffee table.

Kathy looked at the ruined phone in horror, then turned to her husband. He was down on his knees, still pawing at his ears, trembling and panting. Finally the hands fell away. He gasped to get his breath.

'It kept ringing,' he said breathlessly. 'Terrible sounds . . . on the other end. I would hang up and try to forget it, but it kept ringing, it kept *ringing*.'

She put her hands on his shoulders and knelt behind him, embracing him, drawing him close like a child. She stroked his head and said, 'It's okay, babe. It's okay.'

It took a long time for him to relax under her hands. After some long unmeasured moment he turned and laid his head in her lap. Some time later his breathing deepened, his shoulders dropped. Finally, he slept.

Kathy stayed with him on the thick carpeting of the living room floor until dawn turned the eastern horizon a grim and chalky gray. Between fitful naps and disconnected dreams, she thought about the phone – the ringing.

There was an extension upstairs, right next to her bed. And she always heard the phone when it rang – she never slept through a call.

It hadn't rung at all that night. Not once. Not a single time.

CHAPTER THREE

'I KNEW it!' George said. 'I *knew* we should have talked about the polygraph tests on the Merv Griffin Show!'

The pain was a hot silver wire in his head, coiling around his forebrain, ringing in his ears. It throbbed brighter and brighter as the phone grew heavier in his hand.

He scribbled furiously on a scratch pad by the telephone – coarse black illustrations of his frustration digging into cheap yellow paper. 'Why didn't the studio release the test results?' he said, scoring the paper deeply. 'They *said* they would!'

Eric Hill, their lawyer on the west coast, sounded less angry but just as confused. 'I don't *know* why they didn't use them,' he said.

'Well, *ask* them.' George rubbed a knuckle against his forehead. *Damn*, it hurt!

It hadn't been an easy decision, agreeing to allow the tests. They had all had serious doubts about *any* examiner's objectivity, after all the publicity surrounding the Lutz family's troubles in Amityville. And since the studio had suggested Chris Gugas, George insisted Eric personally check the polygraph expert out.

George remembered the meeting with Eric when they'd decided to go ahead. Gugas, it turned out, had been a polygraph expert for thirty years. He'd been involved in over twenty thousand cases, including some highly publicized ones, every bit as sensitive as Amityville. His peers considered him to be one of the best in the country – maybe the world.

It was decided that George would be examined by

41

Gugas. Kathy would be turned over to Michael Brown, an equally respected examiner. They would run the tests three times, and even record all the sessions; thereby clearly documenting every step of the procedure.

'Hell, if they'd been bad, even *borderline*, I could understand keeping it quiet,' George said. 'But they verified our story *completely*. So why weren't they used in a major wire service release? Why didn't they come out when the film opened? Why haven't they even *spoken* to us, Eric?'

There was no answer on the other end: Just a distant, empty hiss.

George felt anger rising inside him. 'Eric?' he said.

No answer.

George's grip tightened on the receiver. '*Eric*? HELLO?'

No answer.

Eric Hill was a thin, light, sharp-faced man. From his office in Beverly Hills, he had over the years handled many complex and sensitive cases. His opponents as well as his friends had always conceded that he had one of the keenest minds in law. Nothing got past him. He was always *paying attention*, and plenty of attorneys had paid the price for underestimating that special talent.

But now Eric's mind was adrift. He was sitting at his desk, looking down at the scurrying traffic on Wilshire Boulevard, and he was . . . floating. Cut loose. In the distance there was a tinny, filtered voice, like the nasal buzz of an insect. There were bright patterns of sunlight streaming through the louvered blinds. There was the brilliant splash of color on the painting opposite his huge oak desk.

But Eric was . . . was . . .

'Mr. Hill,' Chris Gugas said in his daydream, 'I've had some hard cases to test over the years. But none of them were able to keep lying to me and get away with it. Not time after time.'

The polygraph expert ran his fingers through his thin,

greying hair. Then he cleared his throat and hunched forward in his chair. He seemed *nervous*, to Eric.

'I checked Michael Brown's test data and evaluation on Kathy Lutz. He checked mine, too. It's the same as George's. There's no doubt in my mind. They were telling the truth.'

His voice cracked on the last word. Eric raised an eyebrow in surprise. 'Are you all right, Mr. Gugas?'

He nodded without speaking. His shoulders hunched even closer, as if holding a burden of increasing weight.

'I don't mind telling you, Mr. Hill, it's given me pause. It's all the truth, you know – the flies, the smells, the – the levitating.'

He faltered again. Then he straightened for a moment and forged ahead.

'I'd never really questioned this before.' He swept a hand briefly across the room – the walls, the window, the world outside. '*All* this. But I tell you: I found myself taking out my family Bible. I found myself reading it regularly again.' He leaned forward, and something in his eyes made Eric Hill draw back. Something in his expression sent a cold touch straight through him.

'You know, Mr. Hill, I've had some doozies. I've examined mass murderers, and child molesters, and out-and-out psychopaths. I've heard things and seen things that made my blood curdle like bad milk. But I have never, *never* had to look something like this straight in the face. And I can tell you, it's changed me. I'm *different* now.'

Eric didn't know what to think. He . . . didn't . . .

'ERIC!'

'Here! I'm here, George. I was just . . . distracted.' He felt the lethargy tug at him again, but he shrugged it away this time.

'What were you saying?'

George slammed a fist down on his desk. The phone, the ashtray, the unopened letters all jumped in response.

'Damn it, Eric!' The pain was blazing in his head like an open fire.

'Take it easy, George,' the voice over the phone told him. I'm not the enemy. I'm on your side, remember?'

George crowded the anger out, at least for a moment. He's just trying to help, he told himself firmly. Shouting isn't going to solve anything.

But the pain was still there. It wouldn't let him go.

'Now, I talked to the publicity people at the studio today,' Eric said soothingly. The old calm and command was back in his tone. 'They said the initial response to the movie is good. They expect it to be a big hit. And they want you to do more radio and TV shows with James Brolin.'

'Uh huh.' George pressed his forehead between thumb and fingers and took a deep breath.

'It's been sold to a whole group of overseas markets. There's even talk of you and Kathy doing a promotional tour of Europe and Australia.'

George stopped breathing for a second. Dread grabbed at him. 'I . . . I'm not sure about that. Kathy's not going to be too happy about leaving the kids again.'

'It's just a feeler. Nothing definite.'

'Hold off on it. I can't decide. Right now.'

Don't leave the children alone said an echoing voice in his head. There had been the time he and Kathy were in Amsterdam and their boy, what's his name, had nearly drowned. What is his name? He couldn't seem to remember. Then there was the cross-country tour when the snakes – no, that had been at home, the snakes had been in San Diego.

The pain was welling up all around him.

'What about the polygraph results?' he said abruptly.

'I'll ask about them again,' Eric continued smoothly. 'But don't get your hopes up. I think we've hit a stone wall on that one.'

'You're probably . . . right. I'll . . . talk to you. Later.'

Intense pain washed over George and he could no longer think clearly about anything.

Eric must have said goodbye. Or agreed to call back later. All George remembered afterwards was hanging up the phone – letting it drop like a stone into its plastic cradle.

That, and the pain. The pain like a hungry animal burrowing into his head.

CHAPTER FOUR

AMY LUTZ straightened her bed clothes, folding the top sheet down over the blanket. *There*, she thought. *Just right*.

She patted the blankets on both sides of her small bed and heaved an exaggerated seven-year-old's sigh – a sound much like one that a hundred year-old woman with the weight of the world on her shoulders might make.

Amy's parents were gone for the night. Terri Sullivan, the family friend who usually babysat when George and Kathy were out of town, had sent her to bed at exactly eight o'clock, just like Mommy had said. Amy had *told* her she wan't sleepy yet, but Terri had insisted.

Well, Amy decided, I won't sleep *anyway*. I'll just lie here and show Mommy and Daddy that I'm *not* tired, no matter *what*.

She flopped onto the carefully made bed and crossed her arms. She stared up at the ceiling and stuck out her lower lip in a profound, experimental pout.

The tiny nightlight near the foot of her bed threw strangely shaped shadows on the walls and ceiling. One big one almost directly over her head looked . . . *familiar*.

It looks like *Jodie*, Amy thought. The pout grew heavier.

Jodie had been her friend. They used to play together all the time. He made things . . . *happen* for her.

Like, he made the rocking chairs rock by themselves, she thought. Sometimes he sat in them and made himself invisible and only *I* could see him.

That's 'cause we were special friends, Amy told herself.

46

In her grandmother Conner's yard, Jodie drove her favorite blue pedal-car around and around and around. He would even stop when Amy said *stop*.

But Mommy and Daddy didn't like Jodie, Amy remembered. That made her pout even more. She'd tried to explain to them that Jodie was her special friend, but Mommy and Daddy thought Jodie did . . . *bad things*.

She told them, 'Jodie wouldn't do anything bad. He's my friend. He's my *good* friend.' But they made her tell Jodie to go away and never come back.

That was 'way back in Amityville, Amy thought. When I was just a little kid.

She smiled lightly as she thought about what happened after she'd told Jodie to go. Her friend didn't *want* to, and Jodie knew that *Amy* didn't want him to go, either. So he stayed hidden. No one but her knew that he didn't really leave.

The smile grew even wider when she thought about the plane trip – about how worried she'd been that Jodie wouldn't be able to come to California. She'd been scared about that a lot, she remembered. Then Jodie told her another secret . . . and when they took that jumbo jet to San Diego, Amy snuck a look out the window.

There was Jodie, sitting on the wing. Just like he said he would.

When they first got to San Diego it was hard for her and Jodie to play. The others were always around, especially in the motel they stayed at. But when they all moved into that new house, she and her special friend got to play every day.

. . . 'Till Daddy found out. Then he got *real* mad.

He made Amy *promise* she would tell Jodie to leave. And she couldn't break a promise, especially to her Daddy. So she did what she was told.

Jodie didn't want to go, and Amy cried a lot. Still, she had to do it. And Jodie *did* go away this time. She hadn't seen her special friend since that day, and that had been a long, long, *long* time ago. *Months*, even.

Amy sighed at that. She was starting to feel tired. Sleep crept over her, and as it came she found herself thinking about her long-absent friend.

Maybe he was sick. That's why she hadn't seen him. And who would look after him if he was sick?

The thought of it stopped her slide into sleep, but only for a moment. Soon she was snoring lightly.

But as she drifted off, she clung to one last scrap of thought – she made one last wish.

I wish Jodie was here, she thought . . . and slept.

The sidewalk outside the movie theater was glistening when George and Kathy emerged. It had rained while they were inside, watching the film.

George turned and looked up at the marquee, hunching his shoulders against the drizzle as he squinted into the light. THE AMITYVILL HORROR, it read. 'They left off the "E",' he said to himself. 'Must've blown away.'

Kathy didn't say a word as they moved swiftly into the parking lot. They passed a long line of people waiting impatiently to get inside for the next show. A few of them glanced in the Lutz' direction. Of course, none of them showed even a glimmer of recognition.

How could they know? George thought. *How could they know?*

The headlights of oncoming cars were sharp and beautiful beyond the wavering windshield. George turned the car onto the ramp that led to the San Diego Freeway, and wings of water rose up on both sides as they passed through three inches of water at high speed.

'Well?' he said. It was the first thing he had said to his wife since the lights in the theater had dimmed.

She looked at him intently, and George couldn't quite tell if it was annoyance or puzzlement or furious thought hiding in her eyes. Finally she looked away and took in a sharp breath.

'I'm still here,' she said, frowning.

George didn't respond.

'I mean . . . I'm still Kathy Lutz. It's – it's *confusing*, George. There's a whole new Kathy out there, a whole different one. The Kathy in Jay's book. The Kathy in the newspaper stories and the television interviews. Now the Kathy in that movie. But *I'm still here*, and I'm not like *any* of those people. I'm . . . *me*. I'm . . . oh, I don't know.'

She crossed her arms and frowned more deeply, and for a moment George was reminded of little Amy in one of her high dudgeons. She was certainly her mother's daughter.

He knew what she was trying to say. It wasn't easy, all this unasked-for notoriety – all the challenges that interrupted having a normal life again. But he hadn't had as much trouble accepting Jim Brolin playing *him*. In fact, he and Brolin had met and struck up something of an acquaintance. Still . . .

'It looks like it's going to be a pretty big success,' he said, trying to change the subject. 'Eric says they think it'll do even better overseas.'

Kathy sighed.

'In fact,' George said, regretting it even as he said it, 'they *might* ask us to make a promotional tour – just a short one,' he added hurriedly when he saw the expression on her face.

Neither of them spoke again for most of the remainder of the trip. They were off the freeway and waiting at the last stoplight before George broke the silence. 'At least we might make back some of the money we've lost since all this started,' he said almost petulantly. '*Maybe*.'

She shrugged. 'You hear so much about movie studios and publishers and – what do they call it? Messing with the books?'

He smiled tightly. ' "Creative accounting," I think.'

'Right.'

'Still, we'll get *some*.' Not enough, he added silently. All the money in the world wouldn't be enough to pay for one day, one *moment* of what they'd gone through.

But reality was reality. There were bills to pay, debts to take care of, a future to plan for. There were problems coming up, and their commonness, their un-supernaturalness, didn't make them any less difficult.

Terri Sullivan burst out of the front door as they pulled into the driveway. Before George could stop and open the door she was at the side of the car, holding open a book, pointing frantically at a picture she had found there.

'Look! *Look*!' Her voice was wavering, unsteady. She sounded ready to crack wide open. '*Look*!'

She was only checking on Amy. She'd done it a hundred times before. That was her *job*, after all. Watching after the kids. Keeping them safe.

She remembered reaching down and turning the knob. The door swung open very gently. She leaned into the room.

The nightlight showed Amy sleeping quietly. It smelled of wool and warmth inside the soft darkness.

Terri smiled and started to leave. She tightened her grip on the doorknob and began to pull the door shut, moving back into the hall –

'Amy?'

Terri froze. It was a deep voice – drawing, almost groaning.

She spun around and looked down the hall.

Nothing.

And in the other direction –

Nothing.

Ammy? It wasn't a shout exactly. More like a question – a drawn-out, dull, insistent *call*. 'AMMMMMMMYYYY?'

She spun and put her hands on the bedroom door. She felt her heart buck like a broken machine.

50

It was coming from inside the little girl's room.

She swung the door open very cautiously. She looked toward the bed. And for an instant, for a fraction of a second she saw . . .

. . . she saw . . .

Something . . .

When she thought about it later – and she thought about it many, many times – she realized, there are things in the world that are not meant to be *seen* at all. They cannot fit into the tidy compartments of the mind – they are just too awesome or too horrible, or both. And when someone accidentally, impossibly, catches a glimpse of such a thing, what she sees is . . . *not right*: A mental equivalent of a sketch, a rendering, a poor approximation. But it's all that the human mind can bear.

In that moment when Terri Sullivan tried to *see* the writhing, roiling, bellowing, horrible thing that hovered above Amy Lutz' bed, her brain shut down. Her body reacted without conscious cue. A segment of time disappeared from her forever –

– and the next thing she knew she was downstairs, standing in the dark . . . in the kitchen.

She was frozen. She couldn't move. The blood in her veins felt as solid as stone; her limbs were like metal. She couldn't blink; she couldn't even *swallow*.

'Are you *okay*?'

The immobility shattered in an instant, as if the sound of a human voice was all it took. Terri reeled and almost fell. She caught herself on the arm of a large kitchen chair and turned slowly around.

Greg Lutz looked alien, bathed as he was in the interior light from the large refrigerator, balancing two giant sandwiches and two glasses of milk against his chest. 'Are you okay?' he asked again, his eyes huge.

'Amy,' she whispered.

'W – what?' The boy's voice cracked.

51

'Amy!'

She rushed past him without thinking. She took the stairs three at a time. She swept open the door to the little girl's room without thinking about what might be inside, what might be waiting for her –

Amy was sleeping soundly in her bed. The room smelled of wool and warmth inside the soft darkness. And there was nothing there. Nothing at all.

Slowly, the fear passed. The roaring in her ears subsided. After a long time, she was able to swallow the lump lodged in her throat and go downstairs. She found Greg framed by the archway in the hall, his arms still full of food, his mouth open wide in shocked amazement.

Before he could say it again, she raised one weary hand and tried to smile. 'I'm fine,' she lied. 'Fine.'

He looked at her for a long beat, then finally shrugged and hurried into the living room. The commercials would be over by now, and Matt always left things out when he told about what had happened, especially when it was one of Greg's favorite shows.

I didn't want to know, Terri told herself. Oh, she'd heard about the Lutz' troubles – of course she had, she'd known them for more than a year now. She'd even seen the book on the newsstands, and read about it and the movie in *The Enquirer*. But it had never interested her. She had never *wanted* it to interest her.

LOOK IN THE BOOK.

Now she was part of it. Whether she wanted to be or not, she was . . .

LOOK IN THE BOOK.

The Book.

She turned towards the bookcase, entirely against her will. It was calling to her, *urging* her –

LOOK IN THE BOOK.

Before she could stop herself, she had found it on the shelf. She was pulling it out. Opening it up. Scanning the pages –

There.

52

In the part about Amy. The part about her special friend. There was a picture of a drawing the little girl had made of –

Jodie. The pig-thing *Jodie*.

And God help her, *Terri Sullivan recognized it*.

Then there were headlights in the living room window, and the sound of the Lutz' car in the drive. And Terri was out of the house, out on the lawn, ignoring the night and the wind driven rain. She was spreading open the book and holding it against the wet car windows, frantically trying to *show* them, to *warn* them of something she didn't want to understand.

'Look!' she said to the white, frightened faces of George and Kathy Lutz, still hiding inside their car. 'Look, *look*!'

CHAPTER FIVE

GEORGE LUTZ strode along a smooth cement sidewalk. The sunshine touched his face, reaching into every pore of his body with a penetrating, almost incandescent warmth. He dug his hands deeper into the pockets of his light jacket, even though he wasn't the least bit cold. Just to feel. Just to *be*.

If only life could be this *cozy* all the time, he thought. The warmth rippled over him, and George concentrated on it, almost fed on the passing sensation with a growing hunger.

But . . .

Something wasn't quite right.

Yes, he thought, I feel warm and safe and happy. But . . . still, something isn't *quite right*.

What? *What*? The answer seemed to dance a fingertip away, just out of reach.

Then he noticed something very strange. The houses were slipping away.

There were familiar ranch-style homes, built back off the street behind tidy green lawns. He recognized them all; he had been this way a hundred times before. But they seemed to be speeding by, somehow – sliding past at an incredible pace.

Maybe, he thought *I'm* what's moving so fast. Much faster than my body. He looked down at his legs and realized that they were taking longer and longer strides. Not stretching, exactly, but covering immense lengths of territory with every step. He was passing houses so fast they were blurring into streams of color, streaking along the edges of his vision to become a wondrous psychedelic border.

Then he lifted out of his body.

It began with an almost startling smoothness and ease. One instant he was walking along the sidewalk, solid and full of weight. The next he was drifting upward like a soap bubble or a camera on a crane.

I am a camera, he thought from the distant, tranquil place his mind was resting. He was gliding backwards now, turning effortlessly, and he thought again of the movies he had seen shot from helicopters or planes.

He looked down on a burly, bearded man walking briskly along a sidewalk, his thick fists thrust deeply into the pockets of his windbreaker.

Sure enough, he thought. There's George Lutz.

And then George . . . *changed*.

The man's outline began to ripple, as if seen through a sheet of water. His features ran together, and the weight – the *substance* – seemed to drain away.

Now the George Lutz that George saw was flat – two-dimensional. The beard and the hair and the khaki pants were all still there, but they were paper thin, cut from a colorful plastic sheet. The legs seem to flicker in and out of existence as they moved, turning edgeways and disappearing, impossibly narrow.

Not me, he thought. But still – *me*. Like a man made of paper. Or an image projected on . . .

. . . film.

There was a blink, a flicker, and –

– he was back in his body, walking along the street again. But it was still a flat body, a *movie* body, he realized. He lifted his hand and wiggled the fingers as he walked. They waved like a paper cut-out, flaps of celluloid that were both alien and uncomfortably familiar. They were *him* and *not him*.

George passed a long American sedan parked at the curb and spotted himself in the reflection of the large glass windows.

It was the film version of George Lutz. A reflection of a reflection, but still –

'No. I'm *me*," he said firmly. 'George Lutz, *George Lutz*!' Confidence filled him like a light in a cave, and with the confidence came weight. Dimension. *Form*. He looked in the darkened glass again, and this time he was whole. He was *real*.

A unique feeling of *being* filled George. He was ecstatic at the sensation he had never acknowledged before – the feeling of simple existence. George prodded himself in the stomach; he felt his arms and face. Strange, he thought, and wonderful. Just knowing I am *me* can feel so good.

He lifted his arms, still light as a feather. He wanted to spin like a top, or dance like a child. He took a deep breath, reveling at the swell of air into his lungs. He turned and –

– the smile froze on his face.

He was standing on the front lawn of a house in Amityville – the house he swore he would never come near again. But even as the fear clawed at him, he felt his body moving forward.

I don't want to be here. I don't want to be *anywhere near this house*!

'Stop!' he cried aloud, hoping desperately that his legs and arms would obey. But the legs kept moving. His feet shuffled forward. He found himself drifting along the side of the house toward the horribly familiar front door.

'Why am I doing this? I don't want to be here, I don't – '

Wait. His mind raced. He felt himself tremble. *That's not my voice*, he realized. I'm George Lutz. I'm thinking these thoughts and shouting into the air . . . but *it's not my voice*.

As his hand reached for the doorknob, he caught a glimpse of himself in the small inset windows.

It's not me. It's the other one – the *movie* one. I'm trapped in a reel, trapped in a *scene*, and I have to go wherever it takes me.

The door opened and he entered the front hall. An elongated, circular mist was swirling there, only a few feet inside. The mist was a deep blue green – a spiraling tunnel that beckoned to him.

George wanted to turn and run, but the movie version stepped forward without hesitation. The blue-green fog closed around him like a swallowing throat, and a bottomless humming blossomed in his breast. He was drifting and falling and flying . . .

George was standing in a room – a red room. *The* red room he realized. In the basement of the house at Ocean Avenue.

He knew that the walls were made of brick and cement. He knew they were only painted scarlet; it only *looked* like blood. Or like –

Flames leapt from every brick. Mortar spurted like lava. The red walls were red with heat, he knew now, *heat*!

And they were closing in.

The tongues of fire licked towards him. The heat pushed against him on all sides. Hot. *Too* hot. His lungs were searing. His lips cracked and split in an instant. He knew he was dying – *dying*. He opened his mouth to scream, and –

A blink. A flicker. And –

He was standing in the sewing room. The door behind him began to move. George lunged for it, shouting –

His fingers brushed the wood as the door slammed shut. And the hand that pawed frantically at the doorknob was ridiculously flat, papery –

Damn! The two-dimensional film character had taken over him again! He/they turned, walked to the window, and looked down on the boathouse below.

Something was buzzing in the room.

My God, George thought. It's a fly.

He tried to move, to get away, but the movie version held him fast. 'Please,' he said to his other self, 'get out of here.' His voice sounded hollow and far away and . . . *not his*.

'*It's only a movie.*' It was a disembodied voice – *another* one, a different one, coming from someplace outside the scene.

'No!' George shouted. 'It's real, it *has* to be!'

The swirling blue-green vortex was back. It floated midway between the floor and ceiling, where the door should have been. George tried to move to it, to use it as a gateway, an escape. But not this time. His feet were pinned to the floor.

Suddenly, chillingly, he knew what was happening. The vortex wasn't a doorway *out* at all. It was there to let something *in*.

The buzzing multiplied and grew louder, and George recognized it as it swelled. It was a sound that had haunted his dreams, a sound he had prayed he would never hear again.

It was the sound of flies, swarming.

He looked into the vortex, down its center, and a living blanket of flies gushed out, hitting him full in the face and chest. In seconds the room was a sea of churning black insects.

He was lost in an instant. His eyes, face, hair were alive and writhing. They swarmed down his throat, inside his nose, along the corridors of his ears. He could smell them, taste their flat metallic bodies under his tongue, hear them booming and gritting inside his head.

George tried to scream, but his throat was coated with a moving furry blob.

His mind shrieked instead. Sanity lifted away on invisible wings, and left him squawling in the humming black.

(There was a voice from the past – a most-loved childhood memory. There was a gentle, grassy Austrian hillside and a woman in a long print dress with a white apron. She was spinning, her arms outstretched, full of joy. She turned to him. She opened her mouth. He expected to hear her sing an old familiar song, the one about the hills and the music. But she opened her mouth and The Voice was there again – the one from the outside, the *other* one, and it had doubled now. There were two voices that he didn't recognize, both coming from the woman, though her lips didn't move –)

'*It's only a movie.*'

A third voice, just as unfamiliar joined in.

'*It's only a movie.*'

And another, deeper and half an octave down, did the same:

'*It's only a –* '

Blink. Flicker.

He was poised at the top of the stairs on the first landing of the Amityville house. His arms were loaded down with clothes. There were pants, shirts, and jackets that looked like Greg's and Matt's, and a small colored jumpsuit that could only be Amy's. His own blue coat and some of Kathy's things poked out from the bottom of the pile.

A tearing scream echoed up the stairwell. Kathy? he thought wildly. He wasn't sure.

He peered down the stairs, into the darkness. Then he was rushing forward. He couldn't remember why; it was all very vague, somehow too dark to understand. But he suddenly knew *he had to get out of here*.

He stumbled down the stairs two at a time and –

It was there again. He remembered now. The ominous, black, oozing, cloud-thing, hovered above the steps and blocked his way.

This can't be happening, George thought from somewhere deep inside himself. It can't be happening because it's already happened. I've already lived through this. I ran the gauntlet. *I got away.*

But here he was again, staring into the evil, seeing the strange twisted shapes once more – the faces, the demons, the monsters.

George knew he should be able to stop this. He should be able to turn away and refuse to continue with the farce. But it didn't *feel* like a farce. It felt full and solid and horribly *real*.

Well, he decided. I made it once. I can make it again. Just do what you did before. Don't touch the thing. Get away. Don't make any mistakes.

He moved forward, easing to the left, trying to bypass the swirling, bottomless *thing* that waited only inches away. Then –

– he was a spectator again, trapped inside the movie version of George Lutz. And the movie version stopped. Turned. And threw itself, *hurled* itself into the boiling blackness of the thing that waited. George tried to scream as his body was swallowed up by the –

Blink-flicker.

'*It's only a movie,*' the voices said together, singing sweetly.

Harry's bark echoed in the darkness.

George and the Lutz' friendly mongrel dog were rushing down the basement stairs as fast as they could go. The urgency was tangible, *tasteable*, but George couldn't place it. Why were they going so fast? Where was the emergency? Why –

The steps disappeared under them. One instant they were standing on solid sturdy wood – the next they were gone.

Harry let out a howling yelp as he and his master fell down into darkness. A putrid smell stabbed at them, and a bare instant later they plunged into a clinging bog.

George bellowed and flailed helplessly, groping for a handhold in the muck. He could find nothing except the matted and stinking fur of the panic-stricken dog.

Keeping his nose clear of the slime was almost impossible; kicking against the muck was like swimming in mud. He tried to help Harry, tried to keep the dog from drowning, but when he heard the miserable howling cut off, he knew it was too late. He held on a moment longer, then sank beneath the bubbling surface with an obscene *plup . . . plup . . . plup.*

'*It's only a movie,*' a small chorus twittered.

'No,' George's mind insisted. '*It's all there is.*'

60

BLINK!

A tall man in his early twenties slowly made his way up the stairs to where George was standing, on the first landing of the house at Ocean Avenue.

There was something strangely familiar about him, but George couldn't quite put his finger on it. He wanted to call out to the man as he came, but the other version, the movie George was back in control. He could only watch the scene unfold before him.

The younger man seemed intent on something as he made his way along the hall. He looks like someone I know, George thought, but the man simply walked by, only inches away, and didn't seem to recognize George . . . or even *see* him.

Then George figured out what it was. He looks like *me*, he realized. He looks like George Lutz. He was younger, true, and built in a different way, but still there was a striking resemblance.

The man opened the door at the end of the landing and entered the room there. For the first time, George saw the rifle hanging at the man's side, and his mind finally made the connection.

He had heard about this man. He'd read about what he'd done.

'No! NO!' George screamed at him, but the words were swallowed by the leaden air.

I know what's going to happen. I know what he's going to do. George fought to hold onto his sanity. It's *sick*! It's a *terrible* thing! Something like this should never have happened, and *it's happening again*.

A rifle blast shook the entire house. The sound grew and grew, in expanding echoes. George slammed his hands over his ears, trying to blot it out, trying to forget what he knew was happening.

The man walked out of the room. The smoking rifle was hanging at his side. Casually, almost matter-of-fact, he headed up the stairs to the next landing.

George tried to scream at him, knowing it was hopeless.

'Stop it! It's not *God* you're hearing. It's not the Lord making you do these things!'

Suddenly George began to move slowly forward, towards the door to the room that the man had just left.

'Oh, no. Oh, please, no, *please*. Don't do this, *please* don't do this.' George was sobbing, but the sound was absorbed in the thickness that surrounded him.

He tried to make the movie version stop. He tried not to look as he drifted through the door, into the room, over to the foot of the bed. But he couldn't keep his eyes closed. The movie version even controlled *that*. He was forced to see the tiny fragile body of the little girl, lying in a pool of her own blood.

Another rifle shot shook the house. From above. Above –

BLINK!

Now George was looking at a teenage boy. He was sprawled face down on his bed. Blood pulsed through a torn wound on the back of his close-cropped head.

George tried to cry, but it wasn't allowed. Not in the movie version.

The rifle blasted *again*.

And again.

And twice more.

After each crashing explosion, George was forced to look at the carnage, helpless to prevent it, out of control. The other boy. The mother. The father.

God, was all he could think. Oh, *God* . . .

George was hovering over the body of an old man when the last blast exploded. The house began to oscillate erratically. The sound echoed louder and louder and *louder* –

A window imploded, spraying shards of glass across the room. A sliver ripped into George's arms like a speeding knife, and the sudden pain made him stagger back. He looked down in mute surprise as hundreds of tiny wounds blossomed along his body.

Pictures fell from the walls. Plaster rained down from

the roof in a powdery shower. The shuddering vibrations expanded, flattened, grew too deep to hear.

The house could no longer stand the attack. It began to come apart at the seams.

George hesitated, taking one last look at the body of old man DeFeo stretched out on the large bed. Then he turned and ran for the door. He was halfway to the hall before he realized that he was free again – able to move when he chose, able to escape. His body was round and whole and solid again, and hope blossomed in him as he rushed for the stairs.

The ceiling collapsed with a vast roar, and George was driven to his knees. He struggled amid falling plaster and splintered wood. Torn electrical wiring still spluttered where current surged. Dust clouds churned and clutched at his throat.

He dragged himself forward on bloody elbows. For a few frantic seconds he thought he might actually make it out, make it into the light –

A huge overhead beam swept down and slammed him across the shoulders.

He was pinned under the rubble of what had once been his bedroom. Settling dust and debris nearly blinded him – he couldn't see more than a few inches. George could only lie quietly and listen, waiting for the voices to come, waiting to be told it was only . . . only . . .

When they didn't come, he muttered it himself. 'So,' he said through gritted teeth. 'This is only a movie?'

He fainted.

Some measureless time later, the darkness came alive around him. George blinked, then blinked again. He was sure his eyes were open and working, but all he could see was darkness. He was alone, he realized, completely –

'*It's only a movie!*'

The voices were a huge chorus now – chaotic, wild, but choral – *musical*, somehow. They filled the darkness . . .

filled his head . . . George could feel them ripple along the skin of his forearms. They surged down his spine and exploded in a cascading warmth at the base of his brain.

As the volume swelled, more and more voices – all one voice, he knew, multiplying on itself – joined the choir. The blackness filled with sound so tangible it took on form and shape.

George groped frantically in the dark, trying to lay hands on the warmth he knew was there. The choir repeated the phrase over and over. Sang it and muttered it and bellowed it back and forth.

'*It's only a movie. Only a movie. Only a movie. Only a –*

– dream!'

George opened his eyes. The echo of the numberless choir was still audible, but even as he strained to hear it, it rapidly faded away. He looked around, his heart pounding.

What *now*? He wondered. What distorted memory would clutch at him this time? He turned to the side, cold with fear –

Kathy was sleeping soundly beside him.

Oh, no, he thought. *No. Kathy's* in this one. Now *she'll* have to relive the pain, and she might not be able to take it. It was almost too much for her when it was really happening, when –

He stopped. He held his breath for a long beat.

Finally George exhaled and looked around very slowly. He was in his bed. Kathy was sleeping peacefully next to him.

It *had* been a dream. And it was over now.

Seeing the movie had done it. The shock and confusion of watching it all over again – the same as before but different as well, horribly different. It had obviously affected them more than he realized.

A cool breeze wafted in the open window. It sighed

64

gently across his face, and George put his hands behind his head and eased back against the pillow, half-relaxing for the first time in what seemed like centuries.

For a few minutes he watched the shadowed reflections of the street lamp that stood just outside his home, as the light shifted and danced beyond the swirling trees, moved by a light breeze.

Soon he was sliding into a peaceful sleep – a sleep without dreams. But on the edge of it, in the warmth and darkness that waited there, he saw the Austrian hillside again, and the pretty woman in the blue print dress. She was singing now. Singing about the hills . . . and . . .

The music.

CHAPTER SIX

AN INSISTENT, icy wind whispered down the manmade caverns of Park Avenue. It rubbed George Lutz' exposed brow and cheeks like sandpaper.

He was almost grateful for the pain. At least it was a sharp sensation, something from *outside*. Not like the constant, dull hammerblow inside his head.

The migraines were back, as horrible as they had been since the days in Amityville. This particular attack had begun on the plane, and intensified with every hour. There were parts of the landing at J.F.K., checking in at the hotel, taking the taxi into Manhattan that were lost forever in a haze of blinding –

A horn screamed in his left ear. Tires shrieked an instant later, rushing towards him from the same direction. George stopped in the middle of the street and turned slowly, very slowly to the side.

'Whaddya tryin' to do?' shouted an enraged cabbie. 'Commid *suicide*?'

The pain was blinding him again. He couldn't see clearly, couldn't think. He tried to blink it away and focus on the yellow cab, and the red-faced driver, and the chorus of horns all around him. All he could manage was a hazy blur and a dull awareness that the front bumper of the taxi was only inches from his leg.

Gotta do somethin' 'bout this, he thought dully. He stumbled back to the curb, barely noticing the cabbie's upthrust finger, barely hearing the new squeal of tires as it lurched away, into traffic.

The pain was a roaring in his ears, a hideous light

behind his eyes. Gotta *do* something, he thought again, but deciding what or how was beyond him.

He stumbled forward for an eternity . . . or was it a second.

Stopping a moment, he focused on the incongruous scene of a snow-covered alpine village high above his head. Then, through the nausea and noise, he dimly saw it was an immense *photograph*, and recognized the sweeping, ornate archway of Grand Central Station.

He almost slipped on the stairs leading downward. He had forgotten where he was, where he was going. He could only feel the pain, filling him. A spiked, slamming, invasive pain.

Annette ('Call me Annie') Ridgway was a militant Samaritan. That's what Father Eduardo at the parish had called her. With her sharp, almost fierce Irish features, her twinkling, intimidating sapphire eyes above an aquiline nose and the network of imposing wrinkles she wore as she stalked into her sixty-second year, she was a feisty force to contend with at Grand Central. 'You need a face like this,' she would say proudly, 'to do what I been doin' for thirty-two years.'

Running the 'candy counter', as she called her busy kiosk in Grand Central, was no easy job. She had seen every imaginable sort of human in her time there: drunken philosophers holding forth on everything from existential-ism to the Stock Market; or indulging in one-sided argu-ments with the air about the great, the really *great* fighters; or making impassioned comparisons of Karl Marx and the Beatles. And she had wept for the broken ones – the drug addicts, the winos, the left-over spirits that society had used up and didn't have the decency to care for.

Annie hated what she saw in them. Not *them*, of course. She was free with advice and the address of the nearby missions – though she drew the line at loans and spare change. Still, she hated what the world had done to them

67

with a passion unmatched in most of her jaded New York compatriots.

Oh, there were a few special ones. Mortie Steinman, for instance. He'd worked behind the deli-counter down the block for over twenty years, and he *never* said no to a wino or junkie. She and Mortie had coffee twice a week, every week, after the day's work was finished, and she couldn't understand how he didn't seem to mind all that he saw. He never tired of talking about his plans and dreams, though Annie knew, and she knew *he* knew, that they were the sorts of dreams that stayed just *dreams*. And Father Eduardo at the mission, there was a fine one. And her own late husband, Sandy, now there was a truly fine one . . .

She was thinking about Sandy and breaking open a roll of nickels when the strange man appeared before her.

No bum, she realized. She prided herself on being able to pick the bums and the odd ones out at a glance, and he was neither of those. But . . . a strange one.

He was dressed for the chilly weather, and shivering far more than necessary she thought. But he was bathed in a fine sheen of sweat, as if overheating. He was a big man, too, built more like a bearded bear than anything else. And there was something in his eyes – something terrified and terrifying both. Something Annie hated, yet felt drawn to.

'Are you okay, mister?' she asked.

He looked down at her and swayed, but he couldn't seem to speak. A fever, maybe? she wondered. Some sort of attack?

'I said, are you *okay*?'

'Aspirin,' George croaked. He was standing at a – magazine rack or drug store counter or – or . . . *something*. He didn't remember where, he didn't remember how he got there. He needed something. He needed.

'Aspirins.'

The hatchet-faced woman behind the counter pursed her lips as if smelling something unpleasant and held out a small white plastic bottle with a blue label. George pulled some change from his pocket and dropped it blindly into Annie Ridgway's palm without counting it.

He clutched at the bottle and tried to open it. The cap clicked and turned in his hand, but it wouldn't come off.

He had never taken tablets . . . not even at the house. But this was – was . . .

Pain blazed heavier behind his eyes. He felt the ground start to tilt, and the edge of the kiosk lurched out and hit him hard on his shoulder. He grunted and twisted the bottlecap again. It wouldn't – it – wouldn't –

It wouldn't come off!

Sick, Annie had decided. The poor man was sick with the *mee*-graine. Taking the bottle back from him was child's play. It almost fell from his fingers when she reached for it, and he looked down at her with puzzled, agonized blue eyes.

'Here, love,' she said. 'I'll do that for you. Silly things can give a soul trouble even if they're *not* in a bad way.' Expertly, she pushed down and twisted, and the lid fell into her hand. 'Now, just –'

He snatched the bottle from her and shook a handful of aspirin into his hand. Then he tossed them down his throat without looking.

'*Wait* a minute, love! You'll choke yourself.'

His throat worked against the thickening glob. He looked about dazed for some way to wash the mass down. The plastic bottle fell from his hand and clattered onto the counter.

Annie was quick. She'd been coping with far worse in Grand Central for a long, long time. In an instant she had her stainless steel thermos up and out, and she poured a generous helping of steaming coffee into the red, plastic cup-top.

'Take it easy, now,' she said, holding out the cup. 'Take yourself a deep breath and swallow this slow, real *slow* –'

He gulped it down hungrily, so fast it made Annie gasp. She knew how hot the coffee was. She'd burned her tongue on it not half an hour earlier. But he didn't seem to notice. He took it all in two huge gulps.

The bear of a man tried on a weak little smile when he handed the cup back. 'I get . . . migraines,' he grated.

She waved it away. 'Not to worry,' she said. 'My husband, God rest 'em, used to get the devils himself. Sometimes lay him out for hours at a time. Have to stay in a room with all the lights off and no sound, not even quiet music – '

He was leaning against the counter now, slowly shaking his head from side to side. But he seemed to be getting better. His eyes were clearer now. More focused.

And Annie could see a deeper pain in them – something fathomless and affecting. Something that touched her heart more strongly than anything had since Sandy had gone to his reward.

She reached out and laid her hand over the big man's own. That was something she never did, *never*. Too many people these days didn't like to be touched. They took it wrong. But something inside this wounded soul, something had compelled her to do it.

The skin of her palm felt unaccountably warm. It tingled with some sort of honeyed electricity – not unpleasant, really, but . . . *strange*. She didn't take it back. She didn't really want to.

The man looked up at her and smiled – really *smiled* this time, and Annie Ridgway knew that she had done the right thing. She cared about this fellow – as she had cared about all her temporary charges as they trundled past her kiosk at the Station – and this time, *this* time it had mattered.

The big man squeezed her hand in his own, very briefly – as if to confirm that, yes, it was happening, that something real and very precious was passing between them. And

70

when he finally let go and stepped away from the counter, straighter, and stronger, it felt as if he was still touching her, still holding her hand.

'Thank you,' he said quietly, and nodded. All Annie Ridgway – talkative, opinionated, downright feisty Annie Ridgway – could do was nod back as he turned away and headed towards the wide stone stairs that led up to the street.

And for an instant, she saw it.

She thought about it many times afterward, in her darkest moments. She tried to remember its shape exactly, the outline of its roiling and bubbling in the empty air above the burly man's shoulders. But it didn't have a shape, exactly, or a color or a face.

It was a *feeling*, she decided after much thought and prayer. A feeling made more real and powerful than any human body had ever been.

She remembered blackness, a foul smell, clutching hands, and red, red eyes – but the *feeling* of them, not the sight. The sensation was hunger, hatred, violence, power, and it was hovering in physical form over the burly man as he trundled up the stairs. It was away from him for the moment, driven off only slightly by the special contact between Annie and the stranger. But it was waiting, *waiting* for another opportunity to drive itself inside like a steel pike.

Annie Ridgway had always believed in Evil as a physical force, as a *real* thing. That was the only time she actually *saw* it in its own incomprehensible clothing. And she prayed to God she'd never see it again.

She tried to call out, but the words caught in her throat. She tried to chase after the poor man, to warn him somehow, to help him. Her legs seemed pinned to the blackened linoleum floor. She could only gesture weakly, try to point. And before she could finish the gesture the man and the – the *thing* – were up and out of the Station forever.

When Mortie Steinman came by at lunchtime to see how Annie was doing, he found her sitting on her padded three-legged stool, staring blankly ahead and breathing

71

very, very slowly. For an awful moment he thought she'd had a stroke. But she looked up when he spoke to her, and he was astonished to see tears on her cheeks.

He took her out for a good stiff drink. It was the first and last time he ever saw her touch the stuff, even on New Year's. And she wouldn't talk about what had happened, what had made her act in that most extraordinary way. By the next morning, she was the old Annie Ridgway again – as sharp-faced, forceful, and feisty as ever. But she never would talk about it.

Never.

George yawned theatrically as the elevator dropped sixty-five floors. He hated the pressure it made in his ears, and the last thing he wanted now was a pain in his head – not after he'd finally gotten that headache under control.

Ever since that woman at Grand Central had helped him . . .

He shrugged it off. Must have been the pills, he thought. Just the pills.

The doors opened into the lobby of the office building that held his publisher's suites. The meeting had been successful. The editor and agent were both just short of ecstatic.

'We've got ourselves a bestseller,' the editor had said.

'An *international* bestseller,' the agent chimed in. He sounded in a state that approached religious awe.

There had been papers to sign, plans to make, and questions to avoid about the proposed trip to Australia and Japan. Those had been hard to put off, but he'd managed – for the moment.

He stepped out of the elevator and zipped his jacket up tightly. Back to the hotel, he thought, and then call Kathy and –

The road was gray and lifeless ahead of him, curving insidiously to the right. The car was drifting under him. His hands were at his side. He watched in mute fascination as the white line passed smoothly from left to right. The lane curved one way and the car went another . . .

The oncoming truck flashed its lights on and off. The air horn bellowed loudly, so loudly George jumped and grabbed at the wheel almost involuntarily.

He was heading right for it, across the grassy divider. It was only fifty feet away.

George jerked in the seat, adrenalin slamming into his system. He heaved the wheel to the right and felt the car slide sickeningly to the side and begin to shimmy. But the truck moved off to the left, pounding by with the air horn still *blatting*.

He heaved to the left now, and the car began to fish-tail. A touch on the brakes. Another correction. Then he was back on his own side of the road, under the speed limit, moving smoothly and controlled to-wards . . .

. . . towards . . .

It was like a rush of icy water along his spine. He felt his muscles begin to seize up again, and his fists tightened on the wheel until the knuckles were white.

'Where am I?' he said aloud. 'What am I *doing*?'

He was driving. A blue Ford Fairlaine. He had never seen it before. But he was driving it, *had* been driving it for some time, and the suburban landscape around him looked familiar, somehow.

Terribly familiar . . .

He glanced at the empty seat beside him, and saw a large folder from a car rental company. But he hadn't rented a car this trip – they couldn't afford it, he wouldn't be in New York long enough to use it.

He passed a group of houses and a small shopping complex that he recognized. Where had he seen it before? What could it mean?

Breathing deeply, he eased his foot off the accelerator

and tapped the brake. He was going to slow down. He was going to have to piece this all together.

I came to New York. I checked into the hotel. I had my meeting with the publishers, the agents. And I –

– I –

I don't remember.

There was a sign less than a quarter of a mile up ahead. He saw it in the dying light of day, but he didn't want to recognize it. He didn't want to *read* it.

The distance closed quickly. He felt panic rising like gall in his throat. The words came into focus and he couldn't help it, he couldn't stop himself:

AMITYVILLE

EXIT 3 MILES

Get away, he ordered himself. *Get away*!

He flashed his left turn signal and glanced in the side view mirror. The lane was clear. He could make it.

He stomped on the accelerator and spun the steering wheel hard to the left. He'd make a U-turn right here, right across the barrier in the center of the turnpike, and get back, get *away* –

Something was very wrong.

He had the accelerator pedal flat against the floor of the car, but the engine was rumbling with the same smooth rhythm.

The steering wheel was fully turned and locked to the left, but the car didn't turn – it didn't even swerve.

As if to confirm its own intent, the car calmly moved into the right-hand lane. It began to steer itself towards the exit.

It was heading straight into Amityville.

Then George heard the beckoning call. And the laughter.

He had heard it before. He knew what it was. He knew it was for *him*. And with the realization came the bone-chilling cold, the hideous lethargy, the soundless voice that told him to give up, give in, let it happen –

'NO!' he shouted. 'NOT AGAIN!'

He wouldn't let go. He wouldn't give that damnable monster the satisfaction. Better to die here, *now*, than to return to the house to be swallowed whole.

He reached down and pulled the key from the ignition. Nothing. The engine rumbled, calm as ever.

He dragged frantically on the steering wheel – one way, then the other.

Nothing.

He stamped on the brake until it lay limply on the carpet. He put all his weight behind the emergency brake.

Nothing. *Nothing* would work.

George turned in the seat, letting the wheel move on its own. He tried the door, tried to roll out onto the highway at sixty miles per hour, but the door wouldn't open. It wouldn't even budge.

He punched at the automatic window controls, but his effort was useless. He slammed his fists against the window glass, and it shuddered under the blows but held.

A tidy yellow Japanese sedan pulled alongside the Fairlane. He got a glimpse of the Long Island housewife making her way home, a bag from Bloomingdales in the seat beside her.

'Help!' he shouted, pounding on the window again. 'HELP!'

She didn't notice. She just kept driving.

Something inside George Lutz burst open – some wall that had been holding back the dread and horror of the house.

He hid his face in his hands, not caring about the car anymore, not touching the wheel.

'I can't go back there,' he sobbed. 'I can't, I *can't!*'

Then a memory flashed through him, almost too fast to comprehend. A chilling, immobilizing bolt of *déjà vu* . . .

It had tried this before. And they'd finally escaped. The night in January, 1976. Amy, Greg and Matt, even the mongrel dog, Harry, were with Kathy and George in their black van. Fleeing town. Escaping from the *thing*.

It had attacked. It had tried to control the car. And they

had defeated it, they had driven it back and gotten away, *escaped*, by –

. . . by . . .

Thick fingers of doubt infiltrated him. George felt his arms grow heavy. His vision dimmed. He could barely see outside of the car now as it approached the Amityville Exit.

1 MILE, the sign said . . .

Prayer.

It came to him like a light in darkness, cutting through the fog. There had been a prayer, a *prayer* they had all recited together, and that thing, that damned *thing* couldn't stand up to it. It had been . . .

. . . it had been . . .

Something smashed into the side of the car with impossible force. George flew out of the seat, away from the wheel, and the car swerved at the impact.

He grabbed at the steering wheel, but it wouldn't respond.

The car fishtailed wildly, squealing as it shook, then righted itself.

Think about it, he ordered himself. Imagine it in your mind.

The van. The night. Kathy and the kids –

Another blow smashed at the car, this time from the right side. He bounced back behind the wheel. His shoulder crunched against the locked door, and a bolt of pain blasted through to his chest.

Ignore it, he ordered. The *prayer* . . .

A dark liquid began to spatter on the windshield. George's concentration broke for a moment despite his efforts. The sky was clear and cloudless, but the ooze was coming from *somewhere*. It was covering his windshield.

And now, *now*, the car was responding. The wheel was suddenly alive under his hands. The brakes were up and working. The accelerator answered to the pressure of his foot. He touched the pedal lightly, just the slightest tap –

– the car leaped forward, careening down the freeway

like a runaway animal. George fought to stay in control, grunting to keep the car in one lane.

But the black muck was thicker now. It was hard to see out. And still, part of his mind was searching for the words, trying to reconstruct the memory of that horrible night.

The *prayer* . . .

A wailing scream came up around him. From everywhere, nowhere, it filled the interior of the car, stabbing at his eardrums.

The windshield was black as tar. He was driving blind, and the speedometer read eighty-five.

'Kathy,' he pleaded under his breath. 'Kathy, *what was the prayer?*'

'*Our Father . . .* ' her voice answered.

It made George freeze in spite of everything. It *was* her voice, *her* voice, warm and alive inside the car.

'*Our Father who art in Heaven . . .* '

Yes! Now he remembered it! How could he forget something so simple?

Kathy's voice was strong now, strong enough to remind him. He was alone in an out-of-control car, only instants from death, but *she* was with him. Joy filled him. Kathy, he thought, *Kathy*!

He joined her in prayer.

'*Our Father who art in Heaven. Hallowed be Thy name . . .* '

The windshield twisted crazily out of shape. It bowed like a sheet of plastic, pressing inwards, backwards, *toward* him, with a splintering, painful, crackling groan –

'*Thy kingdom come . . .* '

It cracked with a piercing thunderclap of sound. Fracture lines raced across it, spiderwebbing the black glass like some bizarre roadmap.

'*Thy will be done . . .* '

It erupted inwards. George was pierced by thousands of tiny black glass bullets, ripping into every square inch of exposed flesh. Arms, neck, face, hands, everything was flayed a thousand times over. Blood flickered from a hundred simultaneous wounds.

'*On earth* . . . '

For an incredible instant, he could see the sunset bathed freeway in front of him as he weaved madly from lane to lane. Cars were sliding and veering to get out of his way. He could hear the squeal of tires, the bleat of car horns, but it was only an instant. Then:

There was pain. And blood. He was chewing on needles of glass. His eyes were bleeding. His mouth filled with blood. The words he shouted were guttural groans now, unrecognizable, but he knew what they meant, he felt them like solid objects inside him:

'Lead us not into temptation! Deliver us from evil!'

He was blind again. The car was filled with wind. He could feel the darkness coming to take him, seeping into every pore. He was cold, *cold*, as the hammering battered at the collapsing roof. The ceiling was coming down to crush him.

'Deliver *me* from evil! *Deliver me from evil*!!'

Tears poured down his face. He screamed the words as the sign came rushing towards him.

AMITYVILLE

'*Deliver me from evil*!'

AMITYVILLE

'DELIVER ME – '

The sun was going down. The Ford Fairlane was intact around him. The clock read 5:49. The radio was playing a pleasant golden oldie on WNOW . . .

. . . and it was over. As if it had never begun.

For a moment George was suspended, held tight in surprise. Then, suddenly, the air gushed out of him and he gripped the wheel, tapped the brake, and pulled to a stop on the shoulder.

He held up his hands and stared at them. They were whole. Unharmed. His breathing eased to a relaxed, gentle rhythm as he looked at the roof and saw that it was in one solid sheet. No rips, no dents. And the windshield. His fingers almost caressed the glass in front of him. No cracks. No holes. Not so much as a scratch.

The sign was five-hundred yards ahead of him. It was the first one he'd seen – or *thought* he'd seen.

AMITYVILLE
EXIT 3 MILES

He pulled the car back into the slow lane and moved rapidly up to fifty-five miles per hour. He drove past the Amityville turn-off without so much as a look to his right. At the first chance, he turned around and drove back again – back towards New York.

He never *did* remember what had happened from the moment he stepped off the elevator in Manhattan and the moment he saw the road sign on Long Island. After a while, it bothered him no more – and no less – than what was to come. But in the car, and in the hotel room, and on the plane that took him back to San Diego, he found himself returning time and again to the ancient, powerful prayer his wife had recited more than six years earlier.

'Our Father,' it began. And now it came easily.

CHAPTER SEVEN

GEORGE WAS finally sleeping. Kathy watched him fondly from the corner of the room as he dozed in his favorite chair.

I wish I could sleep half as well, she thought glumly. Ever since he'd left for New York, she had spent the nights tossing and turning. And she kept having the same dream, over and over.

She kept reliving those first moments out of the house. The time in the van. The impossible, pounding attack by huge, invisible fists.

And the prayer. The prayer had been nagging at her the whole time. She loved the feeling it brought – she needed that feeling, now more than ever. But it had been ringing inside her for days like an insistent bell, keeping her awake, invading what dream she could steal in those rare seconds of sleep.

It had faded, quite conveniently, when she had picked up George at Los Angeles International, just that afternoon.

She was looking forward to that night – the first night back with her husband in a long ten days. An *eternal* ten days. Just to sleep with him beside her again . . .

The doorbell rang.

Kathy saw George flinch in his light sleep, but that was all. She tiptoed quickly to the front door before it could ring again, thinking *Let the man sleep; he needs it. We all need it.*

She opened the door just as a thickly gloved finger was about to poke the bell a second time. Her eyes followed the line of the finger up a velveteen arm, across a shoulder made wide by a florid purple epaulet, and finally came to rest on a painfully thin, hawkish face that framed a set of protruding and intimidating slate-gray eyes.

'Mrs. Lutz?' the man said. 'Mrs. George Lutz?'

Kathy nodded. She felt somehow stunned.

The man whipped a stovepipe hat from his head and folded into a low, awkward bow. He was wearing a pair of tight bell-bottom trousers with sequined serpents running up the sides, a black velveteen tailcoat with deep purple cuffs and epaulets, a paisley vest and a deep black ascot held in place by a stickpin in the shape of an ankh. His hair was white blond and almost shoulder length, and there were pockmarks of teenage acne on his cheeks. All in all, he couldn't have been more than thirty or thirty-five, though he was doing his level best to look twice that age.

'Greetings,' he said, plopping the stovepipe hat back on his head. 'Doctor Quentin W. Cosmos, at your service.' There was a flip and a flash of hand movement. Kathy flinched. Suddenly he was holding a deep black business card between his gloved fingers. They were thick white gloves, Kathy noticed dazedly, like the ones Mickey Mouse wore.

She opened the screen door just a crack and took the card. The white, expensively embossed lettering said *Quentin W. Cosmos, Psychic Investigator and Ghost Hunter*. It had a post office box and two different office phone numbers, one for Fort Wayne, Indiana, and one for Dallas, Texas.

Kathy swallowed. 'What . . . can I do for you?'

He smirked and scratched the side of his beaky nose. 'It's not what *you* can do for *me*, dear lady,' Quentin Cosmos replied. 'It's what *I* can do for *you*.' He leaned so far forward that his froggy eyes were only inches from the screen that separated them. 'You need my help,' he whispered urgently.

'I . . . don't . . . think so,' Kathy said slowly. She glanced over her shoulder and caught a glimpse of George, still asleep in the living room chair. 'Look, I don't know who you are, or why you think we need you, Mister –'

'*Doctor*' he insisted. '*Doctor* Quentin W. Cosmos.' He toyed with his fingers and tried to look casual. 'Oh, I know all about you, Mrs. Lutz. You and that house in Amity.'

'Amity*ville*,' Kathy corrected without thinking. She immediately regretted it.

'Ah! Yes!' Cosmos beamed. 'Amity*ville*. Believe me when I tell you I know about such things. *I* am one of the chosen. I was *contacted*. Hearing the call, I traveled from my headquarters – at my own expense – to help you.' He gestured behind him, at a huge black car hunched along the curb. 'Of course, I brought my *limousine* with me to further impress upon you how *important* I think your case is. As my thousands of clients and followers know, Dr. Quentin V. Cosmos spares no expense when the call comes.'

Kathy listened, almost hypnotized by the musical rise and fall of his oratory. Her eyes followed the pointed glove and she was stunned all over again.

It was a limousine – or at least it had been a limousine *once*. It couldn't have been more than a year or two old, but Cosmos had modified it somehow.

The hardtop roof had been converted into a raised dome, and mounted on the dome was what appeared to be a very expensive reflector telescope. The hood had been extended and decorated with rhinestones in the shape of constellations, and the grillwork between the two pitted frog-eye headlamps had been spray-painted with a flecked metal substance that looked for all the world like it might be real gold. A solid silver ankh, almost three feet tall, had been welded to the center, and Cosmos' name, complete with angel wings and hellfire, had been painted on the side. Something like a rumble seat had been cut into the back where the trunk should have been.

The entire effect was undeniably garish, and yet also a little awe-inspiring.

What in the world would a ghost hunter need with a rumble seat? she thought. And she started to giggle.

Cosmos smirked all over again, completely misunderstanding. 'I'm not surprised you're impressed. It's not

often that I venture from my headquarters to work with
. . . well, with *regular* people. But in your case, now, *your*
case interests me.' He put two dainty gloved fingers on the
screen door's handle. 'May I come in?'

'No!' Kathy hadn't intended to say it so sharply, but this
strange man with his strange car made her very uncomfortable.

'Don't be frightened, missy,' he said, shaking his head
and nearly losing his top hat in the process. 'I represent
the forces of God.'

'Kathy? What's going on?' George's voice, thick with
sleep, was coming from the living room.

'You want to come here a second, honey?'

'What?'

'I said *come here*, George.' She was feeling just a little
hysterical.

George appeared in the doorway, as broad shouldered
and scruffy as a bear disturbed during hibernation. The
strange man outside unexpectedly brightened. 'Ah,' he
said, his protruding eyes afire, 'You must be Mr. George
Lutz himself?'

George looked suspicious. 'What if I am?'

Kathy gave him the elegantly printed card. 'This . . .
ah, *gentleman* says that we need his help.'

George looked at Cosmos. Then he looked at the card.
Then he looked at Cosmos again.

'How did you get our address?'

'That is of little importance,' Cosmos said. 'What *is*
important is *me*, Mr. Lutz, and how I can help you rid
yourself of the evil that has plagued you. *I*, and I *alone*,
have the power to free you, and your wife, and your
children.' He suddenly looked worried. 'You do have
children?'

Kathy said, 'Yes, but – '

George said, 'Get out of here!'

Cosmos smirked again. Kathy was beginning to hate
that smirk. He raised his gloved hand and tried to calm
them. 'Please, please, don't be afraid. I know I can be

rather . . . *imposing*, shall we say! But I assure you, the power I control can work in your favor! Oh, yes it can!'

'Sure it can,' George said. 'And how much is this "power" going to cost us?'

'Why nothing, of course. Not a penny.' Cosmos looked a little offended at the thought. 'All I ask is that certain representatives of the media – reputable men, I assure you – might accompany us to your house in Amity so that – '

'That's enough! Get off my property, Dr. Whatever-your-name-is.'

'Cosmos. Quentin W. – '

'Get off my property *now*, or I'll call the cops.'

Cosmos was still trying to calm him down. 'Please, Mr. Lutz, open your mind to the infinite.' He put his hand back on the screen door's knob. 'If you would just let me come in – '

George had taken all he was going to take. He threw the door open – nearly severing Cosmos' ample nose in the process – and seized the man by the arm of his suit. He had him turned around and trotting down the driveway in an instant.

'I don't know how you got this address,' he said as he hustled the 'ghost-hunter' back to his bizarre conveyance, 'and frankly, I don't care. But I'm warning you – get the hell out of here and *don't come back*. Next time I won't be *nearly* as polite.'

They were standing next to the mutated limo before Cosmos had the presence of mind to pull away from George's hand. 'See *here*, young man!' he said, straightening his outfit.

Young man? George thought. This weirdo is no older than I am.

'I know you must be terrified of the power of Satan nipping at your heels and all, but – '

'I'm giving you ten seconds,' George said with frightening calm.

Cosmos pressed on. 'But if you'll simply give me your permission, I will enter your house in Amity and face the

Devil himself. We will wrestle, we will battle, we will fight it out toe to toe, as it were, until I, and I *alone*, emerge the victor.'

'You better get your tubes checked, buddy. We haven't owned the house for months.'

Cosmos goggled, but only for a moment. 'Well – well, then – what about the things that have happened since you left the house?'

That stopped George cold, and Cosmos was cunning enough to read the surprise in his face. 'Aha!' he crowed. 'So things *have* happened to you!'

George jerked open the car door and nearly threw the man inside. 'Get the hell away from here,' he said. 'You make me sick. You and your costumes and your funny cars and your bullshit – '

The man pulled away again, and quite suddenly there was a look of naked, unadorned hatred in his thin, pock-marked face. 'I knew it all along,' Cosmos hissed. 'I *knew* it was a hoax! You *had* to be lying, you *had* to be! I – '

George pushed him into the car and slammed the door on him. Cosmos barely got his fingers and top hat out of the way before the door whammed into place, and as the engine roared to life, George turned away and started up the driveway, muttering to himself about fanatics and moneygrubbers and publicity hounds.

'Where in Heaven's name do they find the money for all this?' he said, shaking his head.

'*You can escape from me, but you can't escape the power of Satan!*'

A grating, electronic version of Cosmos' voice came from the locked car. George turned and gaped at the limo.

'*Think about it, Lutz! You can't comprehend my position with the Lord!*'

George cursed at the car and shook an angry fist at the hidden P.A. system.

'*There is wheat and there is chaff, Lutz! Don't be caught on the far side of the bar when Judgment Day cracks!*'

George couldn't take it anymore. He threw himself at

the limo and *kicked* at the passenger door as hard as he could. It made a satisfying clanging sound and caved in.

Cosmos barely missed a beat. '*And – and there shall be demons of blood, Mr. Lutz, as the sheep are separated from – from the goats –* '

'Get out of here!' George kicked at the limo's fender twice as hard as before. It made an even better sound and almost flew free.

I knew this martial arts training would come in handy someday, he thought gleefully.

Cosmos got the message. The car started to ease forward, but the amplified voice blared on. '*Remember, George Lutz! Remember when Quentin Cosmos came to save your soul, and you turned away! Remember!*' George threw one last kick at the limo's rear end, and hit it squarely in the rumble seat. One hinge broke off and the door dropped, hanging below the bumper. It scraped and sparked on the asphalt as the limo took off, its P.A. still blaring at him.

'*You don't know what you're doing! You don't understand!*'

George shouted, 'Go on! Get out of here! *Get out of here!*' until the limousine was completely out of sight.

After a long moment, Kathy crept out of the house to join him.

'Do you feel better?' she asked.

George turned on her, wild-eyed. 'What?'

She burst out laughing. 'It looked like you got a real thrill out of that. Didn't it make you feel better?'

George grinned and laughed himself. 'Yeah, it did, actually. I feel a *lot* better!' He grabbed her in a massive hug. 'Don't you?'

She threw her arms around his shoulders. 'Yes,' she said, 'as a matter of fact, I do!'

They walked back to the house arm in arm, laughing.

CHAPTER EIGHT

AUSTRALIA, GEORGE thought as he pulled to a halt at the stop sign. The street signs read *Rhododendron Way* and *Elise Court* – pretty, meaningless names in a pretty, meaningless sub-subdivision.

He glanced at the address on the slip of paper taped to the dash. 2047B, it read. Felicia had been very emphatic that he write it down and repeat it to her.

Now he could see why.

Australia, he thought again as he crawled the car past an endless stream of identical red brick houses with the same concrete porches, the same mansard windows, the same green lawns, the same adolescent birch trees and planters.

He and Kathy had never been 'Down Under' before. He still didn't like the idea of leaving the children – not after what had happened last time – but he had to admit it sounded interesting.

'A quick ten days,' Eric had assured him earlier that day. 'That's it. You'll do a few interviews, the Don Lane Show – very big over there, George, believe me – and interviews with the newspapers, *The Sydney Morning Herald*, *The Australian*, and one or two magazines. One short photo session, and you're back home. Promise.'

George remembered grinning slightly at that. 'Just in time to talk about the trip to Japan, I suppose.'

Normally, Eric would have laughed at that. This time he just stared dully at this client and said, 'Pardon me?' He hadn't looked well, George realized now. Not well at all. Almost as if he had a headache – one of *those* kinds of headaches . . .

Ah. 2047B. He pulled up to the curb and parked behind a red Audi. As he turned off the engine he heard a door open somewhere, and the sounds of an afternoon party swelled suddenly – the tinkling of glasses, the babble of conversation and the soft strains of music thrumming behind it all.

He did not want to do this. He did *not* want to suffer through another party. But Felicia had insisted. 'Sandy Dennison and Cal Steiner are interested in talking to you about a possible mini-series,' Felicia had said. 'So I thought it was worth a small get-together.' Her voice was low, confidential. As if it was all part of some grand master-plan. 'Intimate, George. Just a few close friends. Buddy-to-buddy, and all that.'

George sighed and got out of the car. Kathy had had the right idea. Pass on the whole thing. But they hadn't made that much on the book, and all the talk about their share of the movie rights was still just that – *talk*. The simple fact was, they could use the money.

He sighed again as he approached the front door. Well, he thought. If it's *too* strange, I'll make an excuse and leave as quick as I can.

The man had an expression like a basset hound with the croup. His soft wet eyes blinked slowly and he shook his head slowly, back and forth until the dewlaps waved like wet banners. 'It must have been a traumatic time for you and your family,' he said, undertaker-heavy. 'Truly traumatic.'

George stifled the fiftieth sigh of the afternoon and nodded without a word. He looked down at his watch, trying to hide his desperation, then glanced around for a phone.

Forty-five minutes, he thought. That's long enough. I'll call Kathy and tell her I'm on the way home, then make some excuse about being needed there. Some –

'I simply can't imagine the *pressure* you must have – '

'Excuse me,' George said. 'Have to make a call.'

He slipped away, sliding between the 'few close friends' that Felicia had gathered. He didn't know a living soul. And after being drawn into a solid dozen insipid, shallow conversations about everything from psychic phenomenon to Post-Modernism, he doubted if these people *had* any close friends outside the confines of their own skulls. Talk, talk, talk . . .

Felicia was a correct hostess, George noted as he made his way to the front hallway and the phone. Her living room was precisely pleasant, with just the right amount of furniture. Colorful trays and plates of snacks lined the large coffee table, and the built-in bar glittered with bottles of wines and soft drinks. There were clots of people throughout the house, all in deep discussion, all ignoring George.

Oh, they were pleasant enough; they even went out of their way to make him feel comfortable. But there was something strange here – something just under the surface. He and Kathy had come up against it before, far too many times: an unhappy combination of scepticism and simple fear.

He saw a middle-aged woman in a middle-aged bouffant following his path across the room with huge, sad, mascara'd eyes. She virtually oozed pity. George almost thought he could smell it on her.

Pity was the last thing he needed. Sympathy wasn't all that much better. And if he heard one more 'It must have been *terrible*,' from *anybody*, he was going to *scream*.

Three more party-goers were standing a few feet from the phone: a tall, thin-faced woman with fiery red hair and a penetrating, nasal voice; an elegantly dressed older woman with a sour expression and eyes so cold they seemed to stay far back in her head, and a burly, long-haired man built as powerfully as George, with an intent expression and an abundance of focused, friendly energy.

George slipped by them with a nod and began to dial the phone. But he couldn't help overhearing as he stared sullenly at the turning dial.

'. . . couldn't *believe* how scared I was when I read *that book*,' the tall redhead was saying much too loudly. 'And *now*, to find out that it's all *true*, I mean my *God* . . .'

George's finger poised over the last number. His other hand gripped the receiver until his knuckles turned white. Here it comes, he thought, here it –

'*It must have been TERRIBLE for them*!'

He slammed down the phone with a tremendous *clang* and turned on them. 'Of *course* it was terrible!' he said, barely aware he was shouting. 'What do you *think*? But why doesn't anybody ask if anything *good* ever came out of it? If we ever learned anything, or – or *shared* anything because of it?'

The two women and the burly man turned as one and stared at George. In the new silence, he realized that everyone within earshot had stopped talking.

And they were all looking at him.

'I'm . . . sorry,' he stammered, turning back to the phone. 'Didn't mean to interrupt.'

He snatched up the receiver and began to dial again. The sound of conversation stumbled like a broken engine, then started up again. After a moment he heard a piercing laugh – the redhead, no doubt.

''Scuse me, mate. Don't mean to intrude.'

George turned and looked into the smiling face of the bearded man in the leather jacket – the one who had been talking to the women. He had a thick, pleasant accent – not quite Cockney; something like Welsh . . .

He thrust out his hand, and the smile grew wider behind his sandy beard. 'John Jones,' he said. 'We can talk later, if . . .'

George put on a smile himself. He was still embarrassed about the outburst; here was a chance to make amends. He took the oversized, thick-fingered hand in his own and shook it firmly. 'Good to meet you,' he said. 'Sorry about the shouting.'

John Jones waved it away. 'Aah,' he said. 'I don't blame

you. But you have to admit, all we've heard so far – about what's happened to you, I mean – makes it sound pretty horrendous.'

George found himself responding to the smile in spite of himself – that and the wide, flat accent that made the man seem downright charming despite his rather imposing physical presence.

The fact of the matter is, he realized, that John Jones looked a lot like a biker.

'But there *was* a good side to it,' he said. 'I mean, we wish none of it had happened – *none* of it. But we got through it. And we got help, too. Help from . . .'

Others were listening again. They were starting to close in. And no matter how engaging this young foreigner was, he didn't feel like being the center of attention all over again.

John Jones seemed to notice it, too. 'Look. I know you must be up to *here* with questions,' he said, marking an imaginary spot in the air well above his head. 'But if you feel like talking about it, I'd love to hear some of the positive things.'

George looked at him a minute. Then, in spite of the people – in spite of the attention, he nodded decisively. 'All right,' he said. 'Let's go over here.' He led Jones to a quiet corner of the room – a spot where the others would have a hard time overhearing without the real risk of exposing themselves.

And he started to talk.

He hadn't meant to do it at all. He'd only planned to answer a couple of questions and get the hell out of there. But he found himself describing the experiences with the figures in white light. He told the foreigner – an Australian, no less! – about his son's rescue from the riptide by the mysterious man named Michael; about his own ability to ward off the thing from Amityville with the power of an ancient prayer.

But the conversation didn't stop there. Somehow George mentioned the plans for visiting Australia for a promotional tour, and Jones was very interested. Talk of

Sydney and Melbourne led to questions about the Australian's presence in the States, and then to a long talk about their mutual passion for music. George had played drums from an early age through college. John said he was still a singer and songwriter.

'I've been working on some new recording here in the States,' he added. 'Lotta good musos and studios in Los Angeles, y'know.'

Talk of Los Angeles led to talk about cars. George had been a fanatic about them since he could remember; John described the odd breed of autos that inhabited Australia, and mentioned a couple to keep an eye out for.

And cars led to cycles, and cycles to touring, and touring back to the wonders of Australia that Jones said the Lutzes would *have* to see – 'stuff well off the beaten track, mate,' he said, grinning.

Neither of them noticed that the guests were quietly leaving. The light was beginning to fail when John casually glanced at his watch and gaped. 'Damn, look at the time,' he said. 'We've been talking for hours here.'

George was as surprised as he was. 'I better get going,' he said, and got to his feet.

'Me, too.' John thrust out his hand again, and George was happy to take it. He realized as he returned the strong grip that this was the first time in weeks – perhaps *months* – that he had had a long, leisurely conversation outside his own home, and *not* discussed Amityville or the entity or the book or the movie for hours at a stretch.

It was a good feeling. He wanted more of it. He wanted more than anything to put the entire experience behind him – behind them all.

'It's been a lot of fun,' John said sincerely. 'I hope we get a chance to do it again soon.'

'So do I,' George said, and he realized as he did just how much he meant it.

Felicia called the next day to thank him for coming by,

even though nothing had come from the talks about the mini-series. She mentioned John Jones in passing, but she didn't have much to say about him – a recent arrival, a friend of a friend.

It wasn't until three weeks later George discovered that John Jones was more than a musician and auto enthusiast. He was a writer as well.

CHAPTER NINE

'Owww!' TERRI Sullivan cried out in pain as an electric shock charged up her arm and slammed into her elbow. Her keys flew out of her hand and clattered onto the wood porch and she jumped back, shaken.

If it had happened a month ago, she would have run to get someone – at least she would have called the utility company or the locksmith.

But that was a month ago. Before that night. Before she saw that . . . *thing*, and everything started to go crazy.

This is what that book is about, she realized. Tiny, stupid, harrowing things like this that make you go a little bit crazier each time they happen.

She rubbed at the muscles in her forearm and slowly bent down to pick up her key-ring. It was dusk, and the shadows cast by the large, comfortably shabby wooden house were deep and thick as velvet.

Her mother would be home soon. They had been sharing this house for a few months now, and they'd worked out a system: it was Terri's turn to make dinner.

She tentatively tapped at the lock on the door, ready to pull back quickly if it sparked or shocked her.

Nothing. No more sick surprises. She sighed heavily, turned the lock, and went inside, hurrying down the long hallway to the darkening kitchen. She felt exhausted, rough-edged and jumpy as a wounded rabbit.

This is what's happened to them, she realized as she flopped into a kitchen chair. This is why Kathy and George have changed. She had seen them slowly distort over the last few months – seen the fear in their eyes, the heaviness that slowed their steps. And she hadn't understood, she hadn't *accepted* it.

Now she did. Now she felt closer to ninety than nineteen.

Ever since that day. Ever since that voice, that shape, the blackout. Something had happened to her in the slice of time she had lost. Sometimes she could almost remember – could catch a glimpse of it, almost *smell* it . . .

She shrugged and stood up slowly, working up the energy to start the meal. If only the craziness had ended there, she thought. But that had been only the beginning.

A few days later, at the office, a water cooler had exploded like a bomb, not two feet in front of her. The shards of glass came at her like a cloud of knives, but no serious damage was done. *It just scared me out of my gourd*, she thought.

The next night she was positive, *positive* someone was following her home. It was a feeling at the back of her neck – like cold fingers tickling the tiny hairs along her spine. But she hadn't been able to catch anybody – not *quite* – and finally she'd given up. Besides, she thought as she worked in the gray semi-darkness of the kitchen, I kept feeling it even when I was in the elevator, all by myself. How can somebody be watching you when there's not anybody *there*?

Then, that weekend, her hair dryer had tried to kill her. She plugged it in like always, careful to be standing on the rubber mat in front of her sink, careful to keep her long wet hair away from the pistol-shaped machine. She was terrified of electricity; if she could have avoided the dryer completely she would have.

Then the long white cord came alive. It snapped like a whip, rucked up like a tail, and *it wrapped itself around her wrist*. She remembered lurching back, trying to pull away. But the cord *jerked* at her. It pulled her off the mat and into the puddle of water from the shower, right in front of the tub. There was a crackle of electricity dancing over the damn thing, icy blue in the fluorescent light, and the pungent stick of ozone. Terri pulled again, harder, as hard as she could.

Someplace in the back of her mind, even now, she knew that it had been very close – *too* close. The hair dryer's plug had pulled out of the socket and the screaming machine had gone dead in her hand, but if it hadn't, if the plug had stayed in place, she was *sure* it would have gotten her. Even now, days later, she was positive it would have killed her if it had had the chance.

She had thrown out the cursed thing after that. And she didn't care if her thick blonde hair *did* look a little frowsy sometimes, she wasn't going to do that again.

But the worst part of all, she thought, is not being able to forget about *that book*. She had been compelled, *forced* to sit down and read it after she'd seen that – that *thing* at the Lutz' house. And now the images haunted her day and night. She imagined every shadow was filled with flies. She heard running water, and thought of the black muck that welled up out of the pipes. And every twinge, every passing pain, was the first sign of a killing headache that would make her go mad.

Stop it, she ordered herself. She pulled open the refrigerator so quickly the jars and bottles clattered loudly on the door shelf. *Stop it*. You're just making yourself crazy, you're just –

Something moved in the corner of the room. Something off to the left.

Terri froze, an eerie silver in the light of the refrigerator door. Slowly, *slowly*, she turned to her left.

Maybe it's my mother coming in. Or a reflection from the road. Maybe a bird got caught in the curtains, oh *please* let it be a bird . . .

There was nothing there. Not even a hint of movement. She felt her heart pounding in her chest and she gulped in air, forcing herself to relax. *No more*, she pleaded. *No more*.

Then it came to get her. The thing she had forgotten about.

At first it was only a nasty smell – the thick, unhealthy odor of something dead and decaying. Terri wrinkled her nose at it and tried not to inhale. Not *again*, she thought, almost annoyed –

– and then suddenly she remembered what her mind had forced away.

The smell. It had been there when the hair dryer came alive in her hand, on top of the cutting ozone, tearing at her brain.

It had clawed at her throat when the water cooler began to rumble and quake. When it blew up right in her face.

In the parking garage. In the elevator. Lurking outside her door. When she thought she was being followed, it was *there*, it was *waiting*, and it wasn't any odor at all, it wasn't just a stink. It was a physical thing, a *force*, that wrapped itself around her throat and squeezed and squeezed and *squeezed*.

Oh! God! *It was in Amy's bedroom*! It came to Terri in a horrifying rush, with the image of the pig-thing, with the forgotten horror. It was part of the thing she was running from – the force of the creature reaching out to strangle her, smother her –

kill her!

Abby Sullivan dropped the bag of groceries on the kitchen floor. It exploded like a bomb, green vegetables and canned goods flying in all directions.

Her daughter was lying on the floor, clutching at her face. She was white and bloodless when Abby came in, and as she ran to her, as she knelt helplessly by her side, she saw the teenager begin to turn blue.

'Terri! What is it?'

The girl writhed on the floor, gasping.

'Terri! TERRI!'

She could hear her mother's voice, somewhere in the distance. But she couldn't answer: She couldn't speak. Everything was spinning around. The smell had become a boundless green and blue *thing*, a cloud with claws, that was ripping her throat away.

God, she thought dimly as the thing wrapped around her. *God, God* . . .

CHAPTER TEN

OMINOUS CLOUDS blackened the cerulean sky above Mission Bay, but George and Kathy Lutz ignored the harbingers of rain, gliding lightly over the choppy water in a rented sailboat.

Kathy tucked herself into the hollow of George's arm as he leaned against the large wooden tiller. Harry, the family dog, was sprawled in the bow of the small boat, eyes closed and muzzle pushed forward, enjoying the breeze that whispered in his whiskers.

'Look at Harry,' George laughed as he pulled his windbreaker more tightly around his chest. He eased the tiller to the right and steered more directly into the rising wind.

'He hasn't got a care in the world,' Kathy said, laughing with him. She looked up at George and her eyes sparkled. 'This was a nice idea, babe. Getting away for a while, just the two of us.'

He smiled, though his eyes never left the sea ahead of them. Kathy knew he was as happy to be here as she was. He loved boats, and they'd had pitifully few chances to get away like this and just . . . relax. To do nothing but enjoy each other.

She could feel the tension easing from his body. She smiled even wider and turned her face to the wind, enjoying the pleasant sting of the salt-spray peppering her forehead, her cheeks, her lips, even the edges of her ears. We need this kind of healing, she realized.

Mission Bay was dotted with small sailboats and larger yachts. The billowing polychrome spinnakers and the scurrying crews stood out in bright profusion against the cobalt sea. As the wind picked up, the crews moved more quickly than ever: trimming sails, securing sheets, adjusting courses. Some of the less hardy sailors turned to head back to shore, but most of the boats stayed out, bucking in the current and rising wind. They looked almost eager to face the challenge.

Darkening clouds swallowed the sun. The wind chilled slightly as it shifted direction.

'Nice-looking craft,' George said, pointing to one of the few cabin cruisers swimming gracefully through the inlet. 'Forty-five footer, I'd guess.' He flashed a mischievous grin at his wife. 'Think you could handle owning one of those – just for fun?'

'Oh, it'd be hard,' she chuckled, 'but I guess I could get used to it.'

A huge drop of rain splashed on Kathy's nose and she jumped. They both laughed.

'Uh-oh! I think we're about to hit hard weather, Captain-Sir!'

'Don't be ridiculous, first mate,' George said in his sceptical captain's voice. He put out his hand palm up.

As if on cue, the cloud split open and the rain poured down in torrents. The surface of the sea boiled in the downpour, and George's outstretched hand was drenched in an instant.

'On the other hand . . .' he said blithely.

Kathy grabbed the large yellow waterproof tarp they had brought along and pulled it up around them.

Harry was on his feet, barking at the rain. He tired of that in a moment and quickly clambered back to Kathy and George, nudging at the edge of the tarp until Kathy lifted it and let him slip under.

'Good boy,' she said. 'Little wet out there for you?'

Harry shook himself off in one long rippling motion. Water flew in every direction, threatening to drown the Lutzes all over again.

'*Harry*!' Kathy's indignation broke into laughter. The dog looked up, tongue lolling, then licked her face. Kathy pushed gently at him until he finally laid down under the far edge of the cover.

'Well, matey,' George said mock-seriously. 'I suppose it's *possible* we might get a little pre-cip-eye-tation. I'll head for yonder small island just in case, eh wot?'

His attempt at an English accent was terrible, but they couldn't keep from laughing. It must have seemed strange to anyone going by, but they didn't care. It was wonderful to be able to laugh. Just to *laugh*.

A few minutes later, the boat was rocking gently at its mooring on the leeward side of one of Mission Bay's many small islands. Kathy and George snuggled warmly under their tarp.

She opened the thermos and poured coffee as the rain played a musical tattoo on the makeshift tent. George lifted the flap and checked the weather.

The rain was already easing. Across the bay, shafts of light broke through the heavy cloud cover, and the water glittered like polished stone.

'Shouldn't last much longer,' he said.

'Let it,' Kathy answered. 'I'm having a fine time.'

She eased down next to him, sipping the coffee, enjoying the feeling of not thinking at all.

'How do you feel about the trip to Australia?' George asked gently.

It caught her off guard. She felt an unpleasant, out-of-scale anger welling up, but she quelled it.

'Just the two of us?' she said, frowning.

'I don't think it would be good for the kids to be uprooted from school and friends,' he said, thinking. 'The publisher probably wouldn't pick up the tab anyway.'

Kathy thought for a moment, then sighed heavily. 'All right,' she said. 'Who knows? It might even be nice.'

George reached out and drew her to him. His broad arms encircled her shoulder as he gently stroked her hair. 'That's what I thought,' he said. 'They have interviews and appearances scheduled for about three weeks. Maybe after that we could take an extra week and just relax.'

'I could call my mother and get Helen and Carrie Innes' number,' she added hopefully. 'It would be nice to see them again. And maybe if we get away from here –'

She didn't have to finish the thought. They both knew what she meant.

The rain whispered more softly against the tarp as they hugged each other tightly.

'How did all this happen, babe?' Kathy asked softly. 'What did we do to deserve it? It sounds silly, I know, but . . . *why us?*'

George had heard Kathy close to breaking down when she'd asked questions like this before. But now she was calm, even relaxed. She sounded more honestly confused than afraid, for the first time in a long while.

'I don't know, Kath. I wish I did. Then maybe there'd be something I could do, something . . .'

His words trailed off.

'I saw a talk show today on television,' she said, changing the subject. 'Two experts in the field – they *said* – and two – I don't know, restaurant critics or something – were arguing about whether things like this really happen.'

George grinned in spite of himself and said, 'Oh? What did they decide?'

Kathy grinned back and tried not to laugh. She'd started out half-serious, but – God, it was so *stupid*. 'They decided it was all a case of mass hysteria,' she told him.

George started to laugh. 'Oh, *really?*'

'– brought on by the publicity things like this get.' She was laughing too.

He couldn't stop now. 'Oh, good!' he said, holding his side. 'Then we have nothing to worry about!'

Now neither of them could stop. They had a full-on case of the giggles. George and Kathy had never actually *joked* about what was happening to them, never actually *laughed*, and even as George wiped away tears and gasped for breath, he knew it was helping them in some unexpected way.

It was a lovely afternoon – the first in a long, long time.

101

Later that night, they weren't laughing.

Amy and Matt were already in bed. Greg was staying over at a friend's house. George and Kathy were relaxing in the living room, watching a Steve Martin TV special.

They both laughed at the opening segment, and snickered at a second, longer skit.

If Greg were here, he'd be in heaven, George thought as he watched. Steve Martin was one of his son's favorites right now – though if he said 'EXCUUUUSE ME!!' one more time, he would lock him in his closet. At the moment, however, he couldn't blame his son. George found himself laughing at the silliness in spite of himself, and Kathy was tittering away in the chair next to him.

Their laughter stopped abruptly as the next skit began.

There was the Amityville house – not their own, but the one the movie had made famous. And there was Steve Martin in a loud sports jacket, standing next to the 'FOR SALE' sign on the house's front lawn, trying to unload it on an unsuspecting couple like a desperate used car salesman.

If they could have looked at it objectively, it probably would have been funny – particularly as moaning started to come from the house, and smoke belched from an upper story, and Steve the salesman got more and more nervous.

But they weren't objective. And it wasn't funny – not to the Lutzes.

George got up and changed the channel without a word. Neither of them spoke as he found an old Humphrey Bogart movie. They sat and watched the black and white images flickering on the screen for a long time without seeing them. George was thinking – worrying.

Was this what we can expect from now on? he asked himself. Was this what it came down to? It was one thing to appear on radio and TV talks shows. And having hosts suddenly introduce some bogus 'resident psychic' who would invariably start questioning their credibility – even that was expected by now. At least it was straightforward and answerable. He and Kathy could respond to their questions. They could tell the truth. And then the audience could decide what they would believe.

But this was different. Ever since the movie had been released, their story had taken on a whole new dimension. It wasn't *real* anymore; it was a symbol, a catchphrase, a set of images that showed up in political cartoons, in stand-up comedy routines – even on TV skits.

Everyone had conveniently forgotten that it wasn't just a scary story. It had *really* happened, to a *real* family. And at the moment, all the skits and stunts and snappy comebacks seemed directed right at them. Pot shots taken at long range.

Kathy looked up from the movie, a worried frown on her face. He pretended to be intent on the film until he saw her turn away.

How do you handle something like this? he wondered. How do you act when your life becomes an international joke?

CHAPTER ELEVEN

THE BATTERED Volkswagen swerved as it turned sharply onto the calm residential street, its balding tires screeching against the asphalt. The engine sputtered as Terri stamped on the accelerator, and coughed again when she bounced unceremoniously into the Lutz' driveway.

George was coming out of the front door, his arms full. Terri was out of her car in an instant, almost stumbling as she ran to him.

George looked surprised. 'What happened?'

Terri frowned and gave a frustrated snort. 'Problems! There was a bad accident on the freeway – a *huge* traffic jam. I was trapped. Couldn't even get to the next exit.'

George put down his two substantial suitcases and flexed his arms. 'That's okay,' he said easily. 'Kathy's just finishing up. We'll make the plane in plenty of time.'

Kathy emerged from the house with a suitcase in one hand and an overstuffed bag hanging from the opposite shoulder. Matt and Greg trooped behind her like dutiful soldiers, both with loads of their own. Amy brought up the rear, struggling with a leather camera case that hung around her neck.

As if on cue, a bright red taxi cab pulled up in front of the house.

'Hello, Terri,' Kathy said lightly. 'We were getting a little worried about you.'

In spite of herself, Terri glanced up at the empty house. A chill went through her, but she shrugged it away. *Remember what Philip Kaufman said*, she reminded herself. *Confront it.* 'Any . . . last minute lists? Notes?' She remembered how flustered Kathy had been just before their last trip, months ago.

Kathy shook her head as she handed her bags to the cabbie. 'Not a thing. You've got all the numbers where we'll be.' Terri saw her steal a look at the children, busily loading up the taxi with George.

The teenager put a hand on Kathy's arm. 'Don't worry,' she said gently. 'I'll take good care of them.'

Kathy put on a brave smile. 'I know.'

Then she said goodbye to her three children very slowly, one at a time. She brushed the hair out of Greg's eyes and kissed him on the cheek. She straightened Matt's collar and gave him a brief, tight hug. Then she bent down and lifted her little girl, camera case and all, off the ground.

'Be good now, okay?' she said to them all, and Terri could hear her trying to keep the tremble out of her voice.

'Okay!' they chorused. George opened the door to the taxi, and Kathy put her daughter down and climbed in without a word, her lips pressed tightly together. George slid in beside her and rolled down the window.

'Have a wonderful time,' Terri said warmly. She was trying to keep the tremble out of her own voice, she realized.

'Don't forget my boomerang,' Greg added.

'Or my bird pictures,' Matt piped up.

'Koala bear!' Amy crowed.

'Oh,' George said, remembering something. 'You might get a call from a fellow named John Jones. He's the one working on the sequel? He might have some questions, so tell him I'll call as soon as we get back.'

'Fine.'

He looked down at the children again, and Terri could see tears filling his eyes. He turned away gruffly, tapped the seat in front of him, and said, 'Whenever you're ready.'

The children and their guardian watched the cab until it was completely out of sight. Then they watched a moment longer. Finally Terri turned to face the house where she would be staying for the next three weeks. *Remember what Philip said*, she repeated. *Confront it. Confront it.*

'Come on,' she said, taking little Amy's hand. 'Let's go inside.'

Kathy watched George check his pockets for the twentieth time in fifteen minutes. She knew what he was doing: feeling for the traveller's checks, the airline tickets, the passports. They were all there. They had been there when he'd checked a minute earlier, and the minute before that.

'Did we forget anything?' he said absently. Kathy looked closely at him and saw how tired he was. *Really* tired.

'I checked everything,' she said in a low voice. 'Why don't you lie back and get some rest, babe?'

'I'll sleep on the plane.' George patted his coat pocket again.

She had hoped this trip would be a real vacation for them. He had been working so hard, trying to find a steady job, negotiating all those silly deals. And then that too-quick tour of the Midwest had come along, delaying Australia and Japan and everything else. It was beginning to take its toll.

At least it's far away, she thought. Maybe even far enough away for us to finally get some peace.

'The feature film will begin shortly in all the aft cabins. To aid in the viewing comfort of all passengers, please switch off your overhead reading light if it is not in use. Thank you.'

The heavy Australian accent of the airline steward buzzed in the overhead speakers of the blue-area economy section on the Qantas jumbo jet. Between the dialect and the amplification, no more than every other word was intelligible.

It was clearer for Kathy. It abruptly cut into the soothing

music that whispered in her earphones. She looked over from her window seat to check on George. He was already slumped in his seat, deeply asleep.

Kathy turned away from the moonlit alabaster landscape of cloudtops beneath her, eased down the window shade and pulled at the small brown blanket in George's lap. It was clean and well-made, but far too small. She pulled the spare from the empty center seat, slipped it from its plastic cover, and draped both of them around her husband.

George groaned slightly and ran his tongue over his lips. She heard a soft clicking sound come from him – a sound he only made when he was fast asleep and dreaming.

Make it a good dream, Kathy prayed. A hostess pulled down the projector from the overhead carry racks and opened the cover on the small screen ahead of them. George barely stirred.

Kathy settled down to watch the film – some spy movie she had ignored when it came to the San Diego theaters. The titles were scarcely finished before she felt her eyes drooping. It was the semi-darkness, and the long day of packing, and the gentle, purring rhythm of the jet engines . . .

George was drifting. Not thinking or feeling or doing, just . . . *drifting*. A soft, throbbing *purr* pulsed around him. He felt oddly content. Even happy.

Without opening his eyes – without really using his eyes at all – he looked out. Not up or down or side to side, just . . . *out*. And, as if in the distance, as if in a fog, he perceived a group of people packed tightly together in a long, metallic tube. Most of them had discs and wires draped around their heads. A few were staring at a flickering square of light on the wall in front of them.

. . . Headphones, he thought. The term drifted into his mind and then drifted out again. Movies. Airplanes. They didn't seem to mean much. They didn't seem to be connected to *him*, somehow.

One of the people looked familiar. She was sleeping in her chair, with a set of headphones half on and half off.

Kathy, he realized. Her name was Kathy. And next to her was . . . *him*. George Lutz. Suddenly, he understood – in a soft, distant sort of way.

He was out of his body. He was looking at the scene from outside – elsewhere.

It felt marvelous.

The soft, thrumming roar of the engines was suddenly ripped, fractured by a deafening sonic boom. The outside-George bounced against it, suddenly jarred and on edge. No one in the plane seemed to notice. Nothing else seemed to change. Except –

– there was something hanging over his sleeping body. Something . . . *grotesque*.

It was a twisted, writhing thing, but it was no cloud, no misty semi-solid. It was real, and hard-edged . . . hideous.

The elongated body was a chitonous black shell. Incredibly long, multi-jointed arms, thin and twisted as the roots of trees, stretched out of knobby shoulders and terminated in – God, George thought, are those *hands*? They were impossibly long and thin. They seemed to bend in six or seven places, bulging with thick, swollen knuckles and glittering with talons or . . . claws.

But the head was worst of all. Shaped like an ostrich egg, completely hairless, the gray and wrinkled flex was scarred and pockmarked, twisted and cystic. Pustulant swellings hung over the cavities where the eyes were hidden. Thick bristles encircled a pair of stumpy tusks on each side of a snout, thick and flat as a boar's, that dripped a foul yellowish liquid. Directly below it an enormous set of blackened, razor-sharp incisors thrust forward and down.

And for all its solidity, all its *weight*, it seemed to George to be a construct of some sort – a temporary form, a transitory phase. Like a hideous moth only half-emerged from its cocoon.

Abomination, George thought. It was a word from the Bible, heavy with meaning for him. *Abomination*.

The thing spread its maw, and a sibilant rattle oozed out. The stick-like arms opened wider. The talons spread.

It was descending. It was drifting toward the Lutzes.

'NOOOO!'

George screamed in fear and horror, and the abomination whirled about to face him. The shout, he realized, should have roused everyone on the plane. No one stirred.

The thing streaked forward, talons thrust out. George's own insubstantial form darted to the side as if under some power of its own, but as he moved he felt a tidal wave of emotion sweep over him. A suffocating gray wave.

Defeat. Doom. Despair. It gushed from the creature like a physical force, and he knew he was drowning . . . drowning . . .

I'm lost, he thought. *I put up a good fight, but I can't . . . can't . . .*

The abomination was directly in front of him. Its shifting, gray-green face was only inches away. And George felt himself staring deep into the bottomless caverns where its eyes should have been. He started to lose hold. To fall . . .

Images bubbled and boiled there – images of a blue-black mist, with icy indigo flames flashing in the dark. There were creatures there – blind, fingerless things that had never known light. And the stink was a sharpened claw, cutting deeply into the brain.

George felt himself being pulled in. With a force far stronger than gravitation, it was dragging at him, pulling him.

Got to get away . . . he thought through the darkening clouds of despair.

He glanced down at his sleeping body.

He was closer to the eyes. He was almost gone.

Got to be a way out!

At his sleeping body . . . sleeping . . .

WAKE UP!

George's body leaped up, lurching forward with tremendous force. He was half on his feet, groping for the seat ahead of him to keep from falling.

But his brain was back in his body. He was wholly, horribly awake now, seeing the plane and the passengers with a metallic clarity.

I've never done that before, he thought, listening to his heart laboring in his throat, trying to calm his shaking hands and get his legs solidly under him. I've always been *trapped* in the dreams before, locked in the nightmare.

But the thing – the abomination – had been different this time. More physical, more *real*, and not just a shapeless pain in his head. It was as though taking on physical form had weakened the entity's hold on George's mind. As if there was some exchange between the mental strength and material power.

Somehow, he instinctively knew, that as their seven-year sentence to Hell grew shorter, the entity itself was becoming desperate. It was *changing*, groping for ways to attack them before time ran out.

George turned to look down at his sleeping wife. She was huddled uncomfortably in her seat, the movie headset pinned under one ear and dangling loosely from the other. The entire cabin, he saw, was bathed in a rapidly changing, kaleidoscopic dance of colors streaming from the motion picture projector.

It was all very peaceful. He thought, for a moment, he could almost fall asleep again . . .

No. He straightened up abruptly. He wasn't ready for that, wasn't ready to face the abomination from his unconscious – or elsewhere. At least not yet.

He stretched mightily and decided to walk – at least stretch his legs in the aisle. Careful not to disturb his wife, he slipped from the seat and turned towards the back of the plane, aware of the confining space and darkness for the first time.

He hadn't realized how empty the flight really was – not until now. The section he and Kathy were in was sparsely seated. But there were only seven passengers in the entire rear section – the orange-area economy section – and all but one of them were stretched out across the four center seats, dozing.

As he passed the rear galley and entered the orange section he smiled at the one hardy soul who was watching the spy movie. She was in the ninth row, center aisle, sitting up straight and completely enthralled by the film. She was about twenty, almost pretty, and her curly blonde hair fluffed out on both sides of the headset.

Like Mousketeer ears, George thought wryly as he moved past the young woman. He smiled as he worked his way back towards the lavatories at the rear of the fuselage. The wide-awake woman was the last passenger to the rear. Behind her was row after row of empty seats, looking lonely and full of shadows in the dim overhead light.

I'll just splash a little water on my face, George thought. Try to get interested in that terrible –

He froze in the center of the aisle. His breathing stopped. His hands grew icy. For an instant even his heart grew silent.

The abomination was floating in the center of the aisle less than ten feet in front of him.

He put his hands over his face and pressed – *hard*. He ground his knuckles into his sockets and looked again.

God, he thought. It's there, *it's there*!

It was nine feet tall, a slimy, glittering gray-green. Its spindly arms stretched out over the empty seats. The fingers crooked towards him.

The maw opened wide. A silent voice hissed in his brain. FIRST YOU, GEORGE LUTZ, it whispered to him. The voice was a congealing rumble of scratch. FIRST YOU. THEN THE WOMAN. THEN THE REST OF THEM HERE.

George stepped back as it raised an arm and swept it out, as if to cover the passengers – to take possession. The creature's shadow, black as bile, passed over George. He flinched at the stinking darkness.

Another chill passed through him. *A shadow*, he thought, and his eyes grew wider than ever. *My God, it's real! IT'S CASTING A SHADOW!*

The creature floated toward him. Its talons glittered in the dusk. BELIEVE IT, GEORGE. A TERRIBLE ACCIDENT. NO SURVIVORS, GEORGE. NO SURVIVORS. NO SURVIVORS . . .

Something broke open in George Lutz. All the fear, all the months of hatred and hopelessness he had locked away suddenly burst open. He threw himself at the creature, arms thrust forward, fingers arced like claws of his own.

It tried to dart out of the way, as George's own mind had done earlier. It couldn't move fast enough.

George's hands clutched at the creature's pulsating throat. His fingers closed around it and he squeezed. And squeezed. And squeezed.

The cutting stench sliced into him again. George bit down on his tongue until he tasted blood and squeezed. And squeezed.

A dark muck oozed and bubbled from the abomination's pores. It gushed over his hands, and the creature wriggled like a huge fish, trying to escape.

George refused to let go. He dug deeper and squeezed. *Die,* he ordered it. *Die, DIE!*

The creature struck back.

It was a blast of sound and black light, a blow so strong he was blinded for an instant. But his hands held. They *held*.

The razor teeth pushed forward, protruding from split lips. Clear venom dripped from their tips and sizzled as it hit the burnt-orange carpet.

And it began to pull free. It began to take George down.

As his fingers started to slip, George knew, he *knew* he couldn't defeat the thing – at least not alone.

He thought of the white light – the energy from elsewhere that had helped him before. Part of him hated the idea – hated having to ask for help again, to be the victim once more. But he had to get free of it, he had to escape.

Help me, he pleaded. *Please help –*

The abomination broke free. With a tremendous *shove*, George's hands flew from its throat and the creature reared back, larger than ever. Its tree-branched arms flailed in the air. The dripping maw gaped wide as it rose, waving, hissing in his mind:

NOW, GEORGE! NOW!

One slashing talon collided with an overhead lamp and shattered it. Plastic caromed off the carpeted wall of the plane, and a new, harsh light shot out. George lurched back, out of range, as a darker, sharper shadow stabbed –

– and fell on the seat where the blonde woman passenger sat.

It made her flinch. For the first time she seemed to notice what was happening only a few feet behind her, and George watched in horror as she peeled the headphones away and turned in her seat to see –

– to see –

The woman froze like a wax figure. Her eyes bulged wide – so wide George could see the ball standing halfway out of the socket, white fully encircling the cornflower iris.

She sees it, he realized. *She sees it, too!* The damn thing is real, and it's coming for me!

HELP ME! he screamed in his mind.

He threw himself on the abomination one final time, and from outside – from beyond himself – the pure, impossible energy he had experienced before flowed into him.

Strength swelled in his arms – *white* strength, pure strength. An all encompassing warmth rippled into his muscles.

Suddenly renewed George's hands were steel clamps. Squeezing. Crushing.

The abomination's chuckling growl cut off as George's fingers closed around its throat. It coughed. It shuddered.

And the weirdling creature began to *shriek*.

This part, George knew, was only in his mind. It made his brain twitch in its skull as if it wanted to explode, but the thing was screaming, screaming in *pain*.

He gritted his teeth against the agony and squeezed on the creature's throat. And squeezed. And squeezed. And *squeezed* –

George Lutz' hands suddenly rammed together. The pain of the blow bolted up his arms. And he fell to one knee in the center of the aisle, all alone. Completely exhausted.

The creature had vanished.

He drew in a long, cool breath of sterilized airline atmosphere. He looked at the palms of his open hands and saw slime – thick globs of muck – dripping between his fingers.

There, on the floor, was a dark stain that stank of death.

There, above him, was a shattered light fixture that the creature had struck.

It wasn't a dream anymore, he realized. Not just a mind-game or hallucination. And though it had always been real to them, now it was real to *everyone* – even innocent bystanders.

George struggled to his feet and turned to face the blonde woman – the new innocent bystander. who had glimpsed the gateway to hell.

She was still staring – staring at the empty place in the air where the creature had hovered. He realized dimly that the whole struggle had taken no more than a minute or two. That the hostesses and stewards in the other sections of the plane hadn't sensed a thing; that the other passengers were still fast asleep.

But this woman. This poor woman.

After a long moment, the passenger's eyes shifted. Her head jerked, moving unnaturally, like a mechanical toy. She looked straight at George, and for an instant he thought he would fall again – into a brand new kind of madness, one of wholly human manufacture.

And then . . . she turned away. She straightened in her seat. She replaced the earphones and looked back at the screen. As George watched tears streamed down the woman's cheeks – painful, hot tears that turned her cheeks scarlet, even in the dim light.

He didn't try to talk to her. He couldn't bear the result if she pushed it away. And he wouldn't blame her for trying.

He left her to herself and stumbled blindly to the nearest lavatory.

The stench from the dark muck, caked on his hands, was becoming unbearable.

Standing at the tiny metal sink in the small lavatory, he scrubbed his hands for the third time, squeezing them tightly together. Foaming on more and more soap.

The slimy mess was gone, flushed down the sink. But George could still smell it on his hands. He realized it couldn't be. The two bars of soap he'd used were heavily scented. His hands were red from so much washing. He realized it was true. Knew it must be true.

But each time he decided that was enough, he would remember the *beast* . . . and then the *smell* . . . and begin scrubbing again.

George Lutz finally left the lavatory and headed back toward his seat.

The blonde girl was sleeping now – probably dreaming horrible dreams that George didn't want to even think about. He padded gently by, and on into the blue-area section.

Kathy was snoring softly as he slipped into the seat next to her, weary beyond words.

Yet the weariness was tinged with a new feeling. He was much too tired right now to try and understand why, but there was a sensation of *hope*.

He laid his head back against the seatcover and sighed. In seconds he was asleep. In the days to come, he would remember that sleep as the most wonderful he had ever known.

CHAPTER TWELVE

TERRI SULLIVAN picked up the empty plastic garbage cans, one in each hand, and hauled them back from the curb to the side of the Lutz' house. *I don't know how Kathy does it*, she thought, putting the black rubber lids on tightly as she wrestled the containers to the garage wall. Handling all these chores, taking care of the kids, and still getting through everything that's happened to them.

–that's happening to me, too, she added unwillingly.

She dusted off her hands as she headed back up the driveway, feeling a mild sense of satisfaction. She was finally getting caught up. The kids were off to school, the house was clean, and her mother wouldn't be by for a visit for another hour or so. That would give her plenty of time to –

A whimpering howl pulled her up short. She turned toward it and frowned.

It was coming from behind the house.

'Harry?' she said, stepping forward. It didn't sound like him, but . . .

The whimpering grew sharper. 'Harry?' she said again. Terri opened the latch on the high wooden gate and almost tiptoed into the wide, neatly trimmed lawn.

Harry was cringing against the back of the house, a trembling black mound of fur.

'What is it, boy?'

The dog didn't move. He had burrowed a shallow rut beneath the foundation; now he was trying to hide in it. But the hole was far too small, and the dog's black rump stuck up into the air. His tail scooped down between his shaking legs, and his back paws scrabbled at the dirt, trying to drive him even deeper into his hiding place.

'Harry, come out of there,' Terri said. 'You know you're not supposed to dig holes.'

Harry's whimper cut her off. She realized there was an entirely different edge to it – an edge of *fear*.

Her hand touched the black fur on the dog's back, and he shuddered convulsively. The legs scrabbled harder than ever, and Terri realized he was trying to dig deeper – to get away.

'It's all right,' she whispered gently, still stroking his matted fur. 'It's all right.' Her calm voice seemed to reach the animal, and slowly he stopped shaking. 'There. That's better,' she whispered, rubbing his back. She insinuated three fingers under his collar and pulled firmly. 'Now come on out. Everything's okay, there's nothing to be afraid of.'

Terri listened to her own words and smiled grimly. Harry had been through things with the Lutzes that she could never hope to understand, she realized. Maybe he knew what to be afraid of a lot better than *she* did.

She'd read about the amazing abilities of animals – even insects and birds. About that sixth sense that let them detect things humans couldn't. Maybe . . .

She turned quickly and looked around the yard. It was empty. Everything seemed normal.

'Come on, Harry,' she told the dog, more firmly this time. 'We can handle it . . . whatever it is.'

Terri tried to put as much conviction into her words as she could muster – as much for herself as for Harry. She knew her energy level was at its lowest ebb. She felt as tired and depressed as she'd ever been, and try as she might she couldn't seem to break out of it.

She didn't even want to *think* about how it had all begun . . .

She'd tried to block it all out. She'd convinced herself that she had just imagined a lot of strange things. Philip Kaufman, a psychiatrist friend of hers, had helped a lot.

Harry just kept whimpering. 'Come *on*, dog,' she said.

'Come *on*.' She pulled sharply at the collar, and Harry backed up a foot, completely against his will. The whimpering turned to a wailing.

Philip had been a teacher when she was in college. She'd met him half-accidentally at the student union one day, and they'd been close friends ever since. When everything in the Lutz' house had become too much for her, Terri had called him and asked him out to dinner.

During the meal, she had started from the beginning and told him everything that had happened – at least, everything she could remember.

Halfway through her story, Philip Kaufman stopped smiling.

By the time she finished, he was frowning like an old man.

'Harry! Come *on*!' She was losing her patience. She *jerked* at the collar hard, and Harry was dragged backwards. He still tried to drive his head into the ground, scraping it painfully in the grass as he yelped and whimpered and cried . . .

'Remember old Professor Sallinger?' Philip had said. The response to her story had brought her up short. Terri remembered blinking in surprise.

'Sure,' she conceded. 'Our prune-faced old instructor from Psychology 101.'

Philip nodded and raised one finger in Professor Sallinger's unique, crook-fingered gesture. He twisted his face and half-frowned, half-grinned, like the eccentric old Viennese emeritus had always done. When his voice grated out, it was an exact duplicate of the teacher's gravelly East European foghorn.

'Never underestimate de capability of de human psyche!' he trumpeted, waving his crooked finger. Terri couldn't help but laugh. It was a perfect imitation. 'Delusion!' Philip continued. 'Delusion is de most powerful and insidious of all psychological dysfunctions, and *vy*? Because de subject truly *believes* – No! In fact, he *knows* dat vut is happening is true, und dere is liddle likely to shake dat conviction.'

Terri giggled, and Philip broke into a sunny, non-Sallinger smile. 'Nein?' he said, and they both broke up.

'Harry, *stop it*!' Terri lost her temper. She grabbed at the dog, tried to straighten him up. There was nothing wrong, nothing *there*, why did he *have* to –

Harry turned on her. He thrust his paws out straight in front of him, braced himself for a leap with his back legs and snarled at her – *snarled* like a wild animal.

Terri backed off fast. There was spittle dripping from the dog's fangs. His eyes were rimmed in red, showing whites all around.

He started to bark – loud, rough barking, unlike any she'd ever heard from him.

'Calm down,' she said shakily. 'Come on, boy, *calm down*.'

He barked louder. Faster. He took two shuffling steps toward her, as if readying himself for a leap, and Terri backed up, suddenly chilled. Was the dog crazy? Did it have some sort of disease?

Louder. Faster. Harry couldn't seem to stop barking. It came out of him in choking gusts, spittle flying, a tangled roar without breath that came faster and rougher and faster and *faster* –

The dog stopped. Stiffened. For one horrible instant he raised off his front paws, lifted into the air as if by invisible wires, twitching like a puppet . . . and fell.

He landed on his side with a sickening *thud*. Terri knelt and put a hand on the dog's side without thinking, and for a long, terrifying moment she could find no heartbeat, feel no breath.

Then Harry's stomach swelled like a balloon, taking in one huge, grateful breath. He started to pant like a puppy, and slowly, very slowly, he lifted his head from the ground and looked at her – a dim, gummy, half-asleep look.

'It's okay, boy,' she said. 'It's okay.' Terri realized for the first time that she was crying. She brushed the tears away with the back of one hand, but she still petted the dog, still kept a hand on him, as if the touch was all that was bringing him back to life.

Harry struggled to his feet, almost too weak to stand. He staggered forward, into Terri, and for an instant she imagined that he was going to attack again, to sink his jaws into her face . . .

Then his tongue came out and licked her across the cheeks – a long, wet, typically slobbery sign of affection. Terri put her arms around the dog's furry shoulders and hugged.

'It's going to be okay,' she whispered to him, pulling him gently behind her as she stumbled through the rear door. 'It's going to be okay.'

Please, she prayed. *Please*.

As Harry drank half a gallon of water and nibbled weakly at an extra helping of food, Terri thought of all that Philip had said – during the dinner, and in a number of meetings afterwards. 'Look at it objectively,' he had said. 'You're working for a family who *says* they've been – what? Haunted? You've read about their experiences. Obviously, you've thought about it a lot, too. Is it really so surprising that you've been caught up in it all? That your own fears and anxieties are being expressed in this weird, kind of supernatural way?'

She had told him what was bothering her – typical teenage problems that had nothing to do with the Lutzes and the house. Boyfriends. Trouble with her mother, though she loved her very much. Worrying about what would happen after college, about money and friends and being lonely . . .

She remembered how firm and serious he had been. 'You better face the truth, Terri, and quickly. There's a real possibility of this becoming an obsession. You could lose track of what's real, and what's purely imagination.'

'It was as real as we are,' Terri had said. 'As real as us sitting here.'

'That's exactly my point.' he had said.

Confront it, he had told her in half a dozen sessions –

'get-togethers,' Philip had called it since he had refused to accept her as a patient. *Confront it*. She had been less than overjoyed when Kathy had called and asked her to take care of the children while they went to Australia, but . . .

'Going back to the house will put an end to it,' he had said confidently. 'It may be the only thing that will convince you that it's a delusion.'

Now she was back in the house. Now she was tired, and drained, and the dog was acting crazy, and she was starting to feel that something, something *awful* was waiting for her.

The dog wasn't eating any more. She couldn't hear him at all. She cringed inside as she called his name and crept timidly into the kitchen.

'Harry? Harry, are you . . . ?'

She found him curled in the center of the kitchen floor, on his favorite scrap of rug. He was fast asleep, snoring peacefully.

He was perfectly fine.

'You look terrible,' Abby Sullivan said when Terri answered the door.

'I love you, too.' Terri snapped back. It was a poor attempt at a joke.

The slim, middle-aged woman put her hands on her daughter's shoulders and looked deeply into her face. 'What is it, Terri?'

The girl passed a hand over her face. 'I'm just . . . tired, that's all. Tired.' She pulled away and moved slowly towards the kitchen. 'Coffee?'

' . . . Sure.' Abby was more than a little worried. Ever since the day she had come home to find her daughter collapsed on the kitchen floor, she'd been concerned. The teenager had tried to ignore it or ridicule it into unimportance, but her mother wouldn't accept that.

She took it up again while she watched Terri move listlessly around the kitchen, trying to prepare a late lunch.

'Maybe you need vitamins,' she said. 'Why don't you go and see Dr. Callendar?'

Now Terri was annoyed. Why doesn't she just leave me *alone*, she thought as she gave a long-suffering sigh. 'All right. *All right*. I'll go as soon as the Lutzes get back.' She plopped down in her chair and stared sullenly into the coffee mug.

Her mother tried to make the best of the situation. 'Oh?' she said brightly, changing the subject. 'What do you hear from them?'

Terri only shrugged and said something about how expensive long-distance phone calls were. It was a long, leaden visit, without much of the joy of intimacy that Abby and her daughter usually shared. Terri kept talking about how poorly she felt, but every time Abby would prod her, the teenager would snap back, shy away.

She's trying to block it out, Abby realized. She didn't hold much with all that psychological claptrap, but she knew well enough when a girl was trying to lie to herself. Terri was working hard to forget everything that had been happening to her – to forget her 'fainting spell' and everything that went with it.

But Abby couldn't forget. She could still see the fear in her half-conscious daughter's eyes the night she had come home to find her. She remembered her own terror when she found herself holding Terri's head, stroking her fine blonde hair as she had when her daughter was a child, and singing her baby-songs to calm the trembling, to quiet the whimpers.

Oh, the girl had come out of it. At times, she seemed almost her old self – full of life, cheerful and bright. But the other times – *most* of the time, she had to admit . . .

Terri Sullivan was simply not herself.

'How can it be tomorrow there?' Amy asked. 'It's still *today* over here.'

George and Kathy had called long-distance from

Sydney, Australia, and though Terri couldn't hear Kathy's explanation, it seemed to satisfy the little girl. In a moment she was giggling at the voice that whispered over the receiver.

After Matt and Greg both said their hello's, the children all wandered back into the living room while Terri talked with Kathy. Their favorite program was on television, they explained solemnly.

'Everything's fine,' Terri told Kathy Lutz. 'No problems. How is it there?' There was a no reason to mention Harry's . . . *problem*, she decided. He was probably just reacting to a high-pitched siren or something. Everything *was* fine.

Kathy didn't believe her. 'Really,' Terri insisted, realizing how hollow it sounded, even to her. '*Really*, it's going fine.'

She had barely said goodbye and replaced the receiver when Harry's sharp and frantic bark lanced through the house. Terri jumped like a puppet on a piano wire and rushed into the living room.

Harry was standing in front of the television, barking madly at the screen. He was shaking again, and hunched against the carpet. *Just like this afternoon*, Terri thought. She felt a chill trickle down her spine. The dog seemed to sense something on the screen – or behind it? In front of it? And though both boys were trying to pull him back, away from the set, the dog's clawed feet were firmly planted. He wasn't about to move – or to stop yelping.

'Harry!' Terri shouted. His high-pitched bark was driving a wedge into her skull.

Harry leaped forward. Only Greg's sudden tug on the collar kept him from smashing squarely into the screen.

'Knock it *off*, Harry!' Greg shouted.

'Take him outside,' Terri ordered. Greg tried to comply, but the harder he pulled on the dog's collar, the more firmly Harry resisted. He *saw* something there, and he wasn't going to budge until *it* did. 'Terri,' Greg pleaded. 'Help me, I can't –'

The picture on the screen flickered and faded out. It was

the only light in the dim living room, almost an hour after sunset, and suddenly the children and their guardian found themselves buried in shadow.

Harry stopped barking. It was as if *he* had been switched off, too, and in the sudden, terrible silence Terri almost wished he would start again. It was so *quiet*.

Harry's head twitched to look in one corner of the room. Then another. He turned tail and looked behind him. He sniffed the air like a tracker.

Then he sat back on his haunches and *howled*.

It wasn't possible for a dog to make such a sound, Terri thought later. It was the lonely, horrible howl of a timber wolf, a wild beast baying at the moon out of hunger and fear. But it was coming out of friendly, dopey Harry – an endless, hollow, piercing call that seemed to encircle them like a living thing.

And it went on and on and on and *on* . . .

The television set sparked and came on. The picture fluttered, flared into a blur, and for an instant Terri was blinded by the sudden light in the darkness.

Then it went off again.

Then on again.

And Harry kept howling – without a pause, without a breath, he just kept *howling* –

– until the television sound blared on, ten times louder than it had been a moment ago. It almost knocked Terri off her feet, and the dog's hideous yowl cut off – in response? Surprise? – and Harry bolted from the room.

Greg fumbled to turn the sound down. It dwindled to a tinny whisper.

'My *God*,' Terri said, feeling short of breath. 'Has he ever done that before?'

All three children shook their heads in unison: no. Never.

Suddenly Amy brightened, as if remembering something. She opened her mouth to speak . . . and Matt elbowed her abruptly.

Her mouth snapped shut. She shook her head again.

No. Never.

Terri turned without a word and went to the back door. She looked through the thick panes of glass set in the carved oak and saw the trembling black mongrel walking a tight circle in the middle of the moonlit yard – walking and walking, as if trying to work out some huge, unbearable energy. Turning and turning and turning . . .

'Well, Philip Kaufman,' Terri whispered as she watched the dog move in a tighter and tighter circle. 'How would you explain *this* away?'

Terri looked over her shoulder for the tenth time in five minutes. As usual, there was nothing there.

There hadn't been anything there the last time she'd looked, or the time before that, but still she looked again. *I'm letting Harry get to me*, she thought.

The dog had taken hours to calm down, but now, finally, he was upstairs with Greg and Matt.

'He likes to sleep at the foot of my bed,' Greg told her. 'Maybe it'll help him stay relaxed.'

Terri had agreed – and she'd been a bit surprised by the boy's serious tone and practicality. She realized that the Lutz' ordeal – *delusion or not, Dr. Kaufman*, she added acidly – had affected the children as much as George and Kathy. They had learned to cope with it, somehow, and it had made Greg something of an adult well before his time.

Somehow, George and Kathy had managed to keep their family strong, she thought as she settled down with a copy of *Time*. They even tried to let the kids still be kids – as much as possible, at least.

She stared at the articles without really seeing them, while thoughts of George and Kathy grey large in her mind. She thought of the strength of character, the outright *love* it must have taken. *If only I'm that good*, she thought, *when my turn comes . . .*

Terri's eyes snapped open. She hunched forward in the comfortably overstuffed chair and came sharply awake, her senses reeling as she tried to remember where she was.

Something was wrong. She didn't know what, or how, but something was *wrong*.

I must have fallen asleep, she thought dizzily. Here in the living room. I should have gone up to bed.

But – but *something's wrong*.

For the first time, a set of wailing screams came from the second floor. *The kids!* she thought, dying inside. She was on her feet and running for the stairs in an instant.

She took the steps two at a time. She almost twirled on the bannister as she swooped around the landing and tried to take the second flight in three long jumps. One . . . two . . .

Icy hands seized her as she touched the top step. That's what they felt like, she thought later – huge, invisible hands, with fingers as strong as claws, gripping the sides of her body from shoulder to waist and *squeezing*.

Terri's heels lifted off the carpeted step. She was an inch off the ground, hovering, and the cold and vibrations were running through her like electrical energy.

She fought for a breath, but the massive pressure pushed it out of her. She felt her ribs pop and creak, ready to break into pieces. The corridor in front of her began to turn gray and distant, and a foreign, quiet part of her mind told her that she was blacking out – slipping away.

She twisted her fingers into tight little fists and beat at the air around her, searching for something to strike at, something to *hurt*. There was nothing there. She could feel the imprint of the vast talons of both sides, but she couldn't find them, couldn't *see* them.

The room was going away. And now, impossibly, she could see her breath, puffing out in clouds as it was driven from her. As if it was cold, horribly cold all around her.

It was getting worse. As consciousness drained away, she could feel the crackle of ice forming at the corners of her mouth. Her eyebrows were turning white and frosty above her swimming eyes. Already she could barely feel her nose. Her cheeks were aching from cold.

Somethin' to fight with, she thought stupidly, trying to push the cold and unconsciousness back. *'F I could just hit it wi' somethin'* . . .

Then she saw the broom. She had left it leaning against the corridor wall that afternoon, along with its matching dustpan.

. . . to hit wi' . . . she thought as she reached out with one shaking arm. *Hit* . . .

Very suddenly, very completely, it became the most important thing in the world to her. She *had* to get that broomstick, she had to *hit* the thing, and then it would all be okay.

Her fingers, numb with cold, wrapped around the broomstick. She couldn't feel it at all, but she could see it, she could *see* that she had it.

With one wild, swing, she slammed at the air where the invisible thing *had* to be.

. . . and the broom hit something hard.

A voiceless squealing split the air. The pressure on her chest eased just a bit, and Terri, wild with triumph, swung again, and again, and again, gasping with the effort.

It was getting easier to breathe. The thing was going away!

She had both hands on the broom now. She swung it like a baseball bat, then like a hoe, beating and beating and *beating* at the thing until it could hold her no longer.

A piercing scream filled the second floor corridor, and in an instant the pressure disappeared with a *pop* – vanished as if it had never been.

Terri staggered under the sudden release. She was free. *Free.*

The teenager fell to her knees, gulping in air. For a moment she felt too cold to move . . . then the impossible temperature disappeared as abruptly as the pressure had, and everything was fine just fine . . .

There was the sound of an explosion downstairs – someplace at the back of the house. A shattering of glass, a tearing of wood, and a long, terrible wail that faded away very slowly.

She heard the children crying. It was what had brought her upstairs, and they were still sobbing, *still*. She hobbled to Amy's door and leaned heavily against it, forcing her unwilling legs to support her.

Why so weak? she thought dimly. *Thing's gone now. I should be* . . .

She stared in astonishment at her hand as it reached for the doorknob. It was covered in frost and blue, *blue* from the vanished cold.

Her legs must be the same. She looked as if she'd just come out of a *blizzard*, for God's sake.

She forced herself to ignore it. She closed her numb fingers over the knob and turned it – opened it on the crying child.

Amy was fast asleep, but still sobbing convulsively. Terri reached out and touched the little girl's forehead, mindful of how cold her fingers were.

Amy didn't even flinch. Terri cupped her hands around her mouth and blew, warming herself, then stroked the child's cheek.

'Wake up, honey,' she said. 'Come on, wake up.'

Amy just cried, her eyes shut tight.

Prickling pain surged up and down Terri's awakening legs as she hobbled into the boys' room. Matt was sobbing just as Amy had been, gulping back tears, his chest heaving. But Greg . . .

Greg called out as she entered the room – a quick, inarticulate moan, as he swiped at something invisible in the air above him. As she came closer, she saw his lips peel back, his teeth gleaming in the dim light. He strained the air between his teeth, wheezing loudly.

He was fighting for a single breath. Fighting – and losing,

She took another quick step to his bedside, and her foot collided with a soft furrry mass on the floor. Terri stumbled, caught herself with a hand on the foot of Greg's bed, and looked down.

Harry was huddled in an immobile mass, knocked halfway under the bed itself. He hadn't yelped or jumped or even flinched when Terri had kicked him heavily in the side. If she looked hard, she could see his sides moving slowly, *very* slowly, but he seemed to be in some sort of . . . *coma*.

Just like the boys. Just like Amy.

Terri reached out, past Greg's flailing arms, and laid her warming fingers against his brow.

At that instant, Matt stopped sobbing. Simultaneously, Amy's cries from the next room cut off.

It's focusing on Greg now, she thought, without wondering what *it* was. She glanced at Matt and saw he was still asleep – and knew, somehow, that he would *stay* sleeping until all this was over.

But Greg's skin was on fire – burning at an impossibly high temperature. His breathing was more erratic than ever, rattling hollowly in his throat. She could see the muscles working violently, as if he was trying to swallow a stone. As she watched, his skin blanched white, whiter than the pillow on which he rested, and long black streaks spiderwebbed down his cheeks, looking like shadows or cracks in the skin.

. . . *like his mascara ran*, Terri thought numbly. She felt giddy, almost cut loose.

What a silly thing, What a silly, silly thing to have your make-up on in bed. What a funny thing to –

No. Her hand tightened on the bedpost and she turned, clamping her jaw against the panic and hurried to the bathroom.

She swept open the medicine cabinet too strongly – stronger than she had meant to. It clanged against the wall, and pain stabbed like glass across her chest.

A broken rib? she wondered, afraid all over again.

She tried not to think about it. *Thermometer*, she ordered. *Aspirin*. *Wet towel*.

She stumbled back to Greg's side, imagining she could see steam rising off the little boy's overheated body.

The thermometer read *106°*.

He's taking his own sweet time in there, Terri thought. She paced the hallway, biting at her cuticles and trying to ignore the pain in her chest. It had taken the devil's own time to convince Dr. Callendar to make a house call in the first place. Then it had seemed like hours before he had let himself in downstairs. And now, *now* . . .

She had held Greg's head while he gagged and retched. She had seen the ulcers break out on his body, then fade just as suddenly, then erupt all over again. She had felt the heat coming off him in waves, so violent that she felt it would sear her fingers.

What could that old quack be up to? He'd looked sour as Scrooge when he'd finally shown up, and –

Dr. Callendar let himself out of Greg's bedroom and closed the door quietly behind him. He had a faint, studious frown on his face, and for an instant – just an instant – Terri hated his kindly old ways and his professional tone and his avuncular bedside manner – even though he had been her doctor since she was a child.

'Well?' she said, biting at her last remaining cuticle.

'The little girl and the younger boy – Matt is his name? They're fine.'

'I know *that*,' she snapped, passing a nervous hand through her hair. 'What about Greg?'

The doctor let a small smile pass quickly between them. 'He's fine, too,' he answered quietly.

Terri's jaw dropped open. 'What . . . what do you mean?'

The doctor began searching his pockets absent-mindedly – an old ritual from his long past pipe-smoking days. 'He's in excellent health,' he said gruffly. 'A perfect specimen of a boy his age.'

'What about the fever! What about the *sores*?' Terri

could hear her own voice reaching too high, becoming too loud, but she couldn't stop herself.

'He hasn't got any fever.'

'*It was a hundred and six*!'

'It's ninety-eight point nine now, Terri,' he said very quietly.

She couldn't believe what he was saying. She could barely even comprehend it. She simply stared at the old doctor in astonishment.

Dr. Callendar frowned more deeply and took her strongly by the arm. 'Come into the light,' he ordered, moving down the hall.

She tugged free, suddenly afraid of the old man. 'I'm fine,' she said.

He looked through her with startling, ice-blue eyes. 'Your mother called me today – or, more precisely, *yesterday* now.' He glanced rather maliciously at the cuckoo clock on the corridor wall. It read 2:45. 'She said she thought you were ill.'

Terri was still thinking about Greg. About the fever and the sores. 'What?' she said, not understanding.

He tilted her chin up into the light and squinted at her face. 'What are those burns? How did you get them?'

'I'm not . . . burned.' She felt as if she was very far away, and drifting farther with every second.

'Don't quibble, young lady. Would you care to explain how you acquired a case of frostbite? In August, no less?'

Frostbite? It didn't even register at first. *Frost . . . bite*?

'Terri?' he said sharply. '*Terri*?'

'I'm tired, Doctor Callendar. I've very . . . tired.'

The doctor glared at her for a long moment, then turned away abruptly and led her downstairs. In the front hallway, he scribbled out a prescription for a salve to ease the pain of the burns, and offered her a second prescription for sedatives.

Terri could barely keep her eyes open. The last thing in the world I need, she thought dully, is a sedative. She declined.

The doctor glanced at his watch, then back at the exhausted girl. He was obviously torn between what was left of a good night's sleep and concern for the teenager. 'You're quite sure you're all right?'

'I'm *fine*,' she said, feeling the last of her patience fray. 'Everything's *fine* now, *please*.'

He nodded and left. Terri closed the door and leaned heavily against it for a long time.

No. Everything was far from fine. Greg *had* been sick. Amy and Matt *had* shared some sort of nightmare. Harry *was* comatose. And she . . .

– pain crossed her chest in a blinding flash. It was worse than ever. She stumbled to the full-length mirror in the front hall and opened her blouse, pulling it away from her tender skin as she worked at each button.

She couldn't believe her own eyes.

Burns – burns from *cold*, she realized – covered both sides of her torso in thick horizontal bands. The skin was angry red and blistering, like her cheeks and her palms.

She spread the blouse wide like a pair of cloth wings. It was obvious it was so *obvious* . . .

The bands formed the clear outline of a pair of giant, clawed hands.

She felt herself start to faint. She bumped against the wall, pulled herself up, and ran stumbling to the kitchen. There was a vague plan in the back of her head – she'd run her head under the water, she'd pour ice on her head, she'd –

Terri Sullivan stopped in the doorway to the kitchen and stared in awe at the nightmare's final surprise. A stiff breeze blew over her. A new chill set in. But she didn't move. She didn't even blink. She could only stare and shake her head, back and forth. Back and forth.

She'd forgotten the sound of the explosion so many hours ago. That huge noise, right after the . . . *hands* . . . had let her go. Glass and wood. A terrible sound.

Now she saw what had happened. She saw that the back door was no longer there.

Bits of oak and shards of glass lay sprinkled across the back lawn – bits not larger than splinters. The door had exploded, *exploded*, until only the twisted bits of the brass-plated hinges were left clinging to the shattered frame.

It had been smashed open, smashed apart, by something *huge*.

Terri stared at it for almost an hour, thinking the same thought over and over – the same silly, stupid thing.

Finally, she said it out loud. 'Well, Dr. Philip Kaufman,' she grated, feeling her legs give out one final time. 'How would you explain *this*?'

CHAPTER THIRTEEN

'IT LOOKS like it's going to fall on us,' Kathy giggled.

'Amazing,' George said, sounding more than a little awed.

'The unique and majestic edifice looming directly in front of you, blocking most of the magnificent Sydney skyline, is the Sydney Opera House. This architectural masterpiece on Bennelong Point is rapidly becoming an international symbol for Australia, rivaling the koala and the kangaroo.'

The tour guide standing next to George laughed lightly at his own little joke, then went on to point out other Sydney landmarks to the ten or twelve people in his group.

George and Kathy Lutz were standing on the rear platform of the hydrofoil *Dee Why* as it skimmed across the sparkling blue waters of Sydney Harbor. They felt the vibrations of its massive engines beneath their feet as it swooped towards Circular Quay docks. The steady, pulsing rhythm of the engines eased off, and the main body of the vessel fell gently to the waves as the wings lifted clear of the water.

Today there had been no interviews or press conferences. The Lutzes were simply being tourists.

Kathy gripped the guard rail tightly and leaned back, craning her neck to get a wider view of the huge white structure.

'It looks ready to take off, doesn't it?' she said, smiling as she took the last bite of her 'fairy floss,' an Australian version of cotton candy.

George nodded and put his arm around his wife. They'd

taken the hydrofoil to Manly, then walked along the streets of the seaside resort with its shops and streetside vendors. Kathy had tried almost every kind of food, and looked in every shop – at least it had seemed that way to George – and they had ended their journey on Manly Beach with their shoes and socks off, splashing in the shallows and running from the waves.

This is the Kathy I fell in love with, George realized. Vibrant, alive, – a lovely and loving girl-woman. It was a special treat to see her relaxed enough to be herself again. It seemed like years since she had been like this.

George took his wife's hand and held it tightly as the *Dee Why* glided towards her berth below the dual-purpose railway line and freeway overpass. He had come to a decision while watching her today. It had been building up in his mind over the last few weeks, and the episode on the Qantas flight had finally convinced him.

They had to get help – and not just help to survive the attacks. They could no longer simply wait, hoping the entity would leave them alone, then frantically scratch for survival when the horror inevitably attacked. They had to *do* something – something positive and constructive.

The thing on the plane wasn't a dream or a vision or whatever psychic researchers – or psychiatrists! – might call it. At least not anymore. The attack didn't end with everything returning to 'normal,' as so many others had in the past.

This time, the thing had taken physical form. Someone else had seen it. The force centered at Amityville was beginning to change its attacks, he realized – to become solid matter. And somehow George knew that this wasn't the last time it would happen that way.

Something else had been different, too. George had been able to *fight back* for the first time. Oh, it had been a feeble attempt at best, he knew. And he had still needed help simply to survive. But he *had* been able to fight. It was no longer just a matter of passive resistance and hoping for the best.

There had to be ways they could arm themselves, he decided – things that would make the fight less one-sided.

The Fight, he thought a second time.

He rolled the word around slowly in his mind. Yes, they *would* fight . . . if it were possible.

In that instant, George Lutz decided to call Father Mancusso, the Catholic priest who had helped them before, as soon as he and Kathy returned to California. Maybe *he* could help them with this.

'Where to next?' Kathy asked, still smiling.

'Oh, I thought we could walk through Sydney for an hour or so,' he said. 'Then we'll stop and eat wherever you want to. That should get us back to the hotel in Kings Cross in time to get ready for the TV show.'

For a moment, George was afraid that mentioning the interview would dampen Kathy's mood. But she didn't seem to mind the thought of all those questions and answers about Amityville. She simply squeezed his hand and as they moved across the wide gangplank onto the wharf, then alongside the high wire fence at the exit, she started swinging their linked hands back and forth.

Before long, they were both laughing like children.

The cab inched slowly along Darlinghurst Road towards the hotel where the Lutzes were staying. It was a busy time of evening here in Sydney so the driver had brought them around past the Wooloomooloo dock area to avoid traffic. But as they entered the main section of Kings Cross, it was back to fitful stop-and-go driving.

The Don Lane television show had been one of the best George could remember. A fitting way to end the business side of their trip he thought as he looked out the window at the centerpiece fountain, in the park. The perfect halo of brightly colored water seemed to hover there, suspended in time as throngs of people hurried by on their way to any one of numerous and varied possible destinations. Now, late at night, this area was one enormous celebration of light. In the day, George knew, it was a celebration of color.

'Is it always like this?' Kathy asked the driver.

'The Cross?' The cabbie smiled. 'Never changes, love. I bin drivin' close to twennie yeahs; like a quid fer every time I drove along 'ere.'

George couldn't help smiling at the Australian's accent. There was something comfortable, almost *homey* about the sound of it. He had recognized the same thing in John Jones when they'd met at Felicia's party, and again later, after John had agreed to write the book, when they had spent three days with him, going over their experiences.

'Preddy colorful, eh, mate?'

'It certainly is,' George said. He stared out the window, marvelling at the passing show.

'I'm glad the work's over,' Kathy said softly.

'So am I,' George agreed.

The next day the Lutzes were tourists again, and it was late in the afternoon before they returned to their hotel. Within moments, they had left it again, for a walk down William Street towards the center of Sydney.

'I think I've walked in this city more than I've walked in my whole life,' Kathy said as they traipsed happily along.

'Well, it can't hurt me any,' George said, patting his stomach. 'I could stand to lose a few pounds.'

A short time later they followed a street sign that read *The Domain*. Twenty minutes later, they found themselves in another huge park.

The city of Sydney seemed to be dotted with them, and George and Kathy had visited quite a few, admiring the fountains and gardens. This one was more an open green area than a landscaped park. Wide expanses of lawn were interrupted only by a network of black tar paths and wire trash containers that most of the visitors seemed intent on using.

Dusk was creeping into the afternoon, but the evening

promised to be soft and warm. The Lutzes walked past a huge Museum, its solid stone structure darkly stained by time. It looked as if it had grown up out of the ground, like some vast natural formation in the middle of the park – despite the freeway on-ramp that ran only a few yards away.

Across the park, George saw a pair of dogs playing – chasing a ball, wrestling, yapping happily.

As the shadows grew darker and longer, George began to feel suspended in time, midway between day and night. He thought about getting a cab and choosing a restaurant for dinner.

The dogs were barking more loudly now – more insistent, somehow, and closer. Neither Kathy nor George paid much attention.

'Which way should we go to get a taxi?' he asked.

'This way, I think,' Kathy said, pointing off to the left.

The dogs weren't playing anymore, but the barking went on. They were less than a hundred yards away, and moving closer.

The Lutzes, arm in arm, retraced their steps across the wide lawn. George had to strain to see the path in the gathering gloom.

'I don't think this is the right way . . . ' he said gently.

'There goes my career as a wilderness guide,' Kathy said, laughing. George grinned and started too –

A wild animal howl filled the park. George and Kathy stopped short and turned together.

'What . . . ?' Kathy whispered.

'Just some dogs,' George told her gruffly. He didn't believe it himself, but he –

It came again – a long, high, piercing wail that cut through the evening like a sharpened blade.

A second call came from another direction. *It's answering*, George realized. *They're in a group – a pack.*

He took Kathy firmly by the arm and started walking fast. 'The road's this way,' he said grimly, not believing a word of it. Kathy's hand trembled in his own. He started to search for lights to guide them toward the roadway – to guide them toward *anything*.

There were no lights – none at all.

Kathy saw it too. 'There's no stars,' she whispered. They stumbled to a halt.

A moment earlier the first lamps were being lit. Lights had been glittering through the trees, and the aura of metropolitan Sydney was warming the far horizon.

Now there was nothing – not even the thin and antiseptic light of a new moon.

Sound had drained away as well. There had been the twittering of birds, leaves rustling in the dying breeze, a murmer of receding conversation. Now . . .

Nothing. *Nothing*.

George looked to his right – at his wife. He couldn't see her.

'Kathy?' he said. His voice caught in spite of his effort.

'I'm here,' she whispered.

Her hand was still in his. She squeezed it hard, *very* hard, as if to reassure them both. 'What do we –'

The howling came again – a dozen of them, now a hundred, screaming in the darkness.

The sounds seemed to encircle them. *Wolves*, George thought. *Or something more*. But . . . wolves in a public park? In the middle of a major city? Did Australia even *have* wolves?

Suddenly a pair of eyes hovered in front of them, insubstantial in the darkness – red, dull eyes, glowing with a light of their own.

Below them a mouth opened, glowing with the same bloody luminescence. White fangs glittered against undulating color.

George backed up two steps, then three, and spun Kathy roughly about. '*Run*,' he hissed. '*Run!*'

The ground was hard and rough beneath their feet – not the yielding turf they had felt before. Part of George's mind groped for points of reference, for any bearing at all.

They could be inches from a wall, moments from collision with trees, but he could see nothing, he could *feel* nothing.

'LOOK OUT!' He dragged Kathy to a stop, skidding on the rocky surface. The eyes were ahead of them again. The mouth was opening wide.

He jerked her to the right and they ran again – faster this time, lower to the ground. George's lungs burned with the effort, but they had to keep going, they had to get *away* –

'I can't . . . keep . . . up.' Kathy panted, stumbling half a step behind him.

He slammed to a stop. He caught Kathy in his arms as she careened into him.

The apparition was there again. Not five feet in front of them.

The first pair of eyes was joined by a second. Then a third, and a fourth. George turned, clutching Kathy against him, and saw the eyes, the mouths, moving closer on all sides.

And now he could hear them breathing – a low, hungry panting. The breath of the beast.

They began to bark – wild, vulpine yapping, high and unnatural. It grew louder and sharper, piercing their eardrums. Kathy tried to put both hands over her ears, but George wouldn't let go of her hand – he couldn't, not in this darkness – and now he could see them, he could *see* the silhouettes of the creatures taking form around the incandescent features.

Dogs – no, wolves. No. Something horribly more than that – something darker and far more deadly. George found himself thinking of Dante's *Inferno*, of the three-headed Cerberus, the Hound of Hell. And these yapping, howling, scrabbling things, each far larger than any hound he'd ever seen –

Hounds from Hell. God, it was *true*!

They started to close in. Glowing strings of spittle oozed from their jaws. Shadowy paws inched forward. Kathy tried to shrink, tried to hide in George's arms, and he thought wildly of the physical threat the thing on the plane had posed – how this time, *this time it wasn't a dream*.

Something snapped inside George Lutz.

Fight, he told himself. *Damn you, FIGHT*!

'*No!*' he bellowed at the beasts. '*Not again!*' Without thinking, he dragged Kathy to the ground and pulled off his leather boots in two tremendous *jerks*. An instant later he was back on his stocking feet. Kathy close behind him. He swung the boots by the straps, swinging them out blindly, heavily, begging to connect.

No more running, he told himself. Never again. Better to go down fighting than to die with a whimper.

The beast directly in front of them lunged. George swung out at it in a short, vicious arc – and the boot slammed solidly into the side of the massive creature. An earsplitting yelp, painfully sharp, screamed out of the beast. It hit the ground on its side and rolled over twice, coming to rest on its back with its head twisted horribly to the side.

Dead, George thought with grim satisfaction. *I killed it*!

Suddenly the dead thing burst into flames.

George gasped and backed up a step – horribly closer to the other beasts. Greenish-red flames spread hungrily over the corpse and gnawed at it. George caught glimpses of smoking skin, of bleaching bone turning black in the heat . . .

He looked away. He turned to the other creatures as they began to move slowly, almost guiltily, towards the burning body.

'Come on,' he gritted, swinging the boot again. 'Come *on*.'

For an instant, the creatures stopped moving. They were frozen, poised, as if waiting a command. George clutched at the bootstrap more tightly than ever. He shifted to shield Kathy from the onslaught . . .

And the hellhounds leaped on the smoking remains of the dead beast. George didn't move. He stared in astonishment as the creatures fell into one massive, boiling ball of fur and flesh, yapping and growling as they tore the dead animal to shreds.

Part of him – *most* of him – wanted to run away – to take this instant to escape, before the beasts turned back to them.

. . . But he couldn't look away. The tangled, tumbling knot of muscle and flesh, spattered with blood, slick with spittle . . . it seemed to be one beast. He seemed to see something else in it, something he couldn't escape . . .

They were like human bodies clawing at each other. Bodies climbing over other bodies, and screaming. Everything in pain. Everything trying to escape, but captured, caught in –

'George!'

Kathy's voice cut through him. He straightened suddenly and turned around.

Kathy had both hands inside his belt. She was dragging him back, tearing him away.

The toes of his stockinged feet were only inches from the dripping rump of the nearest creature. It was still feeding hungrily on its fallen leader. He had been going to them. He had been about to . . .

Sacrifice himself? Join them! *My God*, he thought, *what am I doing*?

'We have to get out of here,' Kathy panted. 'Please, George, *please*, let's get *out* of here!'

His head cleared in an instant. He gripped her by the arm and turned away, shoving her in front of him.

'Go,' he said. '*Now*!'

They stumbled away from the horror. Only a few footsteps off, the light began to bloom. A few more and sounds trickled towards them – the park, the busy roadway, people in the distance talking.

Grass was under their feet again, soft and welcoming. Lights flared, full force and together they emerged from the shadows of a tree-lined path.

There were less than twenty feet from the road to the Harbor Bridge.

Exhausted, still terrified, they stumbled together onto the tarmac.

A blaring horn pulled them up short and two cars shot by, only inches away. George pulled his wife back to the edge of the road. A taxi slowed as it approached, turning on its vacant sign as it came.

The Lutzes piled inside, still gasping from the run. 'King's Cross,' George panted as he collapsed into the seat.

The taxi pulled swiftly away from the shoulder, and George let himself relax for the first time. *At least I fought it*, he thought. At least I got one of them, *part* of it. He knew with a cold certainty that the others could have killed them both quite easily, if they hadn't turned on their own kind. But he'd fought, they'd escaped again.

Still, he knew they needed help, and soon.

He rubbed his forearm across his eyes and blinked rapidly, realizing how close he was to unconsciousness. For the first time, he caught the worried look of the cabbie, glancing repeatedly at them in his rear-view mirror.

George suddenly realized he was still clutching his boots – or what was left of them.

They were shredded – bits of leather held together by threads and bits of padding. A greenish-red liquid was smeared across the material, and it dripped onto the floor of the cab as the remains turned into a twisted, unrecognisable mass.

George dropped them on the floor of the taxi and tried not to think about what the hellhounds would have done to human flesh. It didn't matter – at least not for the moment. They were safe. They had escaped.

But he dreamed about it later. Over and over again.

CHAPTER FOURTEEN

TERRI WAS watering the garden when she spotted The Invaders From Mars.

At least, that's what they looked like when she first glanced up and saw them: four tallish, thinnish, very pale humanoids in black suits straight out of the 1950's. The three males wore thick hornrimmed glasses, all in the same out-of-date style. The fourth, a woman, in a dark, conservatively cut suit of her own, had pale blonde hair turning iron gray, pulled back in a severe bun. She seemed to be wearing orthopedic hose.

No, Terri decided, they must be door-to-door evangelists. Or fund-raisers. Maybe both. She looked quickly down again, back to the threadbare garden that she and Abby had been working over since early Spring. It wasn't much – a few pale tomato plants, some scruffy lettuce, a long line of cheerful marigolds and one lonely rosebush remaining from the nine they had originally planted. But it was their own; they'd come to love it in spite of all the work . . . or maybe *because* of all the work.

Uh-oh, she thought. The four strangers were coming straight towards her. When she looked up guiltily, she saw their expensive shiny black sedan parked half a block down the street.

'Mrs. Lutz?' the oldest man asked. 'One of your neighbors told us you were visiting out here . . . '

'No,' Terri said. 'Kathy and George are overseas. The children are staying with –'

Wait a second, she thought. What did these people want

with the Lutzes! Especially if they didn't even recognize Kathy when they were looking for her . . .

'What can *I* do for you?' she said suspiciously.

'We must see them,' one of the younger men said, adjusting his horned-rim glasses.

Something wasn't right here. She could feel it. Terri casually moved the spray of water a few feet to the left, until it gurgled at the roots of a bush just inside the gate that separated her from these . . . *people*.

'Exactly who are you?' she said, trying to sound polite – and not doing a very good job of it.

'That really needn't concern you,' the older man said condescendingly.

'It concerns me *plenty*,' she said, feeling herself getting hot. 'Are you here on some sort of official business?'

'You could say that,' the third man said, nodding solemnly.

'Police?' she demanded. 'The government or something?'

The older man – the leader, she realized – waved the question away. One pale hand reached up to open the gate.

In one swift movement, Terri twisted the nozzle on the hose and directed a heavy stream of water at the wide wooden gate. It splattered against it with a loud, hollow *tungtungtungtung*, and the four suits took one startled step back in unison.

'If you're here on official business,' she said, 'show me your I.D.' She pointed the hose down to fill the planter on the left side of the gate – still well within striking distance.

'Please, Mrs. Lutz,' the leader said. 'I assure you, we have only your best interests at heart.'

'I *told* you,' she said, losing her patience. 'I'm *not* Kathy Lutz. *Now what do you want*?'

Suddenly the woman stepped forward and jutted out her sharp chin. 'Are the children here?' she demanded.

Terri gaped at her.

'The children *are* here,' the woman said decisively. 'I

can sense them.' She turned to the other three and spoke with an almost military tone. 'We must help them,' she commanded.

The leader stepped up to the gate again, eager to re-assert control.

'Young woman,' he said sharply, 'If you *must* know our personal business, know this: we are associates of Dr. Quentin W. Cosmos, and he has directed us to see these Lutz children, *immediately*.'

Cosmos? Terri frowned. That name rang some sort of distant bell. Quentin W. –

Cosmos! That was the crazy-man who'd been harassing the Lutzes! She and Kathy had laughed about the time George had kicked in the side of that loonie's limo!

'I'm going to give you one minute,' she said grimly, readjusting the hose, 'and then I'm going to turn the water on you.' A wicked part of Terri's brain hoped they'd call her bluff. It would be a pleasure to douse these self-righteous sickos.

'We are here to help!' the woman said severely. She sounded as if she was scolding Terri. 'We have come to cast out the devil from you and your husband, and most important to *cleanse your children*!'

'But –'

One of the men turned and walked along the fence while the woman shook her finger over the gate. 'We *have* to *help* the *children*, before Satan's minions consume them completely and strike out at the world, can't you *see* that! *Thus will the anti-Christ truly be born, the Scriptures tell us*.'

'I don't need to hear the Scriptures quoted to me by a bunch of freaks like –'

The healthy stream of water from the hose abruptly turned to a trickle. Terri looked at the nozzle, dumbfounded, then turned to follow the hose back to the spigot.

The youngest of the black-suited men was hanging over the fence. He had turned the water off at the source.

146

'How – how *dare* you?' Terri said. The old-fashioned phrase sounded strangely stilted in her mouth, but somehow appropriate. 'How *dare* you come barging in here like this, after the way your – your *boss* was treated! Didn't you get the message? *You're not wanted here.* You – people have to *want* your help, dammit! You can't force it on them!'

The older man swung open the gate and stepped quickly inside. The others followed.

'We don't expect you to understand,' he said, as if talking to a child. 'Believe me, you will thank us later.'

'Thank us and *join* us,' the woman said shortly.

They brushed past her, almost sauntering up the sidewalk to the porch.

'You take one more step and I'll call the police!' Terri shouted.

Things had been going so well since they'd left La Costa. She couldn't let something like *this* spoil it. The children had forgotten – or at least they had pretended to forget – all about the sickness of that one horrible night. Her mother had welcomed their visit with open arms; even *she* had let up on Terri about going to the doctor despite the frostbite burns that had long since faded. Hell, even *Harry* was doing better, sleeping like a puppy on the front porch –

Ah-*ha*, she thought.

'Harry!' she called. 'Wake up!'

The dog lifted his head, ears raised and alert. The four unwelcome visitors stopped in their tracks, midway between gateway and front door.

You're not going to bother those kids, Terri thought determinedly. Not when thing are going so well.

'N-nice dog,' the older man said hesitantly. 'No one's going to hurt you, b –'

'Get 'em, Harry! Sic 'em!'

Harry jumped to his feet and stood stiffly in front of the door. The muscles in his leg tensed. The hair on the nape of his neck bristled and stood on end.

The severe woman spun to confront Terri, no more than three feet away. 'Call the beast off,' she demanded.

'Get off my property,' Terri told her.

The woman seized the teenager by the arm and shook her sharply. '*Call that dog off*!' she shouted.

That was all the encouragement Harry needed. He hurtled off the porch and headed straight for the woman who was shaking Terri's arm. One of the men – the quietest of the three – called out in alarm and tried to get in the way.

That was fine with Harry. He sunk his teeth into the thick black cloth that covered the man's thigh and bit down. *Hard*.

The man howled in pain. The other two men backed up towards the open gate, scuttling towards the safety of their sedan.

The gray-haired woman backed up as well, one long, thin arm leveled at the dog. 'The beast!' she shouted. 'The beast of the Apocalypse!'

'Leggo! LEGGO!' The howling man shook Harry loose and ran for the car, with Harry hot on his heels, yapping and barking like an attack dog.

The woman was still backing towards the car, almost chanting as she moved, crablike, into the back seat. 'And he shall appear in many forms,' she chattered, 'and his number shall be Six-Six-Six, and he shall be legion, and vicious upon the earth. Yea, and shall blood wash – '

The older man slammed the door in her face as soon as she was inside. Harry put his paws up on the window, standing on his hind legs, and barked straight into the woman's face as she cursed him silently behind the glass.

A moment later the black sedan lurched away from the curb. Harry gleefully gave chase, still barking furiously. He was halfway down the block before Terri, laughing hysterically, called out to him.

'Harry!' she said, trying to sound stern and failing miserably. 'Harry, that's enough! Come here!'

The dog called off his attack and trotted happily back

to the teenager's side, his huge pink tongue lolling casually from the side of his mouth.

Terri went down on one knee and hugged the dog, giggling as he licked her face.

'Good boy, Harry,' she said, patting him on the head. '*Very* good boy.'

The tall black taxi lumbered down a main thoroughfare in North London. In the rear of the ancient vehicle, George and Kathy Lutz gazed at the sights with equal parts delight and surprise.

'I love these old-fashioned English cabs,' Kathy said, hugging her husband's arm.

He nodded. It was something like being in a big, squarish limousine – but better, in many ways. The high ceiling and incredible amount of leg room made it possible for George to stretch out completely. That was a rare luxury for someone as large-framed as he was.

It was good to be back in England. After all that had happened in Australia – on the plane, in the park – neither of them had felt much like staying Down Under. Helen and Carrie Innes had been disappointed, but they had tried to understand, and George had managed to convince the publishers in New York to reroute their trip home through London.

It was time to talk with Rev. Timothy Johnstone again.

Johnstone was the Anglican priest who had exorcised them many months earlier, and George was convinced that his dangerous, desperate act of faith was all that had given them those months of rest and recuperation. But the rest was over now, and they needed the reverend's help again – his help, and access to his nearly unequalled library of books and papers on the occult.

If anyone can help us, George thought, it's him.

The taxi turned into Church Square, and they passed into the charcoal shadow of St. John's spire.

As they climbed from the cab, Kathy and George felt

the power of the place wash over them again. They hesitated for a moment, standing in front of the wide, tall brick cathedral. Memories of what had happened there fluttered past and brushed against them. So much –

'Well, hullo there,' Timothy Johnstone said. He emerged from the shadows of the rectory doorway, his pale and gentle face alight with welcome.

There was a special bond between the three of them. They had endured an experience that few people would ever know, and they had emerged from it stronger and more whole than ever. The confrontation with the force from Amityville had nearly destroyed the church itself. It had exhausted George and Kathy and literally aged the priest by years. But at its end, the cleansing had lifted a great weight from the Lutzes, all because of this gentle, almost timid, supremely powerful man.

'Hello, Reverend Timothy,' Kathy said. She hugged the minister tightly for a long moment.

George took the reverend's hand in both his own and grinned. 'It's good to see you again,' he said, and the same understanding, the same energy as before, passed between them.

'Come in,' the reverend said. 'Come in. I've just brewed a fresh pot of tea.'

'Oh, dear,' Timothy Johnstone said, brushing crumbs from his vest, 'I was afraid something like this might happen.'

They were seated in his cluttered, sunlit study, sipping their second cups of hot, sweet tea.

'But it *has* receded a bit, hasn't it?' he said, frowning.

Kathy nodded. 'For a long time after you . . . *helped* us, it stopped completely.'

The pastor tapped his upper lip with two long fingers. 'Ah, but not for long,' he said absently, lost in thought.

'There are longer gaps now, between the attacks,' George said helpfully . . . then he realized that it was true. It wasn't a day-to-day ordeal any longer. There were weeks, sometimes even months, between episodes. And more: 'I think I felt something change in the . . . encounters recently, too. On the plane to Australia, for instance. It – I don't know how to explain it, exactly. There's a kind of decrease in – in power levels, or something.'

'Could it be losing interest?' Kathy said hopefully.

'It's more likely that its ability to sustain attacks at long distances is weakening,' the reverend muttered. 'But you mustn't be fooled. We have all felt its power. I cannot believe it will surrender without a serious struggle.'

George nodded and clenched one fist. 'So we need to know *how* to fight it,' he said. 'That's why we came here. I can resist it a little now – I tried to, on the plane and again in the park in Sydney. Still, I felt – I don't know, *helpless*. At first I would be free to act, I could *hurt* it. And then I'd hesitate at the wrong second, or look at the thing in the wrong way, and . . . I was lost. It would suck me in, convince me I'd already lost, somehow.' George's frown deepened. 'I hate that helpless feeling,' he grated. 'I don't want – I can't – '

He broke off in mid-sentence, too twisted and confused to continue. His hands opened and closed in impotent fists, as if searching for the words.

Reverend Johnstone nodded gently. 'Let it come,' he said softly. 'I understand.'

George closed his eyes for a moment and took a deep breath. Then he explained.

He told the reverend everything that had happened – how he had tried to resist it, how it had felt to try. He told him of his conviction that there was something, some *way* to do more than just survive the creature's attacks. Some way to drive the thing off forever. To kill it, if need be.

Kathy volunteered to wash out the teacups, and while she clattered in the reverend's tiny kitchen, George asked one last question in barely more than a whisper. 'Look,' he said. 'We've been told about the seven years over and over. Seven years before it goes away. Seven years of . . . horror. Well, time is running out, reverend, and I've got to know: is the thing likely to make one last grab at us? Are we going to have to face it head-on, one last time?'

The reverend's bright blue eyes were filled with worry and love. 'I'm sorry, George, but I feel it's very, very likely you *will* face one final onslaught. And it will be a serious and deadly affair. Of course, I will do everything I can to help.' He brightened suddenly. 'Perhaps if you could come to England during those last few months. If you were here, with me, I might be able to help in some small way.'

God, George thought. He's willing to go through it again for us – *with* us. They had met some remarkable people in their years of ordeal, he thought, but no one even remotely like Father Timothy. No one.

'I don't think that will be possible,' George said. He felt his eyes fill with tears. 'But thank you, Reverend. Whatever happens – thank you.'

Kathy was back, purse in hand. The reverend stood as she entered and spoke with an almost businesslike briskness. 'Well, then. I'll get those books I mentioned for you to take home.' George could see that the reverend was uncomfortable with the Lutz' strong emotions of thanks . . . and love. He smiled as the man bustled out of the room, hiding his own deep feelings.

They were standing beside the cab and shaking hands before Timothy Johnstone spoke about the entity again – for the last time. 'You're right, George – more right than you've ever been. You will have to fight the beast. It cannot simply be avoided or resisted any longer. And you must do more than simply drive it away. *You must destroy it.*'

George swallowed a lump in his throat. For the first time, he fully confronted the prospect: hand-to-hand battle with the creature from Amityville. A battle to the death.

The reverend still had his hand tightly in his own. His piercing blue eyes seemed to reach straight to George's soul. 'But remember, George. Remember: if you can fight, *you can win.*'

George nodded and started to pull away, but the aging, wiry, intense little priest wouldn't let him go.

'George!' he said sharply. 'I am quite serious! *You can win.*'

CHAPTER FIFTEEN

JOHN JONES walked from the underground station towards St. John's Church, enjoying the noise and the bustle of North London as much as he always did; not knowing yet, that he'd missed Kathy and George Lutz by only two days.

He had been in London many times – he had even lived there once, for a short time. Santa Barbara, California may be home right now, he thought, but I never stay too long in one place. And I wouldn't mind coming back here one bit.

He passed row after row of old brick tenement houses, some no larger than a storefront. The structures shared common walls, forming almost endless lines of masonry and mortar that stretched to the horizon like red brick caterpillars. It was a warm, uncommonly dry day for London. The walk was something to be cherished.

I've done some pretty unusual things in my time, John thought as he walked, but writing this book has to be one of the strangest. He had really only intended to merchandise the book rights for the Lutzes. Some of his associates were well-connected in publishing; he had been sure all along that a book deal was a real possibility. But when it finally came together, John realized that he knew more about what had happened to the Lutzes than anyone else involved. It seemed unavoidable: he would have to serve as writer as well.

Now he was glad it had worked out that way, but before he submitted the final third of the book, he knew he had to visit London and meet with the man who had 'exorcised'

Kathy and George. If he could squeeze it in, he might fly to Amsterdam as well. The Lutzes had told him about some unusual experiences there, too.

But . . . *exorcism*? he thought. That was still a pretty hard concept to swallow.

Not that I'm a non-believer, he thought as he reached the church courtyard. More like a Doubting Thomas with an active imagination.

He liked Timothy Johnstone the moment he met him – even if he did hand him a cup of tea.

Actually, John had never liked tea, and he had always felt a little guilty about it. He was an Australian of sturdy British heritage; there was an almost ancestral obligation involved. Still, he grimaced at the oversweetened brew as he listened to the reverend ramble. He was a talkative man who required little prodding, and what he had to say was fascinating . . .

'. . . I've been called many things,' the soft-spoken Englishman admitted, patting at his thinning hair. 'I suppose "reverend" is fine. Actually, I had a rather large parish here at one time, but my other work slowly took precedence.'

'. . . Yes, I have given some help to people with nowhere else to turn. I like to think it's been some small help to them. It's . . . a gift, I suppose.'

'. . . It's nothing I do. I am simply a conduit. I act as a channel for the power of God to come through and heal those in need.'

Timothy Johnstone talked unselfconsciously into John's miniature tape recorder. As he did, John thought of the Nikon camera in the carry-all at his side. Photographs of the church, inside and out, would be valuable resources as well.

'Can you tell when people really need your help?' John asked.

'Do you mean, am I able to tell if I'm being hoaxed?'

155

the older man said, smiling. 'Quite simply: yes. There was a young girl once brought here. She seemed to be possessed by a demon of some sort – there seemed no other explanation. She raved and frothed at the mouth; screamed obscenities. Quite impressive. But the *feeling* around her didn't match her actions. So I simply told her I knew she was having me on, and that she should stop worrying her parents so.'

Timothy Johnstone paused to sip his tea.

'I understand she left off with that nonsense straightaway. She's had quite a normal life since then.'

John couldn't help but smile. That lovely British sense of understatement.

'What do you mean, "*feeling*"?' he asked.

'It's rather a . . . it's something I *see*, John. Something I *feel*.'

'See?'

'Yes. A darkness. A *presence*, you might say.' The usually articulate preacher was groping for terms. 'You,' he said, taking another tack. 'Now, you look perfectly fine – you *feel* perfectly normal to me.'

'What about the Lutzes?'

'Oh, the Lutzes had an awful darkness around them. It actually seemed to be swallowing them whole. I saw it *and* I felt it the moment they came through that door. I could see immediately that they needed help, and I told them so. Kathy seemed quite open to it, really, but George was another matter. He was most adamant at first. Insisted it was a dreadful waste of time.' Again, he sipped his tea, remembering that day. 'Finally, I managed to convince him to come into the sanctuary. I believe I was able to help them, at least for a short while.'

'By exorcising them.'

'Yes,' Johnstone said.

John leaned back in his overstuffed chair. 'Tell me about exorcism,' he said, frowning slightly.

'It is a cleansing ritual, really. As old as the Church itself. You can read about it in your Bible; it's mentioned many times there.' The reverend absently brushed flakes of dandruff from his sweater.

'Is there an actual ritual?' John asked. 'I mean, a particular set of words you have to speak to make it work – like a spell? Or will any quote from the Scriptures work?'

'Well, it's not *just* the words,' Johnstone said, suddenly awkward again. 'The actual words are only part of it. But I do use a passage from the Scriptures – one that was taught to me by a very great man. I've always used them.'

John leaned forward. 'Look,' he said, 'I know this might be asking too much, but . . . could you say the words for me? Just as you would in an exorcism? Here, into the microphone. I mean – I'll be writing about it; you know that. I wouldn't want to misquote something as important as this.'

Johnstone thought it over for a long moment.

'I don't see any harm in that,' he decided. He turned his chair slightly away from John, focusing his attention on the tape recorder for the first time. He glanced back, suddenly rather nervous. 'As I said, it's not *only* the words.'

'I understand. It's just a resource.'

The reverend nodded and took a long deep breath, composing himself. Then he began to recite the words with a clarity and intensity that surprised John. They were obviously part of something this man did not take lightly.

'I *bind*, by the True God, the Living God, the Holy Ghost – in the name of the Father and of the Son and of the Holy Spirit – any evil force; that it may not intrude, interfere, disturb, or distort your life!'

The reverend's voice swelled to fill the room . . .

. . . and John Jones suddenly felt extremely ill.

Johnstone continued, unaware that his interviewer had lost all interest in the ritual.

What the hell's going on? John wondered. It felt as if the top of his head was being pulled away. His stomach was twittering and jumping; he was ready to throw up.

It must be the tea, he told himself. Or maybe some

157

psychosomatic thing. I know what happened when he did this before; I'm psyching myself into it.

The reverend was continuing. John Jones could barely comprehend a word. He was fighting to keep his food down. Without meaning to, he brought his hand up to cover his mouth.

Timothy Johnstone stopped. 'Are you all right?' he said, looking closely at his interviewer.

John looked back at him with bleary eyes. He hadn't heard the question clearly.

'What is it?' Johnstone said sharply. He could see something, John realized. Something . . . *new*.

The reverend stared for a long moment, then turned back to the tape recorder to finish the recitation. This time he didn't take his eyes from John. This time he watched very, very closely.

The reverend began to speak again . . .

. . . and John Jones fought to keep from sliding out of his chair and falling to the floor.

His head was spinning. He couldn't see at all. The pulling on the top of his head was worse than ever. He thought he could hear his hair tearing away; the bones in his neck were crackling like popcorn, and a huge fist was closing on his stomach, tighter and *tighter* . . .

The reverend turned and shouted the words of the ritual straight into John Jones' face –

– and stopped.

John struggled for breath. A chill passed through him, from fingertips to toes. And slowly, horribly slowly, he felt himself returning to normal.

'I'm sorry,' Johnstone said, putting his hand on John's clammy wrist. 'Something's simply not right here. When you came in, you seemed quite fine to me. But now there is a darkness – remember the presence I described to you? It's hovering all around you, John.'

John palmed the sweat away from his eyes with the heel of one hand. 'I'm fine,' he said. 'It's the English food. The jet lag.'

'No,' Johnstone said flatly. 'There is something wrong here, *very* wrong. I think we should go into the church immediately. I think you should let me clear you.'

John gaped at him. '*Exorcise* me? You're joking!'

'No, I'm not.' The reverend stood, ready to lead him to the sanctuary. John wouldn't be moved.

'No way. No. I came here for an interview, that's all. That's all. Not this. Not –'

'John,' The Reverend Timothy said soothingly. 'What better way for you to see what I do first-hand? As a writer – a *researcher*, John. Surely personal experience is the most rewarding for you?'

John Jones stared at him blankly for a moment, groping for a response. But the queasiness was coming back again, worse than before. He couldn't think clearly; he didn't even want to try. He just shrugged and struggled to his feet. They walked the short distance to the church close together, as if the reverend were ready to catch John if he fell.

Johnstone opened the small side door to the vestibule and went inside. 'Come along,' he said, hushed.

John looked up at the immense structure and shrugged. He put one foot across the threshold –

– something slammed into the top of his head with impossible force. A wave of pain sliced through him, down his arms, through his chest, past his groin and thighs and calves in one horrible, convulsive *twitch*. He was on fire. For one terrifying instant, *he was on fire*.

Then it was gone.

Later, John realized it was in that instant he changed. With the passing of the shockwave through his body, he was no longer a Doubting Thomas, active imagination notwithstanding.

For the first time in his life, John Jones *believed*.

He knelt unsteadily on a small pad before the altar as the reverend donned a crimson mantle. Then he approached

159

the railing where John was hunched. He held a small bowl of holy water in one hand and a delicate, soft brush in the other.

Johnstone turned to face the altar, and John watched him, blinking back inexplicable tears. He couldn't seem to get a good look at the reverend – it was just a gold and white blur. And . . . *candles*, he realized. There seemed to be hundreds and hundreds of candles.

The reverend stood stiffly, legs spread wide, and began the ritual in earnest. Later, John would remember the entire scene with crystal clarity. When it was happening, he could barely follow it at all.

He felt something touch his forehead, and a warm sensation washed through him – tingling, comforting, fulfilling.

It paused for a moment . . . then came again. John opened his eyes and looked up, straining to focus.

The reverend was painting a cross on his forehead with the brush. He had dipped it repeatedly in the holy water.

Then, as John watched, Johnstone put the bowl and brush aside and gripped John's head between his hands – a firm, solid, somehow protective gesture.

'I *bind*, by the True God, the Living God, the Holy Ghost – in the name of the Father and of the Son and of the Holy Spirit – any evil force; that it may not intrude, interfere, disturb or distort your life!'

Images.

Images twirled behind John's eyes. There was a figure bathed in pure white light. It was singing to him – a song that sent him hurtling through a sky that was studded with stars – towards the bright white coin of a full, expanding moon.

As he rushed towards the sphere, it exploded into a million shimmering slivers. Each shard spun past; each sang the same wondrous song. John streaked forward, through the clouds of shattered moon. Beyond it, beyond it . . .

The sun – a monstrous, awesome, honeyed gold. The

song was coming from there, and it was pulling him, it was drawing him willingly, joyfully.

Somewhere far away, he could hear the vast and bottomless words of the ritual, echoing across the sky. But the song was so lovely; the glow was so painfully beautiful. He had to go. He had to touch it. He reached to the golden sun, *through* the sun itself, to –

– darkness. *Darkness*.

And the figure bathed in light swooped out of the black and gathered him up like a child. The song was still there as they flew – the song was still there, and he realized it was inside, *it was coming from within*. John joined in the living, eternal melody as they streaked through the endless darkness, towards . . .

. . . towards . . .

A blade of light cut through the shadows in St. John's Church.

The reverend put a gentle hand on John's shoulder. 'How do you feel?' he asked.

John didn't answer right away. There were no words.

Finally he swallowed and opened his mouth. 'I feel . . . good,' he grated.

The words seemed ludicrous. *Totally inadequate*. There was no way to explain what had happened. No way to – to –

He rose to his feet and followed the reverend back to the rectory. They shared a pot of tea.

Strange, John thought later. It tasted good.

CHAPTER SIXTEEN

JOHN JONES looked at the object in his lap with a mixture of befuddlement and horror. *How could I do it*? he thought. *How could I do it*?

The London-to-Los Angeles British Airways flight was passing the half-way point. The jet roared around him, grumbling steadily over the Alaskan waste lands towards home. A few moments earlier, he had been looking down on a rumpled comforter of clouds thousands of feet below, enjoying a smooth, seamless fog of self-satisfaction – a strangely lazy state of mind that had enclosed him since his . . .

He still flinched when he thought of it, but that didn't make it any less accurate. He'd been feeling this way since shortly after his *exorcism*.

It had begun with the pictures of St. John's. He'd shaken hands with Rev. Johnstone, thanked him for everything – *everything* – and gone into the sanctuary to take a few shots.

Even now, he remembered holding the camera up to his eyes, and seeing the glittering white and gold altar in clear and precise detail. His finger had paused over the shutter button . . .

. . . and the scene through the viewfinder faded to black. John walked dumbfounded as the light meter's level sunk to '0'. Then he took the camera away from his eye.

Everything was fine. The cathedral was as full of light as ever – not so much as a cloud over the sun had changed it.

Must be the battery, he thought, knowing even then that

the battery had nothing to do with what he saw through the viewfinder. That was when the *disconnection* had begun, he realized. He should have known even then that something strange was going on – that it was starting again, as it had before the exorcism. But that eerie, edgeless sense of self-absorption had stolen over him, and . . . it didn't bother him.

It just didn't bother him.

He remembered shrugging and putting the camera back up to his eyes. It happened again. The picture was bright and clear . . . and then it dissolved like a film clip fading to black.

So he took the pictures anyway. He contentedly snapped and posed and framed the photos, without even thinking about how they might come out.

John Jones was a man who valued the power of his own mind. He didn't like the idea of losing track, of letting go. But this time he didn't care.

He just couldn't get himself to care.

The jet hit an air pocket and the cup of coffee on the seat-tray in front of him jounced unceremoniously. He steadied it with one hand, gripping the object in his lap with the other. Just touching the damn thing made him flinch.

He remembered taking the camera to a repair shop in Picadilly Circus. He remembered explaining what had happened.

'Impossible,' the Cockney behind the counter had said. 'It's a single reflex camera, mate – what you see is what you get.' He made an imaginary camera with his hands and clicked his tongue like the sound of a closing shutter: 'Tch-tchk.'

For a moment – just for a moment – the fog cleared and a chill went down John's spine. *He's right*, he thought suddenly. Something's going on here, something . . .

. . . something . . .

'Thanks for everything,' John said suddenly. He snatched up the camera and left the shop – without a repair, without fresh film, without resolving a thing.

But it didn't matter. He didn't mind. He just went back to his hotel and stored the camera under the clothes in his suitcase, filled with contentment on a job well done.

John looked back out the window of the jet, and shook his head. Maybe he could have chalked it up to absent-mindedness. Some kind of deferred stress from the cleansing.

But what about later that night? What about almost drowning on a street in Soho?

He remembered sitting at the bar of the warm and friendly pub in the West End, waiting for Andy Frame to show up. He even remembered how the dark wood walls and the glittering shelves of liquor seemed to turn gray in front of him, and get farther and farther away . . .

'You awright, luv?'

John straightened up abruptly. He was starting to slip off his chair, and he hadn't even realized it.

'Wha – ?' He struggled to wake up.

A wrinkled, gray-haired Englishwoman was leaning over from the seat two stools away. She had a lighted fag in one hand and a half pint of bitter in the other. 'I said, "you awright, luv"?' she repeated, looking closely at him. 'Yu've been nodding' off there. Thot y'might fall an' 'urt y'self.'

'I'm fine, thanks,' John stuttered.

'Sometimes a bit stoofy in 'ere,' she said. 'Sometimes it kin get a mite close.'

'You're right, love,' John said, standing up slowly and rubbing at his face. 'I think I'll get some air.'

She nodded decisively. 'Fix y'roit up,' she said, grinning.

He remembered walking towards the door of the tiny West End pub. He remembered the sudden, welcome gust of moist night air, and thinking how Andy's talk about music and songwriting would be a welcome break from the questions about Amityville

He remembered opening the door. Then –

' – you doing, mate?'

John woke up. He tried to breathe. Water gushed down his throat – cold, gritty water – and he doubled over, coughing like a drowned man.

Water spilled out of the sides of his mouth and splattered on the ground. Andy Frame slapped his old friend on the back and repeated himself.

'What are you doing?' he said. He grabbed John under the arms and half-pulled him into the shelter of the pub's entrance. It was pouring rain – a thick, incessant torrent that had been going on for almost an hour.

John looked stupidly at his coat and clothes. They were soaked through – so wet that the shirt and jacket were transparent. He could see his chest and arms clearly beneath the cloth.

'Sorry, mate,' Andy said nervously, not sure exactly how to take this scene. 'I was held up. I tried to call, but you weren't here yet.'

No, John thought days later, shuddering as the British Airways jet began its descent towards Los Angeles International. No, I wasn't in the pub. I was standing out in the pouring rain, with my head thrown back and my mouth wide open, filling up with water. I was upright and completely unconscious, trying to drown myself on a public street.

He looked down at the camera that was sitting in his lap. He swallowed hard. Timothy Johnstone had called him just before the flight back to Los Angeles – after the sidetrip to Amsterdam, after John's return to London.

'Have you been all right?' he had asked worriedly.

'Fine,' John had said. 'Why?'

'Sometimes there's – there's something of a delayed reaction,' the reverend had said, 'I was concerned.'

A delayed reaction, he thought now.

He put the Nikon up to his eyes and looked down the length of the 747. Even in the dim fluorescent light, the picture was clear and sharp. The light meter's indicator hovered right in the middle – ready to go.

He never had the camera fixed. He never got more film. He had no pictures of Johnstone or the church or Amsterdam. All he had was one roll of possibly under-exposed film.

When the Los Angeles film processor called three weeks later to apologize, John wasn't the least bit surprised. They were very sorry, they said, but they couldn't find that roll of film anywhere – not *anywhere*.

John just smiled to himself and told them it was fine. He would be glad to accept their offer of a free replacement roll.

CHAPTER SEVENTEEN

THERE IT is again. Terri Sullivan spun on her heels, banging her shin painfully against the chrome crossbar of the grocery cart. The family-size box of toothpaste clattered to the floor.

A colorfully dressed old lady wearing too much make-up and a strong, cheap perfume had shuffled by her a few moments ago. But now the aisle was empty.

But – I *felt* something, Terri told herself. She'd felt it a few minutes earlier, in the produce section, and before that in the parking lot.

Something's watching me. Something's stalking me. It wants to reach out and touch m –

'Stop it,' she said to herself. 'Just *stop* it.' Ever since that night in the Lutz' house, when she had – when she –

She forced herself to take a long, deep breath and exhale slowly. 'You're going to be all right,' she promised herself. 'All right.'

She looked up to see a woman in a pink-and-blue flower print muu-muu staring at her through thick lenses. *Great*, she thought. *Now I'm talking to myself. Even the weird people think I'm weird.*

She decided she could get the rest of the groceries tomorrow, when it wasn't one of *those* days. At least that was enough of an excuse for her to hurry out of the supermarket as fast as she could.

Abby Sullivan was tired. She leaned against the wall of

the downstairs corridor and lifted one foot, rubbing her instep, then her heel, in a slow circular massage.

Now that Terri was sharing the house with her again, Abby only had to work a part-time job. But even three days a week seemed to exhaust her these days. It had been wonderful to have the children here, but it had been a draining job. Being a mother has always been hard, she thought as she moved towards the stairs, but I don't remember it being *this* hard.

She sighed as she climbed the stairs, looking wearily at her stockinged feet as they worked their way up, one step at a time. She wondered about whether it was time to get a new pair of pumps. These seemed to pinch her all the time. She was thinking about her paycheck, and Terri, and the housework that was waiting for her . . .

. . . So, Abby Sullivan didn't see a thing until it was too late.

'Come on, baby,' Terri said, and turned the key again. The Volkswagen engine coughed and whirred, then paused dramatically.

Terri pressed on the accelerator, then pumped it again. The engine roared and she popped the clutch fast – it had worked before – and the bug jumped forward with a jerk.

She raced down the parking lot, past Long's Drugs and Korb's, afraid to apply the brakes just yet. 'That's it,' she said. 'Come on.' She wondered distantly if everyone who owned a Volkswagen talked to it like an old friend. Then she cut across the empty parking places painted on the blacktop and headed for the street.

It happened so fast that she never really saw it. It was in front of her only for an instant, for a fraction of a heartbeat, and only later, after the blood and terror, could she bear to examine the image that was etched behind her eyes.

For a single, destructive instant, a huge tentacular arm appeared in the air in front of her car. It was attached to nothing at all – a vast, dripping thing thrusting through from another world, with a line of talons along the bottom and a stabbing claw as big as a mammoth tusk at the end.

It was coming straight for her.

Terri felt a horrible impact and the car flew five feet to the right. The sound of tearing metal, more terrible than a scream, filled the air around her. The car's engine rattled with the sound of metal ringing against metal, then stopped with a loud crash.

There was nothing in front of her. Nothing at all.

For a long beat, Terri sat staring into the parking lot. Cars came and went. People loaded paper bags and started engines. No one else seemed to be sharing her nightmare.

She wasn't even sure she believed it herself. After a long moment, Terri got out of her car . . .

. . . and stared in horror at what she found.

The first sweeping slash shattered a five-foot section of the balustrade behind Abby Sullivan. Broken pieces of carved wood exploded, clattering against the opposite wall, more than ten feet away.

The second strike whistled through the air only inches from Abby's head and punched through the plaster like a battering ram. The wallpaper dissolved. The lath exploded. Even the timber beneath was snapped like kindling.

Abby was frozen at the top of the stairs. The blows had come in front and behind – she couldn't move, she didn't dare. She could only stand and stare at the thing that hovered only a few feet away:

An enormous, multi-jointed arm with sharp spines along one side and a viciously curved claw at the end. A writhing appendage that terminated in . . . nothing. In the empty air.

The apparition wriggled, cobra-swift, barely three yards before her. She could smell the foul stench of the thing. She could see a gray-green ooze dripping on the carpet.

A wide, wailing moan filled the house – not coming from the thing, but coming *with* it, emanating from every corner of the second floor. An envelope of frigid air encased her, and Abby felt her muscles grow tight and stiff inside her. Tiny icicles crackled on her eyebrows. Her breath escaped in steaming billows with every exhalation. She felt frost building up at the corners of her mouth.

Part of Abby was screaming at the sight of it. Part of her would never forget. And another part, the larger part, refused to acknowledge what she saw before her. Like a broken tape machine, it wouldn't record. She could only stand, and stare, and wait for the horror to pass her by.

The bodiless arm attacked again. The air before it shrieked with the approach, and Abby flinched away without thinking.

The claw at the end missed her only by millimeters. The wind from the blow pulled her hair like a hand. Distantly, vaguely, she heard it shatter the wall to her right, and when the thing reappeared, its scales and spines were encrusted with brightly colored wires and strips of twisted metal it had dragged from the wall.

Abby took one step back. It was all the initiation her frozen mind could muster – all her paralyzed reflex for flight could do. She took one step back –

– and found empty air.

In that instant, she knew what would happen. She was standing on the stairs. She was going to fall back. And the thing on the second floor would slither down to kill her.

Too late, she realized. *Too late . . .*

She fell backwards and hit the stairs with both shoulder-blades. Her legs flew up over her, stark against the ceiling. She rolled over backwards and heard the vertebrae crunch in her neck. Then it all came apart in a tangle of arms and legs and deep, indelible pain.

She bounced like a ball down the twenty-five steps – steps she had counted a hundred times over – and landed in a crumpled heap on the hardwood floor of the hallway.

She remembered nothing more.

Terri didn't dare touch it. She was afraid it would turn out to be real.

The VW's engine cover was gone. She couldn't even find its crumpled remains. The body of the battered red car was gouged as if by huge claws – five parallel lines that ribboned the sheet metal for more than three feet.

The engine was an impossible mess. Cables hung like hair. Bright silver grooves had turned metal parts into scrap. And down beneath the broken arms, the snapped springs, the bits of shattered plastic, even the engine block was battered out of shape, as if someone had spent an hour with a ten-pound sledge going at it again and again.

All in an instant. In less than the blink of an eye.

'What in God's name . . . ?' she said very softly. But she knew. She knew exactly how it had happened.

And in a sudden, sickening flash, she knew what it would do next.

She left the car where it was and ran towards the main street, shouting. She would flag down a cop, hitch a ride, call a cab, *something*, but she would do it *now*.

Terri was suddenly frightened for her mother.

She threw a five-dollar bill at the cab driver and jumped from the car. The front door was ajar, and she burst through it without thinking what she might find.

'Mom? Mom, are you –'

Her mother was lying at the foot of the stairs. She was very, very still.

'MOM!' Terri threw herself at her mother's side and seized one wrist.

She couldn't find it. *She couldn't find the pulse*.

Something tickled between her ribs. She ignored it and felt for the beat in her mother's neck – for any sign of life.

– and the feeling came again. The feeling of being

watched, so strong that it seized her like an insubstantial fist and made her stop short.

She set her mother's wrist back on the carpet, slowly and gently. She turned from the body and rose from her knees, almost graceful in her terror.

She was halfway to her feet when she felt it: a flimsy ripple in the air, directly in front of her.

Darkness – oily thick clouds of blackness – gushed from an invisible hole in the middle of the air. She raised one hand to ward it off, and in a heartbeat it had her. She was swallowed by the black before she could speak.

'Mom . . . ?' She whispered. She had to find her, she knew. Drag her out of the stuff. She slid out her foot, feeling the floor where her mother laid.

Nothing. The ground was barren and uncharacteristically rough, more like a natural stone surface than the overpolished hardwood floor of their home.

Either she has moved, Terri realized. *Or I have*. She put out her arms and groped at the air. It was empty and cold, and growing colder. She could find no railing, no walls, no welcoming substance at all.

She moved her arms faster and faster, flailing at the air, pinwheeling like a madwoman –

– and she smacked it. She found something solid, uncommonly solid, and instantly she clutched at it with both hands.

It was soft and pliable beneath her digging fingers. Despite her desperate hold, it slipped and slided in her hands. And the tighter she closed on it, the wetter it got. Wetter and . . . stickier.

Even as it moved against her, Terri's sense of equilibrium returned. There was a floor beneath her feet. There was something sharing the darkness. Something cold and slimy. She hesitantly took one hand from her hold and brought it to her face, sniffing suspiciously –

– and reared back, gagging. It was a horrible stench, like something three day's dead. The intensity made her eyes water and her stomach churn. For a moment she felt ready to faint.

'My *God*,' she choked.

And the thing in the darkness twitched away.

Abruptly the darkness thinned. Gray, directionless light sifted up from all sides. Terri braced herself, locked her knees, and faced the thing she had touched.

And she screamed.

Her left hand was only inches from a wrinkled, inhuman face. A boar's snout thrust down over row after row of shark's teeth. Vicious, impossible tusks poked out of its prognathous jaw, and it's preternaturally crafty eyes glittered like green stones at the bottom of its blackened pits. There were too many legs for her to see, dancing and writhing without touching the ground. And the torso, as thick as an oak, was snake-smooth and oozing. Oozing a vile black pus that was all over her hands, all over her *face* –

She started to back away, still screaming. A voice in her mind cut the shrieking like a switch.

NOWHERE TO GO, LITTLE ONE.

It cut like fishhooks at the crown of her head. A voice from outside her, pulling her back.

YOU CANNOT RUN. CANNOT FIGHT. THERE'S NOWHERE TO GO.

Terri fought to escape it. She grabbed for a handhold, a wall or a doorframe, *anything* to keep from being pulled to the thing.

It opened its lipless mouth. Its gray-green tongue flickered and flattened, and strings of spittle escaped.

WHY FIGHT ME? it purred. I BRING YOU PEACE. DON'T FIGHT ME.

'Liar!' she shouted. '*Liar!*' But her feet were dragging her closer and closer.

Her mind ran screaming from her body, to hide in the corridors of the past. She thought about the dog that had attacked her – about that man who grabbed her when she was only ten.

173

She had thought that he wanted her Emmy – her favorite pink doll. The bad man had tried to be friendly at first, he'd talked to her pretty, but he was *big*, he was *evil*, and he grabbed her arms, he grabbed her Emmy –

– Gramma had given her Emmy. Gramma had made the huge hat with the pink ribbon that shaded her soft little nose, and painted in the puffs of rouge that never wore off. She made her the little plaid dress and the black cloth shoes and put on the solid gold, *real gold* chain that *her* Grammy – Great Grammy – had put on a doll all her own.

'Remember,' the dying old woman had rasped, 'Keep this necklet around Emmy's neck all of the time. It belonged to my mother. It kept her safe. You should keep little Emmy with you always.'

The creature's claws had gripped her. They were dragging her closer and closer to the flickering tongue. And all she could think of was dead Grandma Simpson and Emmy, poor Emmy, with the cross around her neck –

WHAT ARE YOU DOING?

The creature stopped moving her. The grip almost faltered.

Terri's eyes flickered open. She focused again. The creature was there. She fled into dreams. She thought of the teeth and the tongue and her grandmother's necklace with the solid gold cr –

STOP IT! STOP IT!

It started to shudder like a construct of paper and glue. Terri felt the image swelling inside her with frightening power. The golden cross. *The golden cross*. It had been blessed by a priest from the Old Country. It had been handed down for years. *The Cross*!

NOOOOOO!

The creature lunged at her, claws in the air. She screamed and ducked away, and a dripping talon sliced into her arm, sinking in three inches like a knife into putty.

Before blood could well up in the livid incision, invisible

174

fingers clamped around her torso and hurled her into the air –

– she slammed with stunning force into the shattered living room wall. Something snapped like wet wood at the base of her brain, and pain stabbed through her in ten different directions.

Something is broken, she thought slowly as pain lanced like electricity. *A lot of things are broken for good*.

DIE, the creature bellowed in her head. DIE DI-EEEEEE!!!

She flew from the ground, straight up in the air. The ceiling smashed against her and she felt her nose flatten, her fingers snap. The floor came back, twice as fast, and it was all pain then, a red haze of pain.

A bookcase. A chair. She saw one rush against her, a blackening blur. The other stabbed out, all angles and edges, and pulled parts of her skin and muscle away.

Blood was flowing from her mouth. Her limbs were twitching uncontrollably.

The . . . Cross. The Cross!

The beast raged at her and readied another attack. Terri thought at him, she *slammed* the image from mind to mind.

CROSS!

Somehow she was on her knees and moving forward. The legs were still working, at least a little. She could move across the floor, an inch at a time, but she kept slipping in patches of slime and blood.

Every second she expected to be lifted from the floor and shattered one last time. Each second she was ready for another cutting swipe from the talons. And she knew she was close to the end of it now. One more fall, one more attack, and she would be finished forever.

She dragged herself to the foot of the stairs . . .

Nothing happened.

She thought of the cross, the cross, *the cross*, and the creature stayed away from her, consumed in a pain of its own.

DON'T FIGHT ME, it gritted. But now she could

recognize fear in its tone. It was pleading with her, *begging* her. DON'T FIGHT ME.

She took the stairs on her knees. Her chin, then her forehead, collided with each step, but she climbed them. She *climbed* them.

The cross, she kept thinking. The cross, *the cross*.

The creature stayed close, a hideous angel only inches away.

Back to her bedroom. Her personal cave. She was leaving a wide red path on the carpet, but she got there. She made it.

The cross the cross . . .

There was a soft pink bedspread. A white French Provincial vanity. A small box for jewelry that played 'April in Paris.' A chest at the foot of her bed with

cross cross cross CROSS CROSS CROSS

STOP IT! STOP IT! It thundered in her brain.

One arm refused to function. The other trembled weakly as she tried to raise the lid of the chest. Blood filled her mouth. She almost collapsed. But she lifted the lid . . . lifted it . . . *open.*

The creature's shrieking filled the room.

She saw the little walnut box with her treasures inside. She put one hand on it. She started to take it –

– and the creature swept out and threw her away. She hit the far wall with a sickening *thud*, and heard the window behind her scream as it shattered.

She slid down the wall in a smear of blood and tissue. She couldn't see the room or the wreckage or the pretty pink spread. There was only her hands. And the creature.

And the little walnut box she was holding.

Terri ripped the lid from its hinges with impossible strength. Her torn muscles cried out, but she was past the pain now, even past the terror.

She pawed through the treasures as the creature writhed and babbled. Her breath was hot and sharp in her lungs. Her eyes were not working. The picture was fading like the image of an old TV . . .

176

CROSSCROSSCROSSCROSSCROSSCROSS

Rose petals. A ticket to the Zoo that her Daddy had got her before he went off to meet God. A bracelet from her mother. A pin from a boy. And –

The creature rose to the ceiling and bellowed. It began to expand, swelling to blot out the light, the sun, the world.

She slipped it over her head as the room began to quake. She wrapped her shattered fingers around it and pressed, pressed *hard*, and felt the sharp edges, the smooth finish.

A wind as cold as death rammed through the room. The one remaining pane in the window exploded. Furniture pounded against the walls.

'The Cross,' she mumbled through bloodied lips. 'Cross.'

She had done what she wanted to do. She couldn't remember what it was, or why she had, but it was done, *it was done*.

The creature screamed again, all frustration and rage.

She was unconscious before it exploded in a blast of fury . . . and was gone.

CHAPTER EIGHTEEN

'BUT HOW, George? How could all three of them get so sick, so fast – and all at the same time?'

George and Kathy were standing in a dimly lit hallway of their home in La Costa. George could hear the doctor moving quietly in the darkened bedroom. He reached out to take his wife's hand.

'Don't worry, babe,' he whispered. 'It'll be okay.'

'But *why*?' Kathy said, her voice even smaller. 'They were fine before, they were *just fine*.'

George started to say something, then stopped himself. That wasn't true. Kathy *knew* it wasn't. When they had returned from England only two days earlier, Terri had taken them out, away from the kids, and told them everything that had happened: the sudden illnesses, the strange smells – even the horrendous night when the thing in the upstairs hall had blown the back door off its hinges.

George thought of the crude sheets of plywood that still covered the shattered frame. Every trip to the kitchen was a reminder of how bad things really were.

Kathy was blocking it out, and he couldn't blame her. It was getting to be too much, all over again.

'Look,' he said. 'Why don't you go downstairs and make some fresh coffee for the doctor?'

'I want to hear what he has to say,' she said, but George could tell from the hesitant tone that she wasn't sure she wanted to talk with him at all. 'I – '

'Mr. Lutz?'

The doctor was standing in the darkened door to the boys' bedroom. The faint yellow light made him ghostly and insubstantial as he stepped carefully into the hall. 'Mrs. Lutz?'

Kathy's eyes widened. She took a step back. In an instant, George knew that she had already heard too much, seen too much, since their return to the States. And he knew that Kathy realized it herself.

'I'll . . . go make coffee,' she mumbled, and fled down the stairs.

The young doctor rubbed at the back of his neck as he watched the woman go. Then he turned back to George, frowning deeply. 'You know,' he said, 'Doctors never say "I don't know." We're trained to tell patients and families things like "We need more tests" or "We'll put them under observation." My favorite one is "It's a virus." Viruses, see, are hard to identify and almost impossible to treat. And most of them go away in a day or two, all by themselves.'

He put his hand on George's shoulder, and they walked down the hall, away from the boys' room. The doctor's tone was low and confidential. George found himself liking the man immensely.

'So I could say "it's a virus." ' the doctor said. 'And actually, I think it is. But to tell you the God's honest truth, Mr. Lutz – I don't know *what* the hell is going on.'

George smiled grimly as they moved down to the first floor. 'Well, I appreciate the honesty,' he said.

The doctor shrugged. 'Sure. But that doesn't make the kids any better, does it?' He glanced worriedly at the light streaming from the kitchen. 'I'm glad Mrs. Lutz left. Fact is, she looks damn close to exhaustion herself, and for all I know, it could be the same thing coming down on her.'

He pulled a pad from the breast pocket of his coat and scribbled on it. 'What the hell. Here's a prescription for some megavitamins you can't get over the counter. They might help. Dissolve them in water or juice for the kids; take 'em any way you want for yourself and your wife.' He tore the top slip off and handed it to George. 'Load the kids up with liquids – and I mean *load* 'em, as much

as they can stand. It's the best thing you can do. And –
George . . .' It was the first time, George realized, that the
young internist had called him by his first name. 'George,
if they're not any better by this time tomorrow, we may
have to take them to the hospital.' A bitter smile played
across the doctor's lips. ' "For further observation." '

George looked down at the prescription and nodded.
He shook the doctor's hand as the younger man opened
the front door.

'I'll check again tomorrow,' the doctor said softly. 'Good
night.'

George stood in the open door and watched the taillights
of the doctor's car flare in the darkness, then dwindle as
he drove away. *I'll have to call Terri in the morning*, he
thought. *Let her know what's happening*. George was
afraid she would blame herself for what was happening;
he wanted to try and change that before it happened.

He realized that, over the months and years, he and
Kathy – and even the children – had developed a kind of
protective fatalism about the unknown. All too often,
there wasn't a blessed thing they could do to change what
was happening, and in a way that fatalism was all that had
held them together during some of the worst times.

But that wasn't enough any more. He wasn't content to
stand aside and let his children suffer for no good reason.
Not any more.

Kathy came up behind him, and they stood in the doorway, in the bright illumination of the porchlight, and faced
each other as they drank.

'He doesn't – '

'I know,' Kathy said, looking down into her mug. 'I
heard.' When she looked up, there were glittering traces
of tears at the corners of her eyes. 'Let's go up and see
them,' she said, and turned away.

She was already halfway up the stairs when George
caught up to her. He took her hand in his own and she
grasped it tightly, squeezing. They went into Amy's room
together.

Kathy's eyebrows jumped in surprise as she laid her palm against the little girl's forehead. 'It's not nearly as hot as before,' she whispered, staring at her upturned hand. She smiled. 'And she's sleeping better. Look.' Kathy knelt by her daughter and stroked the girl's fine blonde hair. 'I think the fever's broken,' she said. George could hear the relief in her voice. 'It's going to be all right.'

In the adjoining room, Matt was tossing fitfully under the covers, still bathed in sweat and as hot as ever. The lines of worry in Kathy's face returned as she moved to touch both boys.

'They're still burning up,' she said.

Greg sat bolt upright, his skin stretched tight against his skull. 'Terri!' he shouted.

George spun to face him. The boy was still fast asleep, his eyes squeezed tightly shut. And before either parent could reach him, he sank back against his pillows, mumbling and whimpering inarticulately.

Terri? George wondered. Is he having a nightmare about what happened here before – what happened to Terri while they –

'*Terri*!'

George spun to look at Matt. Now he was sitting up, shining with perspiration. His head was thrown back, chin almost pointing to the ceiling, as he called out the name again. '*Terri*!'

Kathy clutched at her husband's arm. 'George . . . ?' she said hesitantly.

They both knew what was happening. They had shared nightmares themselves, when the entity had visited. They could guess what was happening in the children's dreams.

Both boys bolted up, their eyes still shut, their hands thrust out in front of them as if to ward off some violent attack. 'Terri' They shouted in unison – they *moved* in unison, as if reflections of a single body.

'TERRI!'

A third voice joined them – a thin, chirping call from the other room.

'My God,' Kathy whispered. 'Amy's caught in it, too!'

'TER – '

It cut off like a switch. The sound stopped in all three throats simultaneously, and just as abruptly, also in concert, the bodies flopped back to the pillows, drained.

For one wild moment, George thought to call Terri Sullivan in San Diego. Maybe it was something more than a nightmare, he thought. Maybe there's something *real* going on here.

Kathy moved quickly from one boy to the other. She looked over her shoulder at her husband and smiled thinly. 'I think it's going to be okay,' she said. 'I think the fever's broken now.'

They were still deeply asleep at nine o'clock the next morning, when the doctor reappeared on their doorstep. He looked drawn and tired as he mumbled something about a double shift at the hospital but he seemed stronger, even healthier himself as he trotted down the stairs after a swift examination.

'Whatever you did, you did right,' he said, grinning. 'They're looking good. Should be up and around in no t–'

The phone rang. George answered quickly.

'Mr. George Lutz? This is Doctor Marsden, at Reynolds Memorial in San Diego. I'm afraid I have some bad news. About your friend – '

Kathy said it at the same instant. She wasn't even listening on the extension, but she said it even as the doctor did.

' – Terri Sullivan,' she said.

Ten minutes later, George was on his way to San Diego.

'I'm sorry,' Terri's doctor said shortly. 'We're doing what we can.'

George frowned deeply at him. *As different as night and day*, he thought. There was the young and friendly doctor in La Costa, honest about his shortcomings, honest about

182

his weariness. And there was this thick, grim brick of a man, well past fifty and hating every minute of his work. He seemed even less sympathetic than the uniformed policeman standing next to him, and for the first time George realized how much they looked alike; one in white, one in black. Both overweight, and bitter, and a little bit bored.

'Are there any other relatives?' the doctor asked, staring accusingly at his clipboard. He had yet to make eye contact with George, even when he shook his hand. 'Anyone we should notify?'

'Just her mother –' George stopped, realizing that wasn't what the doctor meant. 'No,' he stammered. 'Not that I know of.'

'Fine.' The doctor turned and walked away without another word.

George stood in the hallway outside the emergency ward's treatment center and stared dumbfounded at the physician's back. *None of this makes sense*, he thought. *None of it*. First the fevers, then the dreams, now Terri *really* in hospital, really *hurt* –

He turned to the policeman who was standing impatiently next to him, flipping through his notes and clearing his throat.

'Apparently the victims interrupted a burglary in progress,' he said. 'One or more perpetrators, as yet unidentified, then assaulted Abby Sullivan and her daughter Terri – ' He glanced up, almost guiltily, and cleared his throat again. 'Not sexual assault, Mr. Lutz. Just physical.'

' "Just"?'

The cop scowled. 'Cut me some slack, will you? We got almost nothing on this except a couple of broken people. I'm giving you our best guess.'

'All right,' George said, feeling very calm.

'We're checking for similar M.O.'s in recent assaults. We're looking into recent releases or escapes from mental institutions in the area. It looks like the work of a sicko – a real psychotic. We'll let you know what we find.'

He flipped his notebook shut and looked up at George with a strange, challenging glint in his eye. As if he was daring him to ask any more questions. As if he almost *wanted* George to pick some sort of fight.

George only gave him a very small, very tight smile. 'Fine,' he said, just as the doctor had. Then he turned and walked away.

His mind was racing. Something was wrong about the entire thing. Something just felt . . . *wrong*. Too many coincidences, too many unsurprising surprises. If only he could talk to somebody about it, if . . .

Abby.

George stopped dead in the hall and snapped his fingers. Maybe she could give him some answers. The doctors had said she had taken a severe fall and was badly shaken, but that was ten times better than Terri was.

Terri could die, he thought with chilling clarity. *Terri probably will die*.

He turned and walked to the elevator with new determination. I'm going to get to the bottom of this, he decided. One way or the other, I'm going to get to the *bottom* of this.

This is fine, Abby Sullivan thought. This is just *fine*.

She was drifting away on a wide flat bed. There was a smooth white ceiling way up over her head. Nothing bothered her. Nothing hurt. But she wondered, from time to time, why her daughter hadn't come home from the store just yet.

(Dorothy Gorman, the Sullivan's neighbor, had seen the downstairs lights on and the front door open. She went over to say hello.

(She knocked. She called. There was no answer. She got worried enough to go inside, and found Abby Sullivan at the foot of the stairs. She ran to the kitchen to call *911*.

(Her husband came over right away. He was the one who found Terri, lying in a pool of her own blood.)

Occasionally people had come in to speak to Abby. She remembered them sort of: big faces on tiny bodies, floating far up in the air. Doctors (the white coats). Policemen (the dark coats). Nurses (with hats) and orderlies (with no hats).

But she was floating. And flying. And feeling just fine.

A big burly man – a handsome man with a full beard and bright brown eyes – came to call. He had a very soft voice. He asked her something, a couple of times, but she couldn't quite hear what it was.

She let it go. Fine, fine, fine.

He spoke to her again, more softly than before. And after a while, he left the room.

He seems like a very nice person, Abby thought. *I wonder who he is?*

She was on the third floor. In room 317. Intensive Care (non-cardiac). Some small fraction of Terri Sullivan was continuously, miraculously conscious. She had heard the nurses talking. She had somehow seen the lights in the elevator, the plaque on the door, the inked-in words on the chart at her feet.

She knew she couldn't move. She was wrapped in a rich and colorless gray, far removed from the third floor. Her body, what was left of it, was held down by some invisible, inexorable weight. She would stay where she was. Maybe forever.

Terri relaxed inside the grayness . . . and something tugged at her. Something started to pull her away.

IT'S NICE HERE, the pressure said – not in words at all. In *feelings*, in promises. IT'S PEACEFUL. WE'RE WAITING.

Part of her wanted to go so badly. To leave the pain and horror behind. To slide away, rise above. Let it go.

A fragmented memory of what had happened at the house thrust itself forward. It ran backwards, from end to beginning: The cross. The creature. The stairs. The hall-way. Her . . .

'Mom?'

She was crumpled at the foot of the stairs. Terri couldn't find her pulse.

'*Mom*?'

TER . . . REE, it whispered. The gently tugging press-ure grew more insistent. TERREE . . .

'Is that you, Mom? Where are you? I can't see you.'

(Out on the third floor, in room 317, her broken mouth began to move. Stitches tore open as she tried to form words.)

CLOSE YOUR EYES, TERREE. GIVE IN TO ME.

'Please, Mom, is it you? *Really*? I have to see you, Mom. I have to *see* you.'

(Nurse Callahan called Doctor Pinelli. They stood on opposite sides of the girl and watched her try to speak.

('Demerol, nurse,' he said, as Terri tried to move inside her restraints. Blood welled up around the stitches in her mouth. 'IM injection, *stat*.'

('We've got to get her to relax.')

GIVE IN TO ME, TERREE. WE WELCOME YOU HERE.

It must be my mother, Terri thought. She's come back to carry me over, just like in those books I read. She died in the fall, and I died from the –

– from the creature –

TAKE MY HAND, TERREE. GIVE IN.

'I don't want to go yet, Momma. Please, not yet.'

TERREE . . .

'I should *fight*! You always told me to *fight*!'

IT'S PEACEFUL HERE. SO PEACEFUL.

'*I DON'T WANT TO GO!*'

It reached out for her somehow. It brushed against her soul. And in that instant of contact, Terri felt an image – a solid image of an insubstantial thing.

She remembered it later as a smell – a putrid, cloying, rancid smell of something dead for a long, long time.

The creature. The thing in the house. It was coming for her one final time.

It isn't my mother, she realized. *IT ISN'T MY MOTHER*!

Something pricked her in the arm. Fatigue rushed into the grayness.

Fight it, she ordered herself. Fight it, *fight it*!

('That's better,' Dr. Pinelli said. He handed the empty syringe to Nurse Callahan. 'Notify me if there's any change – any change at all.')

The darkness was coming to swallow her up. But it wasn't the creature – it wasn't *his* death, she knew.

Terri Sullivan had decided she was going to fight.

I won't go without giving it my all, she decided. I'll fight to stay alive.

If after she'd given her best, death still came to claim her – as well it might – there was little she could do about that but face it, as best she could. But the *creature* wouldn't get her.

She clung to the fragments of thought as the drug took effect.

Do you hear me? she shouted from deep in her mind. And again she called in defiance. *You'll never get me! Never!*

CHAPTER NINETEEN

GEORGE LUTZ stopped dead in the middle of the front hall of the Sullivan house. The late afternoon sun came through the open door in rich gold bars, littering the floor and making the walls glow warmly. There were children playing nearby, and the roar of a jet plane overhead, and the distant backfire of a motorcycle, but George heard none of it . . . *felt* none of it.

He only saw the gouges in the wall – the thick, deep marks that were identical to the wounds he had seen on the flight to Australia.

Something about this whole tragedy had felt *wrong*. He was sure of it at the hospital, and again after he had tried to talk with Mrs. Sullivan.

That had been a waste of time. She was cut loose from the world – by drugs or by her own desperate state of mind, he couldn't tell – but she didn't seem to hear his questions. Didn't even know him.

He had actually been on the freeway, heading back to La Costa, when he had decided to try one last thing.

He turned around and headed back to San Diego – to this house where Terri and Abby Sullivan lived.

The police hadn't even bothered to lock the front door. He half-expected to see the chalk outline of a body on the front hall carpet when he went inside, but that was missing, too. It was as if nothing had happened here at all. Nothing –

George dared to take a step closer to the marks on the wall and part of his mind realized that he was in the same place at the same time of day as the Sullivans had been.

Almost exactly twenty-four hours earlier, in this spot, the abomination had tried to murder two innocent women.

The edges of the grooves still glittered with something thick and sticky. Slowly, hesitantly, George put out one hand and touched the marking. Bits of plaster flaked off and stuck to his fingers. The slime clung to his skin.

He moved the hand back and took a small, cautious sniff.

The same smell. The same hideous, disgusting, decaying smell of –

George staggered through the open front door. He barely made it off the porch before he threw up.

'I want it over with,' George said angrily into the phone. '*Now*.'

The deep and familiar voice on the other end tried hard to sound soothing.

'Think about what you're saying, George. Calm down.'

'I don't want to calm down! I don't *want* to take it easy! Damn it, Father, I want it finished! I want to fight it *now*!'

The anger had been building in him since the moment he had left the Sullivan's abandoned home. The attacks had been going on for more than six years – *six years*! – but it had never been like this.

He was going to do what he'd promised himself for months. The moment he pounded through the front door of their home in La Costa, he called Father Mancusso at his parish, thousands of miles away.

He was grateful now that Kathy and the children were already asleep. He didn't want them to hear him shouting like this – not now, not with Terri in the hospital, and their own health in jeopardy. But he was *mad*, damn it, he was *mad*. And he wanted to put an end to the horror once and for all.

'Father, I've had it,' he said. 'I want you to tell me how to call this *thing* up – I know there's a way to do it! – and I want to fight it now. *Tonight*.'

'George, stop. Just *stop*. You've been shouting since the moment you called, and it's not getting you anywhere. Do you understand? *This is the way it wants you to act. This is when you're weakest.*'

George stopped pacing. For a moment, he took the receiver away from his ear and stared at it. The Father was right. He was exactly right.

He put the receiver back to his ear again. He sat down in his favorite chair, the one near the unused fireplace, and took a huge breath. 'Okay,' he said to his old friend. 'Okay.'

'Now start from the beginning,' Father Mancusso told him. The priest was still in control, still guiding George after all these years. 'Tell me what's been going on.'

George told him. He began with the attack in the park months earlier, with the new nightmares, the attack on the plane. He described the hellhounds in Australia and what Terri had told him of the attacks in La Costa while they were gone. He repeated what Reverend Johnstone had said, and he ended, almost half an hour later, with the horror of finding Terri Sullivan in the hospital, and the evidence of the abomination still naked and reeking in her empty home.

'Father,' he finally said, his throat raw, 'it's different now. It was bad enough when the attacks were only aimed at us – when they were mostly mental. I mean, we lived through the worst times then – the sickness and the dreams – '

'I know,' the priest said very quietly.

' – But now the thing's more *physical*, somehow. Its attacks don't end with everything going back the way it was. *Think* about it – my burns, the jet plane, my boots – the back door right here, it's *still* blocked off. And Father – the innocent people. It's not just after my family now. It's attacking our friends, the people we love – '

'It's always done that, George,' Father Mancusso said. 'Have you forgotten?'

For the second time that evening, the priest had stopped

George in his tracks. Yes, he realized, he *had* forgotten. In the heat of his anger, in the immediacy of his pain, he hadn't remembered what Mancusso himself had gone through in the beginning – an exposure to the evil force from Amityville that was still taking its toll on this good and holy man.

'I'm . . . sorry, Father. I . . . '

'George, I can understand what you're doing. I can feel your pain.'

'I know you can.'

'And you're right. Something *is* different now. The entity has changed its tactics. But don't make the mistake of thinking that it's weaker – or even that it can be defeated at all.'

'But if I call it up myself,' George said impulsively. 'If I can fight it on my own – my own territory, my own *turf* – '

'It doesn't work that way, George,' he said grimly. 'If you call it yourself you give it more power. You acknowledge it. You *welcome* it. And whatever happens then, whatever horrors enter your life, are all the more devastating because *you asked for it to come*. Can you see that?'

George covered his face with his free hand. A wave of despair and weariness washed over his face. 'Yes,' he said. 'I know what you're saying. But it seems so hopeless. I just . . . ' He trailed off. Tears of frustration filled his eyes.

'No, George,' the priest said sharply. 'Don't play into its hands like this. There is hope. There is *always* hope. But you must be *guided* by it, not by fear, or desperation, or even your righteous anger.'

'Father,' George whispered. 'There's *got* to be a way.'

There was a long pause on the other end. George listened to the hiss of the long distance line, feeling half-dead and empty inside. 'We have all been through a great deal since that day I came to bless your house,' Father Mancusso finally told him. 'I have come to think of you all as my family. And believe me, George, if I thought it were possible to call up this – this *thing* – ' he stumbled over the word, and George realized how difficult it still was for the priest to even talk of it. ' – If I could, I would call it up and banish it forever.' There was another pause on the phone. When Mancusso spoke again, he sounded farther away than ever before. 'But I can't do it, George. I simply cannot do it.'

George was nodding. 'I know,' he said softly. 'I understand. But what should we do? What *can* we do?'

George heard a sharp intake of breath as the priest pulled himself back together. 'Hope and pray that there *is* no final confrontation,' Mancusso said more strongly. 'And still be prepared for the worst. I will send you a Bible that has been blessed. It's one of my most precious possessions, but – well, you need it more than I do at the moment. I also have a picture of Padre Pio that might help. The English reverend – Johnstone? – I think he is exactly right. You need symbols to focus on, things to channel your strength. Gather the letters that you have received, and keep them close by. But remember, George – the strength comes from *you*, from your family. Not from inanimate objects, as profound as their effect on you may be.'

George agreed to do it. He thanked the father for his help. 'I know how hard this is for you,' he said. 'Maybe I'd forgotten it when I called, but – '

'I'll do what I can, George,' Father Mancusso said. 'I will help you prepare in any way I can, so if you *must* fight it, you *can*. I just pray it won't come to that.'

George swallowed hard and nodded. 'So do I, Father. So do I.'

Images swirled in George's mind as he replaced the telephone receiver in its cradle. It was late – very late – but he knew he wouldn't sleep that night.

He thought of Terri in her tangle of tubes and wires. He thought of the sickness that was hiding in his house. *Again*, he knew, *again*. He thought of his children, and his wife, and the indescribable power of the entity that continued to stalk them.

He came to realize that he was working with risky assumptions: that there was a time limit at all, for that matter; that the entity's change to more physical forms made it weaker, when it might simply be a change in approach that was as unfathomable as the entity's motives had always been; that even though physical evidence was growing, even thought he *was* able to battle the thing in a concrete, understandable way didn't mean that it was ultimately vulnerable at all.

As the sky above the Pacific turned the color of flint George Lutz came to a decision.

They would move again. They would leave this house, leave La Costa. He would take the advice of Mancusso and Johnstone and hope for the best as they prepared for the worst. And maybe, just *maybe*, it would never come to a final confrontation at all.

Kathy came down at 6:30 in the morning. She found her husband fast asleep in his easy chair. The phone was still sitting in his lap.

CHAPTER TWENTY

'IT'S ANOTHER hot summer day here in gorgeous Tucson Country,' the gravel-voice announcer crooned. 'Keep your dial right where it is, and we'll keep the music comin' atcha.'

An old Charlie Pride song filled the car. Bursts of static broke it to bits. George Lutz reached from behind the wheel and turned the radio off. Someone had broken off the Ford's antenna weeks earlier, and he knew right where the signal would start breaking up – right about here, three miles from their new home.

He looked across the desert – past the rough brown hills dotted with scrub and saguaro cactus – that rolled to the south and east as far as he could see. The new development, where they had finally found an affordable home, was farther into the natural desert than most of the city. But he had come to like it that way, he realized. He slowed the car and took the new road off to the right.

He focused on the dusty collection of homes that squatted on the horizon and thought about the move they had made. It had been hard on everyone at first – particularly on the children. But after a few months, they had grown to love the desert. The silence here was a rich, inviting sound all its own – a thing of subtlety and shape. He had never encountered skies exactly the color of these – white and brown simultaneously, like rich and finely woven cloth. Even the heat of the desert was different than he had imagined – different, even than Southern California. It was intense, of course – but clean, somehow. A healing thing. He sometimes thought the heat itself had as much to do with their weeks of tranquility as anything else.

Maybe Terri can come and stay for a while when she gets out of the hospital, George thought. That was only a few weeks away, and it would certainly be a change from the cool, antiseptic walls of Reynolds Memorial.

He'd talked to her doctor – not *that* first doctor, thank God! – only a few days earlier. He'd told George that there was measurable improvement every day; that the muscles were rebuilding at a steady rate, and the physical therapy was progressing ahead of schedule. 'She'll be on her way out of here in no time,' the doctor had said, sounding absolutely jolly.

That was the only thing that bothered George about him. He had never trusted people who sounded *jolly*.

Still, he wondered about the state of Terri's mind. On the one hand, he could feel a steely determination emanate from her with every encounter. This young woman wanted to get better, she wanted to *live* so strongly that her resolve was a physical force. But there was very little joy in that resolve. The last time he had seen her in person, just before their move to Tucson, she had seemed . . . empty, somehow.

George couldn't blame her. He had felt that way himself all too often. And why had Terri taken the brunt of the entity's attacks? Why *her*, an innocent nineteen-year-old?

Twenty, he corrected himself. She had celebrated a birthday while she was still in intensive care, many weeks ago.

He remembered the day with equal parts pain and pleasure. They had gotten special permission from the hospital administrators to go together – the entire Lutz family (minus Harry) and Abby Sullivan. Abby had seemed fine by then – she'd been out of the hospital for weeks. There was simply a blank spot in her memory, from the moment she walked into her house until she came out of her tranquilized haze three days later. She would probably never remember, George thought. And that was probably just as well.

They had all gathered around Terri's cake, perched precariously on a rolling table next to her bed, and blown out the candles. They sang 'Happy Birthday', and talked about how she would be getting out soon. But Terri had been very ill; her eyelids scarcely fluttered during the entire visit. Abby was sure she had missed it all. The doctor had assured them that it was doing her a world of good, and Amy, of all people, had agreed.

'She's here,' Amy had said very seriously. 'She liked it *a lot.*' Then she had taken her father's hand and looked gravely into his eyes. 'Daddy,' she had said, 'if I was ever sick like this, would *you* still have my birthday?'

The question had sent a chill through George that lasted a full week. It still bothered him when he thought about it, even now.

Thankfully, that was all behind them now. Terri's 'busted' body was slowly healing, thanks to her amazing sense of purpose.

But how was she feeling *inside*? With the moving and the settling and school about to begin, they hadn't talked with her in weeks.

It was time to get back in touch. A call would cheer them all up – in Arizona and California.

The colorful pile of paperback books on the seat next to him caught George's eye: *The Amityville Horror II*. John Jones had finished it quickly, and the publishers had rushed it onto the market in record time. It had been a strange feeling, seeing it high on the New York *Times* Bestseller List so soon after its release. They had braced themselves for calls from the publicists about speaking engagements and promotional tours, but, oddly, no requests had come in.

How could it sell so many copies, he wondered, and be virtually unpublicized at the same time? Sometimes the world of media confused him no –

The radio exploded with sound – a screech far louder

than it had ever made before. George jumped in surprise, almost losing control of the car. One hand groped out to turn it off – at least to cut the volume.

It was switched off. The knob obstinately refused to turn any farther . . . but sound *still* gushed out of it, more deafening than before.

He twisted the tuning knob, trying to find a dead place between stations, trying to change the screeching any way he could. The sound kept on, cutting deep into his ears – and then over it, even louder, a crack of thunder exploded, jarring every inch of the Ford.

George looked up into a clear blue sky. There wasn't a cloud from horizon to horizon –

– and torrential rain poured out of it, so thick it came in streams instead of drops. It pummeled the car, rattling louder than the radio.

In seconds, he couldn't see three feet in front of him. George stopped the car and set the hand brake with one tug.

But he still felt movement – a sliding, sickening sensation, as if the Ford was waddling in a direction different than the wheels pointed.

'What the hell – ' George said. He couldn't hear himself over the radio and the rain.

It seemed to be getting louder – impossibly loud. He slammed his hands over his ears, gritted his teeth against the noise and –

– the radio cut off. The light on the dial went dead.

George breathed deeply and lowered his hands. His eyes were watering. His ears still throbbed. But the pounding of the rain from a cloudless sky seemed restful after that . . . *noise*.

The rain on the windshield was a constant sheet, as if a firehose was being played across it. George leaned forward to rub the condensation from the glass and peered through.

A vague shape was rising up out there – a dim black mound barely visible through the downpour. It heaped up in front of the car, growing darker and more solid every moment. Then it seemed to widen, to spread its arms and embrace the mid-size Ford.

It was reddish-brown and boundless. It seemed to be swallowing everything.

Mud, George realized. It sloshed over the hood in a thick, gelatinous wave. In moments it had covered the windows, and the interior was bathed in a deep red light.

'Mud!' he said out loud, into the moist, hot air of the sealed interior.

Moments ago, the sky had been clear. Now an impossible wall of mud was lifting the Ford off the ground. He could *feel* the movement, forward and to the right, like a rubber bath toy in an emptying tub.

And suddenly it was getting very hot in the front seat. George shoved the lever on the air conditioner all the way to the right, but it didn't change a thing. Sweat was running down his back. It was getting harder and harder to breathe.

The car lurched heavily as the current grew swifter. The mud beyond the windows swirled and shifted. There was a dry riverbed less than a mile from their new home, George knew. Maybe it had come from there, somehow. Maybe it was flowing back there now.

George felt a flat hand press against his chest. He gasped again for air, and a sudden wave of claustrophobia swept over him.

Suffocating, he thought with growing panic. *Too close in here, too hot*!

He had to get out of the car. He gulped the seething air again and pulled on the door handle, half-expecting it to be locked. He was almost surprised when it moved easily, and a loud *click* sounded as the latch came loose.

There's thick mud out there, he thought dimly. It's trying to trap me in here. Seal me in a tomb. He braced his shoulder against the door and gave it a huge heave –

– and the door swung open wide, cutting through the soft brown fluid as easily as air. George tumbled forward, away from the car, thrashing and spinning in the sucking current, blind and choking in an instant.

He struggled to the surface, spitting out mud. Even treading it like water was impossible. He had to keep his lungs filled with air to stay buoyant enough to float – and getting breath in the torrential rain was almost as hard as trying to swim.

He looked around blindly, his nose only millimeters from the mudflow. *It doesn't act like mud*, he thought distantly, still thrashing through it. The huge drops of rain barely indented the brown, moving mass. When his hand sliced through it, there was no splash or ripple. It just opened up, somehow, and swallowed him whole. It was something like swimming in half-solidified jello . . . or . . .

. . . *or blood*, he thought.

He saw the Ford out of the corner of his eye, bobbing in the current like a cork on a fishing line. An instant later, the same flow took him as well. He felt his body hurled forward, gathering speed.

The muck seemed ten feet deep, or more, swirling around shrubs and cacti in unnatural eddies and swells. There was something alien about the flood. Alien and . . . *alive*.

His shoulder slammed into a solid and sharp object just beneath the roiling surface. Skin sliced away from his shoulder and arm. George gasped at the pain, and for a moment he stopped moving with the current, pinned against the thing he couldn't see. Then a brown wave eased him back, lifted him and rammed him forward again.

It was a giant saguaro cactus. Thorns like animal claws tore at his skin as he slid along one side.

George groaned at the spreading pain and threw his feet forward. They scrambled uncertainly against the trunk as the thorns ripped and caught at his chest. Then he found purchase and shoved back, *hard*.

He lurched away from the cactus, away from the pain. He was back in the rippling current again.

The muck was trying to drag him down. It sucked at him with unnatural power, turning him head over heels, completely submerged. He clawed at the darkness, searching for something to give him his bearings. His lungs began to ache with pressure, but in the twisting slackness he couldn't tell which way to swim.

Go, he ordered himself. *Swim!* He drove his legs in thrashing kicks and groped forward, sweeping his arms. The alien mud wouldn't let him go. It sucked at his hands, pulled at his legs. He was sinking with every heartbeat. *Sinking.*

His throat was clogged. His lungs were on fire. Every capillary in his head was ready to explode. *Fifteen seconds,* he thought, *and I'll be dead.* And at that moment something brushed his hand, something solid and real. He clutched it and pulled it close, almost laughing despite the muck, almost mad with relief.

It cut him like a thousand tiny knives. *Cactus!* he realized. Another tree-trunk covered with sharp claws.

It didn't matter. He couldn't let it go. He had to stay with it anyway. George wrapped his arms around the stinging trunk and pulled it close, shuddering as the thorns bit into the muscles of his chest and arms.

He started to climb up – up, out of the darkness.

He went at it hand-over-hand. His head was spinning with pain and oxygen starvation; his hands were slick with his own blood. But finally, finally he broke free of the muck.

Air. Moist, rain-choked air. He gasped it in, swallowed it whole, choking on the water that still spilled in buckets from a clear blue sky.

The limb beneath his hands broke off. For an instant he was caught again, floating back into the red tide. Without thinking, he shot out his legs and wrapped them around the trunk of the cactus.

The pain was impossible. It sliced at his calves, his thighs, his groin, and he bellowed into the rain as he threw himself forward, hugging the cactus, embracing the agony. Anything, *anything* was better than drowning.

He shinnied up another foot. The living mud sucked at his submerged legs harder than ever. He could *hear* it pulling at him – a long, obscene whuffling sound, a pressure that seemed to be stripping the skin from his thighs.

'I'll never let go!' he screamed into the rain. 'NEVER!'

The Ford tumbled by, end-over-end, completely in thrall to the rushing red mud. In one desperate lunge, the mud rose again, past his waist, and sucked at him, pulled at him, dragged with every ounce of pressure it had.

George locked his arms around the cactus. He crushed his cheek against the thorns. It felt like a million microscopic fingers, pulling and tugging and pinching the skin from his body . . .

. . . and then it was gone – fallen away in a sudden, complete subsidence.

After a moment he opened his eyes and tried to blink the crust away. The rain was still coming in transluscent sheets, but through the silver haze, hundreds of yards away, he saw the red-brown lip of the mudflow disappear into a gully – the same dry riverbed that passed only a mile from his home.

Five seconds later, the rain stopped – cut off with mechanical precision, as abruptly and completely as it had begun. With its disappearance, the sun beat down again, as dry and hot as ever.

George didn't come down from the cactus for a long while. Not when the mud stopped. Not when the rain stopped. Even after the light, warm breath of the desert dried his ruined clothes, he didn't move for almost half an hour.

Then, finally, he pulled himself free of the cactus. He heard his clothing tear as it came away from the spines. He felt hair and skin pull away in clumps with small, acidic detonations.

His ruined boots touched the ground with a dry and dusty *scrunch*. George stopped and knelt. He laid one hand against the desert floor.

Dry as bone. He couldn't believe it.

Exhausted, dazed, George walked slowly back to the

blacktopped road only ten yards away. Then he crossed it unsteadily and moved towards the dry riverbed.

The sun shone brightly. Sparrows flitted from cactus to undamaged cactus.

All in my head, he thought numbly. *Like always, all in my . . .*

He stopped and looked down into the gully. He wiped the sweat and filth from his eyes and looked again.

The Ford sedan was standing up. It was buried in the hard, dry earth from its nose to halfway up the back door. Its blunt back bumper glinted dully in the afternoon light, five feet above the ground.

He stumbled down the slope, shaking his head. For the first time he saw that his clothes were in tatters, perforated with rips and tears no larger than the blades of knives, and crusted with mud and blood from a thousand small cuts. His hands were a ruin. His chest was a mass of pain. And his legs, his poor legs . . .

He touched the half-buried car. It was dry and cool beneath his fingers. *I was driving this half an hour ago*, he told himself. He would have to keep reminding himself, he knew, or he would believe that the car had been out here a month, or a year.

He climbed up the incline to the roadway again, and slowly, too slowly, his head began to clear. This would be hard to explain, even to Kathy. And they had been through a lot together.

Worse than that, he wondered. *How will I explain the Ford's 'condition' to the tow truck driver who will have to get it out of the riverbed?*

So this is what it's like to be brought back to life.

Terri got out of the wheelchair – that cursed, damnable wheelchair! – and turned to face the white, windowless facade of Reynolds Memorial. It had been her home and her prison for more than six months. She had dreamed of this moment, had tasted it on her tongue, a million times.

She was going home. She was finally going home.

She turned to approach the waiting taxi, twenty yards away. One leg still moved a little slower than the other. There was a twinge between her shoulderblades that the therapists told her might always be there – massage, they said, and certain exercises would keep it from getting any worse. Whole portions of her skin felt new and hairless and far too soft. But she was healthy. She was *alive*.

She remembered what had happened to her. She was still reliving it in nightmares almost every night. Curiously, it always happened backwards: *the cross, the creature, the stairs, her mother*. A strange little litany, recited in reverse. She even remembered the black and nameless creature that returned in her coma and tried to lure her into its arms forever.

She had resisted. She had *won*.

Terri had tried to talk to her mother about all that had happened. It didn't take long to realize that the doctors were right. Abby Sullivan had forgotten it all. She had blocked the entire impossible afternoon from her mind. Her alternatives, Terri decided, were simple: amnesia or insanity. Given the choice, she was glad that her mother had left it behind.

Why didn't *I* do that? she asked angrily. Forget it – forget it *all*.

The taxi seemed a long way off. It was taking her hours to reach it. She found herself thinking of Kathy and George and the children she loved so much. They had faced this evil for years. They had somehow learned to live with it. But they had never been physically hurt, not like Terri – not even like Abby. *It's as if I'm vulnerable*, she thought. *As if it can get to me more easily* . . .

Someone was waiting in the taxi for her. She moved a step closer, away from the hospital she hated and loved.

George had told her their story. In half a dozen talks while she was still semi-conscious, he had described it all. '*You deserve to know*,' he had said.

He talked about the house back in Amityville, and about

the nightmares and dreams that had plagued them since. He told her of Father Mancusso's ordeal, including details that weren't in the books – horrible things, impossible things. He explained his own feelings, and the decisions he'd made about moving.

She hadn't heard from them for a long time. For a moment a sudden and terrible sense of dread bolted through her. *Maybe they've been hurt*, she thought. Maybe they *couldn't* contact her, as they couldn't be contacted by Father Mancusso, in Amityville. How long had it been now? Weeks? A month?

She stopped for a moment on that long walk to the cab. She forced herself to breathe deeply. No. Someone would have said something. She would get back to her house, back to her room, and she would call them herself. It would be all right.

But Terri Sullivan knew one thing for certain: it wasn't over for the Lutzes. And with all that had happened to Father Mancusso, to the Reverend Johnstone, to the lie detector expert and Jay Anson and now even the new writer, John Jones, she knew that it would never be over for any of them until it was finished for *everyone*. Until the Lutzes were free . . . If they *ever* were.

The door to the cab swung wide, pushed open by a gloved hand from within.

'Hello, Mom,' she said. She climbed in carefully, already tired, and the taxi drove her home.

CHAPTER TWENTY-ONE

'I am Mr. Matsumi,' said the dapper, slim little man in the horn-rimmed glasses. 'Welcome to Japan, Mr. and Mrs. Lutz.' He wrapped his tongue carefully around the *L* in their name. George couldn't help but appreciate the effort. 'If there is anything you may need during your stay with us here, please be kind to ask, and it will be my honor to arrange it.'

His diction, like his attire, was impeccable. And the politeness seemed sincere to George and Kathy – a real enthusiasm for the work, and not just a necessary part of the job.

Mr. Matsumi moved their bags through Customs and their bodies through Immigration with almost alarming speed. 'I have done it many times before,' he said modestly, as he opened the door to the Nissan Cedric that was waiting for them at the curb. George examined the car with interest. It was a beautifully built, fully outfitted sedan that would barely qualify as mid-sized in the United States. Here in Japan, it was the height of luxury.

As they darted along the outskirts of the capital city, Mr. Matsumi described in joyous detail the long string of interviews, autograph parties, and television programs that had been scheduled. George only listened with half an ear – he was fascinated instead by the colorful stream of Tokyo's enormous population that sped around them – on foot, on motorcycles and scooters, in parti-colored cars that seemed no larger than toys by American standards. He had heard about Tokyo traffic jams that lasted for hours. Now he could see why.

Kathy was exhausted. The instant they climbed in the car, she laid her head back and closed her eyes. As Mr. Matsumi finished his dissertation, George tried to look bright and attentive, but his eyelids insisted on drooping.

'May I suggest you go directly to your hotel?' Mr. Matsumi said as the Cedric negotiated a complex series of traffic intersections. 'I have taken the liberty of ordering a small snack to be sent to your room after we arrive. There also is a marvellous restaurant at the same hotel, should you feel the desire for something more substantial.'

Kathy was completely asleep. George smiled wearily. 'Thank you for your consideration,' he said. Mr. Matsumi positively *beamed*.

The trip to Tokyo almost hadn't happened. First it was on, then it was off, and then it was on again. Finally they had left with only a few days notice. And even then, with no other alternatives in view, George had thought long and hard before he had called Terri Sullivan and asked her to come stay with the children.

It seemed a cruel thing to ask after all that had happened. And he had been surprised when she had said yes with only the smallest hesitation.

Still, there had been something different about her. He could feel it even over the phone. Something distant and empty – almost desperate. He couldn't blame her for putting up walls like that, he decided after he'd finished the call. He knew what she had been through. Knew it wasn't burglars or psychotics who had done such harm to her body and mind.

She arrived in Tucson a week and a half before the Lutzes were scheduled to leave for Japan, and immediately George sensed the same reserve and wariness he had felt over the phone.

At first, he had let it pass – had been forced to. There were other problems to face first; problems much more mundane but no less serious.

They were pennies away from insolvency. Money had been an acute problem since their first flight from New York years earlier, when in their haste to free themselves of anything to do with Amityville and Long Island, they had sold the family business for a fraction of its worth. Since then, George had tried everything he could imagine to stay out of debt, but now, after more than six years of struggle, he was at the end of his tether.

In a way, he realized with some bitterness, it was as much a part of the Amityville Horror as any of the apparitions and abominations. If only those people who keep accusing us of making the whole thing up for a few easy bucks could get a glance at our financial statement, he thought, I'd have the highest credibility in the country.

The facts were simple and painful. Unless something changed quickly and completely, George would be filing for bankruptcy when they returned from Japan. It was that bad.

Finally, however, in the last few days before their departure for Tokyo, he had taken Terri to a Mexican restaurant near their home to talk about their trip – and about what had happened to her before. Kathy stayed home with the children. George knew she was glad to avoid the entire discussion.

The meal went slowly at first. It seemed a physical effort for Terri to make small-talk. She barely picked at her food. Finally, over coffee and *flan*, she could hold it in no longer.

She looked up at George with tears trembling in the corners of her eyes. 'It *did* happen, didn't it, George? I – I'm not crazy, am I? I really *saw* that thing, I swear, I *saw* it!'

She hid her head in her hands and started to sob – quiet, tearing sobs that made her shoulders tremble.

George quickly slipped from his side of the booth and slid in beside Terri; then put his arm around her and pulled her head to his shoulder.

'It's all right,' he said, his cheek against her hair. 'You're not crazy. And you're not alone either. Not anymore.'

She clenched her fists against the front of his shirt and let it come. George held her tightly until the storm passed completed.

Alone, he realized as he held her trembling shoulders. That was what the distance, the coolness was all about. This poor girl had been handling it all herself, without support, without understanding. She couldn't go to her own mother with what was happening inside her. Abby Sullivan had flensed it from her memory, simply to survive.

The loneliness and fear was what had made her agree to come to Tucson so readily, he realized. So she could have someone to talk to about all this – even at the risk of having it happen again.

As the tears began to subside, as Terri's clenched fists began to open, George began to talk to her. He talked about his family – about how they had survived as long as they had, as well as they had, only because of each other. 'There was always someone to be strong,' he whispered. 'When I couldn't do it, Kathy could. Sometimes we both fell down, and the kids helped us up – those incredible kids. Even our old dog Harry is part of it.'

Terri gave a sniffling laugh, and nodded.

'But you, you poor kid. You've been doing this all by yourself. You don't have to do it that way. We're here to help you now.'

She nodded again and straightened up, and for the first time since she had arrived, George saw her old smile – the bright, open, hopeful smile that had been a constant part of her in the days before the attack.

She wiped at her cheeks with the back of both hands. 'Sorry,' she said. 'I guess you must think I'm a real wimp.'

She giggled again, and George smiled at her. 'You're not a wimp at all. And you've got nothing to apologize for.'

She straightened herself in her seat and sighed deeply, her cheeks puffing out with the effort.

'Do you want to talk about it?' he asked softly.

'Yes,' she told him. 'Please.'

It all came out then: the months of pain, the nightmares and memories. The disembodied voice that coiled inside her coma, seducing her into self-destruction.

George told her about his own confrontation with the physical entity: *Abomination* to him; *Creature* for her, he discovered.

She couldn't believe that he had faced it himself – that the same manifestation from Amityville had appeared in different places, at different times.

'The only person I confided in,' she said, 'was that psychiatrist friend of mine, Philip Kaufman.' George nodded. 'But he kept trying to convince me that I'd imagined the whole thing. He kept insisting that the burglars – the muggers, whatever – were *real*, and that I was creating this whole surpernatural thing because I couldn't face what actually happened.'

'He meant well,' George said,

'But he made it *worse*,' she said, her voice trembling again. 'How can I convince him that it isn't some figment of my imagination?'

'You can't,' he told her. 'And trying will only make it hurt more. You can't *force* someone to believe what they can't believe, Terri. They'll always find some way around it. They *have* to, in a way.' He smiled again. 'Actually, I'm not sure I wouldn't have done exactly the same thing myself, before . . . ' He waved from side to side in an all-inclusive gesture.

He didn't have to explain. They both knew exactly what he meant.

George and Terri talked for another hour – about all of it, about everything that had happened. When they left the restaurant, she looked much better – lighter, somehow, George decided. And younger again.

Maybe now, she can finally begin to heal, he thought. To heal on the *inside*, where it matters.

The hotel in Tokyo was magnificent – a magical combination of the modern and the traditional.

Kathy had brightened, suddenly alert again, as they stumbled into the lobby. And they had only been in their enchanting suite long enough to freshen up before she insisted on an exploratory walk.

They visited the huge Japanese garden between the main office buildings and the guest rooms – an endless, meticulously maintained fantasy of order and perfection. 'Look at *this*, George,' she had gasped in awe, kneeling beside a delicate and beautiful *bonsai* pine. Then she was up on her feet again, peering into a small fish pond bordered by flagstone. 'Look at *this*!' she said again, pointing to a huge rainbow-colored carp that swam lazily in the shadows. The pond was connected to a spiderweb of delicate waterways that crisscrossed the entire garden. Graceful bridges spanned the ponds. Thousands of tiny golden lights twinkled like fireflies in the softening dusk.

She was flushed with excitement and discovery when they returned to their high-ceilinged, spacious suite. 'Look at *this*,' she said one final time when she found the bedclothes turned down and two matching kimonos laid out for them, along with two pairs of Japanese slippers.

George had been grinning for most of the walk. She was her old self again – questing, constantly smiling, full of astonishment and joy. And now she couldn't *wait* to try on her new clothes, while George sat on the bed and looked through their schedule for the next day.

'It's going to be a little strange,' Kathy said thoughtfully as she tied the sash around her waist. 'Talking about the first book and movie, now that the second one's been out for a while.'

George nodded. 'At least we can clear up the crap about that second movie. Everyone thinks we had something to do with it. I'm always having to set that straight.'

'Every chance you get,' she said lightly.

'I mean, it's not even *about* us. It's not even about the *Defeo's*, really. It's just a lot of – '

Kathy turned like a model in her new costume, a swirl of cobalt silk and flying hair. 'How do I look?' she said, giggling.

'Great,' he said. 'Absolutely *great*.'

He tossed the schedule away and pulled her onto the bed.

CHAPTER TWENTY-TWO

'I'M FINE, Mom, *Really*. Please don't worry. I'll talk to you in a couple of days. 'Bye.'

Terri cut the connection as quickly as she could, with a finger against the button on the top of the phone. She let out a long, slow breath and released the plastic plunger.

A dial tone. Good, she thought. I just couldn't talk to her anymore. She *oozes* concern.

Terri started to replace the receiver –

TERREE . . .?

She froze, the receiver halfway between her ear and its cradle. It was a buzzing, barely audible voice.

And it was coming from the phone. From *inside the dial tone*.

TERRREEE . . .?

She slammed down the receiver and jumped back. 'Oh,' she said – less a word than a small whimper, far back in her throat. 'Oh, *oh*.'

She turned and walked blindly to the Lutz' kitchen. Harsh mid-morning sunlight, fresh off the desert, scoured the counter in front of her.

Don't think about it, she told herself. *Don't think about it*.

She'd been alone with the children for almost two weeks, and everything was running smoothly. It was fine, just *fine*. But *now* –

Don't think about it!

She turned on the tap in the kitchen sink and bent over, splashing a handful of cold water on her face. Then she straightened, leaning heavily on the thick porcelain rim.

Deep breaths. Deep breaths.

She steadied very slowly and turned away from the counter. The phone glistened blackly, huddled on the table in the far corner of the living room. Just a phone, she told herself. A stupid old phone.

She walked briskly through the kitchen and into the living room, crossing to the sliding glass doors that led to the back yard.

She couldn't help it. She took a wide detour to the far side of the room – opposite the phone. It sat there, without a sound.

She stood just inside the glass and watched the children playing in the pool outside. Amy and Greg were pushing and prodding poor Harry into the water while Matt urged them on from the waist-deep water. The dog looked less than enthusiastic. Terri could hear the *skrik* of his claws against the concrete, as loud as the giggles and shrieks of the children.

Finally Harry gave in. He yelped half-heartedly and leaped in the water . . . and once he was in, he actually seemed to enjoy himself, splashing and gamely treading water.

The dog paddle, of course, Terri thought to herself, and smiled.

She sighed heavily, feeling something like calm return. It looked like fun out there in the water, but she was glad to be inside with the air conditioning. Her skin grafts were still a little tender, and she simply wasn't used to the temperature – 'dry heat' or not.

Music, she decided, trying to keep her mind off the phone – the *voice*.

She punched on the stereo. It was set on *FM*, and a twangy country-and-western song reeled out. Terri grinned and thought *good old Cowboy George*.

She spun the dial and watched the red needle travel across the numbers. There – the driving bass beat of Pink Floyd.

Sounds appropriate, she decided. '*Another Brick In The*

Wall.' She avoided the implications and lowered herself into the overstuffed armchair the Lutzes had brought from California. George had placed it in a strategic position – midway between his two huge stereo speakers, each almost half as tall as Terri herself.

Listening to music was just what the doctor ordered, she decided. She hummed along as the verse ran through, then sang in a low, husky voice when the chorus began:

    '*We don't need no education*,
    '*We don't need no thought control.*
    '*No dark sarcasm in the classroom.*
    '*Teacher leave your kids alone.*
    '*Hey, teacher! Leave . . .*'

The music faded abruptly, in the middle of the song. Terri opened her eyes, surprised at the sudden interruption. *Now what*? she wondered. What would the d. j. find that was better than *that*?

TERRI (*Terri*)?

It was coming from the speakers in perfect stereo separation: a deep and droning voice, like the one that had called Amy long ago. Like the one she had heard in the house. Like the voiceless voice inside her coma. The voice of – of –

TERRI (*Terri*)?

The echo rumbled over her, impossible to escape. She tried to get up. She tried to *run*. But she couldn't move – her legs wouldn't budge.

TERRI(*Terri*)?

It was louder now. A plaintive, questioning, stereophonically balanced abomination.

That's what George had called the creature: *abomination*.

She heard herself whimpering. 'Oh,' she said softly. 'Oh, *oh*! George? George, *what do I do*?'

TERRI(*TERRI*)! TERRI(*TERRI*)!

The fear built to a paralytic crescendo. She couldn't move. She couldn't scream. It was the bandages. The restraints. The weight of the plaster casts, the drugs made her –

No! You're not in the hospital! Not anymore! You can move now!

You can run!

Terri lurched to her feet and staggered for the patio doors. Her last shred of reason let her tear open one panel instead of slamming through it. She had to get *out* of there. To *escape*.

The blast of desert air hit her like a moving wall. She didn't care. In an instant she turned and dragged the door closed behind her.

Pink Floyd was playing on the radio again. She didn't care. She couldn't go back in there, not now. Maybe not –

'Come in with us!' Amy called from the pool.

'Yeah!' Greg shouted happily. 'Come and get wet!'

Terri turned to them, her back against the cool glass of the sliding door. 'I . . . don't have a suit on,' she said, trying for a smile. Her voice sounded tinny and weak in her ears.

'Well, go *get* one,' Matt said, making her sound like the stupidest person on earth.

Terri looked over her shoulder, through the sheet of glass. The living room looked cool and inviting inside. She could feel the vibration of the rock-and-roll coming through the window.

And for an instant, she imagined she could smell that horrible smell.

She glanced down at her white cotton shorts and her bright yellow jersey. What the hell, she thought, and ran to the pool with as much grace as her healing legs would allow.

'Look out!' she said, trying to keep from crying. 'Here I come!'

She jumped and dived, cutting the water cleanly as she fell . . .

CHAPTER TWENTY-THREE

'OH, NO,' Mr. Matsumi insisted, gentle but firm. 'You *must* go. The Shinkansen train trip is exhilarating and the ancient city of Kyoto is one of the most magical places in my country.'

The baggage was already being loaded. Mr. Matsumi was pushing the tickets into his hand. George knew there was no point in trying to change their host's carefully laid plans now.

Besides, he decided, it might be fun after all. The interviews and personal appearances were over. They were no longer required in Tokyo, and Mr. Matsumi might be right: a few days just relaxing may be exactly what's needed to calm down, to smooth out.

They had talked with Terri at the beginning of the weekend, and she had seemed fine. The children, too, sounded content in their not-so-brand-new home.

'All right,' he finally said, taking the tickets and smiling. 'Thank you.'

Moments later they were in their seats – and none too soon. As Kathy and George settled in, the car jerked abruptly.

They were underway.

Mr. Matsumi waved furiously from the platform and called out something George couldn't quite hear.

'What a beautiful man,' Kathy said.

'What?' George had been paying attention to the rising roar beneath their feet; to the rumble of a thousand wheels against smooth steel tracks. They were already picking up speed. He could feel the power building.

'Mr. Matsumi,' Kathy said, staring past George, looking out the window.

'Oh. Yeah, he's made the whole trip terrific.'

It wasn't as noisy as he had expected, and the feeling of speed was noticeable, but far from unnerving. It was very much like being on a jet plane, George realized as he settled back into his seat. The same comfortable bellow, far away. The same sense of slowly increasing weight, as if gravity itself was growing stronger.

He put his head against the seat and stretched briefly. He could feel himself being pulled back into the cushion, as if by a wide, insistent, invisible hand.

God, he thought. *We must be going faster than I thought.* The pressure on his chest was increasing, pushing him farther and farther into the chair.

He opened his eyes, and the car seemed to jiggle around him like a scene from an unsteady camera. And the weight, the *weight* –

The skin of his face billowed and lifted, stretching back from his skull. It tugged at the roots of his hair, dragging and pulling, *squashing* him.

George tried to sit up. For a moment his shoulders moved up and away from the seat –

– and then he was shoved back, *slammed* by a wall of pressure.

He felt the air whistling from his lungs. He opened his mouth, jaw dropping much too far, and gasped for breath. He could feel his heart laboring in his chest, straining for new oxygen, but it was hard, so *hard*.

Slowly, painfully, he turned his head, feeling the lids actually peel away from the eyeballs.

Kathy looked horrible. The same thing was happening to her. Her features were flat, pressed out of shape as if by a sheet of invisible glass. Her teeth were bared, and the lips stretched back, cutting deep into her cheeks. Her teeth and gums to the back row of molars glistened in the flickering light.

And as he looked at her in horror, her misshapen skull

217

turned to him. Protruding, glittering eyes focused on him. *Help me*, they said, too strained even to blink. Tears ran madly from her cheeks, and flew back into the hair at the nape of her neck. *George, please help me!*

He tried to call out. He tried to escape. And he saw in the mist of receding awareness, that the others on board were perfectly fine.

A British couple were happily snapping photos through the window next to them. A Japanese family of ten or twelve were chattering all at once and pointing at the scenery as it flew by. A steward strolled past them without so much as a glance, looking clean and comfortable.

George tried to thrash himself free – to *force* the pressure to release him. He slammed his head one way and the other, working his fingers, pounding against the incredible weight –

– and then he saw it just outside the window. Saw it reaching towards him through the glass.

Long ago, in a hotel room in Amsterdam, a venomous cloud of darkness had tried to swallow them whole. It had nearly succeeded. It had wounded them badly. And now the same cloud – that same evil, roiling oily black – was clinging to the window of the bullet train.

Kathy had seen it already. Her flattened lips worked towards a scream, but no sound escaped. *No air*, George realized. *No air*.

He flexed his head back to the window with a crunch of compressing vertebrae. There was something *wrong* with the cloud – something unexpected. It seemed to skitter almost nervously against the glass, falling back to reveal a bit of Japanese landscape, surging forward to almost overshoot the window itself, then hovering unsteadily where George had first seen it, directly outside the window.

It was having trouble attacking, George realized, feeling his awareness begin to crumble. It couldn't quite get to them here.

But he saw it was trying. He saw fingers of the darkness

working their way around the glass, penetrating the seal somehow. Reaching and stretching, coming to touch his paralyzed hand . . .

The wind slammed at them – gusting, ripping, deafening wind, flailing like whips across them. George could feel his eyeballs rattle in their sockets. It whistled through his teeth, traveling backwards, into his throat. It tore at his hair with a thousand vicious fingers, pulling up clumps from his scalp, rubbing it raw.

He was seeing things differently now. Without his own eyes. He was feeling the roar of the wind like a constant explosion on every side, but from *inside* the darkness. He was *with* the black cloud now. *He was part of it.*

And he was hungry. He wanted the man; he wanted the woman. He was ravenous, with an appetite made deeper and sharper by the months of denial and pursuit. It would swallow them up. It would finally feed on the sweetness of their energy.

The small part of George that was still surviving realized then, for the first time, that this part of the entity – this version, at least – consumed the Lutz' life like a nourishing food. It sucked at their defiance as well as their despair. It consumed their fear, and their anger, and even their hope. But most of all it hungered for the innocence inside them. For the children . . .

With a sudden, jolting *pop*, George was seeing with his own eyes again. But it was different this time – horribly different.

He was looking through the window *into* the train. He could see quite plainly the seat that he had occupied. He could see the shuddering shadow of his wife, still paralyzed, only a few feet away.

He was clinging, incredibly, to the side of the bullet train, travelling at top speed.

The wind was an endless wall of force, a fist without fingers as big as a building that slammed and slammed without pause. His clothing cut furrows in his flesh. His hair shrieked and whistled, flat out behind him. Even the

219

hairs of his beard were like lashes, snapping at the skin of his throat.

His hands were welded to a tiny projection that sprung from the smooth and silvery side of the train. It was a physical contact, an anchor to matter, but it couldn't be keeping him here, he knew. The cloud-thing was holding him up. The entity was hanging him in a hurricane.

The consciousness of the bubbling blackness enclosed him again, more complete than before – more horribly. He thought as it thought. He knew what it knew.

It was the closest that George Lutz ever approached the abyss.

There was . . . confusion. Bewilderment, anger. He wanted to feed, but the movement was new to him. Velocity, somehow, was an alien thing. *The children*, it echoed, and reached through the train, penetrating metal like mist. Here *and* the children, at once if need be. *Hungry. Need it. Time running out. But the moving, the moving, the move* –

He was back in his body. Back on the train. And the billowing evil was far behind them, rippling now as it disappeared in the distance.

They were safe. For the moment, he knew, they were safe. But he had touched the creature's mind, he had *known* it, if only for one horrible instant.

Panting, coughing, George turned to face his wife. She was sitting stiffly, as if in a trance. Her cheeks were scored with deep creases from the wind, disappearing even now. Her hair was a torn and tangled mess. Even her clothes were impossibly rumpled – a network of miniscule rips and wrinkles. *I probably look just as bad*, he thought distantly. *Like we just walked out of a hurricane.*

He reached out to take her hand –

– and she jumped, twitching with electrical suddenness, and turned to him.

He knew in an instant that they had shared this experience. What *he* had felt, *she* had. What he had learned from the creature, she had learned as well. The confusion. The hunger. The lust for –

'The children!' Kathy said breathlessly. 'George, *it's after the children now!*'

She started to jump to her feet, but George pulled her back, almost forced her into the cushions. The British couple looked back and across the aisle for the first time. The man scowled deeply. The woman raised an eyebrow. Then they turned away together, muttering suspiciously.

'There's nothing we can do until we reach Kyoto,' George said to his wife.

'The children,' she whispered again, clawing at her tangled hair. 'What are we going to do, *what are we going to do?*'

'We'll take the first train back to Tokyo. We'll get the next flight out to California.'

'We have to call Tucson,' she said, clutching at his arm. 'As soon as we stop!'

'Yes,' he said. 'As soon as we stop.'

He could feel it building. He could see it on the horizon. The moment they had dreaded – the final confrontation – was approaching as fast as the bullet train itself.

They had to get home to their children. They had to face the evil together. It was their only chance to survive.

I only hope we can get there in time, he thought. *There's so little of it left.*

CHAPTER TWENTY-FOUR

SHE COULDN'T avoid it any longer. They would have to go back inside.

Terri had made up as many games as she could remember or create to keep the children interested in splashing and chasing through the water. But the sun was low in the western sky now; the gray-green shadows of the lawnchair and the beach umbrella stretched from one end of the yard to the other. And the kids were getting hungry.

She swallowed hard. 'Okay, you guys,' she said. 'Why don't we go inside and – '

Amy was out of the water in an instant. She snagged a towel as she ran to the sliding doors, her small feet slapping wetly against the concrete. 'Dibs on the hall bathroom!' she shrieked, and threw open the doors.

The boys were up and moving in a sudden flurry of arms and legs. As Greg lunged through the open door, Matt snapped him with a towel, and his brother yowled in good-natured rage.

Matt reappeared unexpectedly in the doorway as Terri was drying herself off. For one instant she thought he had found something, or seen something, or *smelled* –

'Can I make a sandwich?' he said, eyes bright.

Terri cleared her throat. 'S-sure,' she said hesitantly. 'But only one. I'll be making dinner in a few minutes.'

'Thanks,' he said, and disappeared into the living room's shadows.

Terri approached the glass door very slowly. She could hear the boys bickering over peanut butter in the kitchen, and Amy calling from the hall about wanting dry towels.

Music was playing softly on the stereo – normal, uninterrupted Elton John.

She took a deep breath and stepped inside.

Nothing happened. Nothing changed. With quick, determined steps she crossed to the stereo and switched off the music with one quick, vicious poke.

Still nothing. Everything was fine.

Then Amy screamed from the bathroom.

She was running down the hall before she had time to be afraid. She burst into the bathroom to find the little girl standing over the sink, her hands at her cheeks, her eyes wide.

A putrid black liquid was swirling in the basin – thick as oil, bubbling and lumpy. And the smell that came off it was almost *that smell* – not the same, maybe, but nearly as bad.

The toilet gurgled as it flushed itself. Terri spun to see the same disgusting muck sucked down the bowl, replaced by a gush of new filth.

'I was just gonna change my clothes,' the little girl said plaintively, backing away from the toilet. 'That's *all*.'

Without a word, Terri took Amy by the arm and pulled her into the hallway. She slammed the bathroom door behind them, loud as a gunshot.

'Use – use the other bathroom,' she said unsteadily. 'This one's not—not working right.'

She turned away from the sound of the thick, flat gurgling. She wanted to scream and run. It was obscene to her, *disgusting*.

'But – '

'No *buts*, Amy! The other bathroom!' It was supposed to sound stern. It came out like a plea for help.

Amy looked at her gravely. 'Okay,' she said quietly. She turned and walked slowly down the hall, pausing twice to look over her shoulder at her trembling friend and guardian.

Get hold of yourself, Terri commanded. *Now*! 'Wait a second,' she said, and Amy stopped and turned. 'Maybe

223

you should use the one in your parent's bedroom. It's farther away from – '

'Would you come with me?' Amy's voice sounded smaller than usual. She clutched her fresh towel and change of clothes against her chest.

And suddenly, Terri remembered reading about the black muck before – how it had appeared over and over in the house in Amityville. That must be bad enough for the poor kid, she thought, her heart going out to the wild-eyed little girl. But to have me falling apart at the same time . . .

'Sure I'll come with you,' she said, putting on a smile. She threw her arm around Amy's shoulder, and they moved quietly down the hall together. 'What would you like for dinner!' she said lightly, trying to quickly forget the affair.

'I don't care,' Amy said. Her voice cracked slightly as she shrugged.

They reached the bathroom off the master bedroom. The door was firmly closed. Terri stepped forward to open it . . . and paused, her hand hovering over the knob.

Do it, she told herself. *Do it, don't be a –*

She flung open the door and every tap in the room exploded. The sink beneath the mirror gushed filthy black ooze. The toilet flushed and splattered muck along the tinted porcelain. The shower door swung open and the nozzle twitched twice, *and* vomited out a long, thick black stream. It hit the grouted tile and clung like stinking mud.

Stiffly, straight-legged, Terri took Amy by the shoulders and led her out of the bedroom and back towards the kitchen. Amy looked up at her with serious, knowing blue eyes, and she saw in an instant that there was nothing she could hide from this bright, frightened young girl.

'Amy,' she said honestly. 'I . . . I have to tell you, I don't know what the heck is going on.'

'That's all right,' Amy said bravely, patting Terri's hand. It was a grown-up, comforting gesture. 'I don't really need to use the bathroom anyway.'

They walked through the living room. Music was playing again, but Terri barely noticed. 'I don't mind telling you, kiddo, it scares the hell out of me.'

Amy smiled at the bad word. 'Me, too,' she said, and hugged her friend. 'Don't worry,' she whispered.

Terri smiled and nodded. 'We'll get through it,' she said, as much to herself as to Amy.

She said nothing to the boys, still fighting over sandwiches in the kitchenette. Forty-five minutes later, Matt visited the bathroom down the hall.

Everything was fine.

After they finished eating, in a ritual they had all come to enjoy, each member of the family trooped from kitchen table to sink to deposit their dishes and glasses and silver-ware.

Greg was the last one to unload. He smiled slyly as he laid them down. 'Wellll . . . ' he said, stretching out the word. Then, in a joyous shout: 'Last one to the TV has to wash the dishes!'

He leaped and turned like a dancer, already halfway out of the room. Matt and Amy howled in protest and ran after him, already losing the race. Terri only laughed and got ready to do them herself.

'*Shit*!' Greg's word echoed from the other room.

'Greg,' she said, only half in warning. 'Better cut out the language.' She dried her hands on a towel and sauntered towards the living room. 'Your parents will have a fit if they think I let you – '

A moving, buzzing black curtain boiled in the archway between dining room and living room. Greg was backing away from it, swatting at himself, kicking his feet. 'Shit!' he said again. '*Shit*!' She could hear the panic in his voice.

Flies, she realized. The buzzing expanded as if it had crawled inside of her. And the living curtain of insects grew, blotting out the other room completely, moving forward to cover the lamp in a hideous, writhing cocoon.

There are thousands of them, she thought dimly. *Millions* . . .

'Get 'em off me!' the boy said, wailing in panic. '*Get 'em off me!*'

Terri snapped out of it. She jumped forward. Something *twanged* in her weakened leg. The faint puckered scar on her right arm tingled, but she ignored it, she pushed it away. In one desperate lunge she laid both hands on the boy and pulled him back, slapping mercilessly at the crawling mass that blackened his chest and thighs.

Greg was starting to babble. She couldn't make out the words anymore. And the flies were gushing forward, in a narrow channel from archway to boy, growing thicker and fatter as they came.

Matt and Amy came rushing from the hallway with wide beach towels flapping in their hands. They began to beat at their brother, screaming at the flies, in a strangely coordinated attack – first one hit, then the other. Then the first one hit again, in synchronized assault. As if they half-expected it, Terri thought. As if they had practiced this all before.

She backed away, then turned and ran to the kitchen. The cupboard beneath the sink banged on her shin as she opened it, but she ignored the sudden stab of pain. She knocked through kitchen cleansers and bottles of bleach, and came up with a huge red-and-white can of insecticide, brandishing it like a club.

She was back at the screaming boy's side in an instant. 'Hold your breath and keep your eyes and mouth shut!' she shouted. Then she thrust the can forward and pressed on the release with all of her might.

A thick jet of poison spewed from the top. She started at the top of his body as the other children jumped back, speechless. She doused him from head to foot, then backwards, from foot to head again.

The flies began to drop as the liquid made contact. In a moment she could hear the sounds of their bodies crackling as they covered the carpet, under the fuzzy, gushing sound of the spray itself.

From top to bottom again. And back up, until the can was empty. The flies were forming mounds and channels on the carpet now. Rising dunes of them covered her feet almost to the ankles.

Greg, still as a statue, stood waiting for it to end. His mouth was clamped shut. One index finger and thumb blocked his nose; the other first lay tight against his chest. He was beet red, cheeks like exploding apples, when Terri finally let the empty can fall from her hand and said, 'It's over, Greg. It's over.'

He let the air out of nose and mouth in a sudden explosion. Terri rushed forward and caught him under the arms before he could fall.

'You okay?' she said, breathing heavily herself and trying not to think about the slimy, crushed bodies squishing under her naked feet.

'Yeah,' he said, coughing. 'I guess so.'

She helped him towards the hallway, away from the drifts of dead flies. 'Go take off those clothes. Get in the shower and wash yourself off – everywhere, Greg. Inside your ears and nose, too.'

'Okay,' he said, standing on his own now.

'Lots of soap! Twice over! Brush your teeth, too!'

'*Okay*,' he said, and disappeared into the bathroom. She could hear the water start. His coughing trailed off.

Terri turned back to confront the other two children. Matt and Amy stood in the archway that had been blocked by flies only moments ago. The tiny blond girl stood frozen, her towel hanging loosely from her clenched fist. Matt's beach towel lay in tangles at his feet.

They were looking at the six-inch mass of dead insects on the living room carpet. 'Weird,' Matt said, very softly. Amy just stared and swallowed.

'You guys okay?' Terri asked, her voice high and reedy.

'Yeah,' they said together.

She reached down and picked up the empty can of insect spray. 'Have we got any more of this stuff?' she asked.

227

'Yeah!' they both said and led the way to the supply closet where two more cans were waiting.

They were sweeping the last of the carcasses into plastic garbage bags when the phone rang. It was George calling from Japan.

Calling to warn them.

CHAPTER TWENTY-FIVE

THE CONNECTION from Kyoto to Tucson, was alive with hisses and clicks. George squinted against the noise and put a finger in his ear, trying to drown out the din of the train station. Kathy was clinging to his side, trying to eavesdrop. She wouldn't be able to hear a word, he realized as he listened to the distant guttural *burr* of the phone ringing thousands of miles away. He would barely be able to hear himself.

They had five minutes or less before the train to Tokyo left the station. He would have to make this quick.

'*Hello*?'

He pressed the phone tightly against his ear. 'Terri?' he said. 'It's George!'

There was a long pause – nothing but the hissing and the clicks. For a moment he thought of the dying phone calls that had plagued them back at Amityville. He prayed that wasn't starting again.

'*Hello*?' It was even softer this time, almost lost in the distortion.

'Terri! It's George Lutz!'

This time she answered immediately – but he could hear the unsteadiness in her voice despite the distance. '*George*? *Oh, George*! *God, I'm glad it's you*!'

'We've had some trouble here,' he said, aware of how loud he had to speak even to be heard. He glanced nervously at the Japanese couples swarming around them. 'We thought we should call and see how you are.'

He checked his watch. Three minutes to go.

Terri laughed without humor. It worried George even more.

'Terri?' he said. 'Are you okay? Are the kids okay?' He was shouting full out now, and Oriental couples were pausing to look at him quizzically. He didn't care.

'*We're . . . fine, George. Kind of shaken up, but okay. How did you know?*'

'I'll tell you later,' he said.

A tidal wave of static nearly swamped the connection. '*– again, George? What was that?*'

'I'll tell you later! he shouted. 'What happened?'

There was another short pause. George had the uncanny feeling that she was trying to pull herself together. '*Too much,*' she said finally. '*Way too much.*'

He glanced at his wife, standing so close he could feel her hair against his cheek. He scowled and tried again. *Damn* the connection! 'Terri, are you *really* all right?'

There was only the hiss of static.

'Give me the truth!' he shouted. 'It's important that I know!'

Finally he heard her speak – a dim, distorted version of a human voice. '*George,*' she said. '*It's starting to feel a lot like it was before. I – I don't want to worry you guys, but –*'

They were announcing the final call for the train back to Tokyo. 'We're on our way home,' George told her. Kathy was grabbing up their suitcases.

'*I though you were staying another week or –*'

'No! We've already called and made reservations. We'll be on a plane in just over five hours.

'*Thank God!*' Terri said, almost sobbing. A chill ran through George.

'Are you sure you'll be okay?' he shouted, not knowing what he could do if she said 'no.'

'*We're fine, we're fine,*' she said, the voice receding again. '*As long as you're coming home!*'

Kathy looked worriedly at the train. 'George . . . ' she said, glancing at the gate where the last of the passengers were boarding for Tokyo. He nodded tightly at her. *Time's up*, he thought.

'*Do you want to talk to the kids?*' Terri called to him.

It pulled him up. God, he wanted to hear their voices – to make sure they were all right with his own ears. But if they missed the train, there wasn't another one for over an hour. And that would mean missing the flight to the States, and there was no telling when another would have an opening . . .

'No time!' he shouted, hating the sound of the words. 'We'll see you all when we get there!'

'*All right*! *Hurry*!'

The train was preparing to leave.

'Terri!' he said desperately, hefting the last bag onto his shoulder. 'Hang on, okay?'

'*We will, George*! *We will*!'

'We love you all! Goodbye!'

He couldn't wait for a response. He slammed the phone back in the cradle and they sprinted for the train, dragging suitcases and tote-bags behind them.

They slipped inside just as the doors closed tight.

They never returned to Kyoto.

'Ready?' George asked as the bellman picked up the last of the suitcases.

Kathy came out of the bathroom and zipped up the carry-on bag. 'Just a second,' she said. She scanned the room with a businesslike eye, checking for last-minute leftovers. Finally she nodded tightly. 'Ready,' she told him, and put the strap over her shoulder.

The bellman nodded and backed out. 'We'll meet you at the taxi stand outside the lobby,' George said. In a moment, the man and all the luggage had disappeared, almost at a run.

George checked his watch for the tenth time that hour. They had alotted plenty of time to the airport, even in Tokyo's impossible traffic. The seats were reserved. The flight was on time and the weather for transcontinental travel was perfect, the ticket official had told him.

But he couldn't shake the feeling that something wanted them here . . . wanted them to *stay*.

He shrugged it off and led Kathy to the elevator. In moments they were leaving the residential complex and entering the endless, magical garden they had explored a few days before.

One jagged path, part gravel and part flagstone, criss-crossed its way through the rock gardens, the high hedges, the bamboo screens, the curtains of silk, and emerged in the lobby where they would check out. They had been this way before– it was the fastest route to where they wanted to be.

. . . and it was beautiful, George realized. In the late afternoon, the misty white light of the city made the garden seem fragile and timeless – there were splashes of deep green and silver, the twinkle of lights and the sheen of fine wood, like a Japanese watercolor, delicate and lovely.

Kathy stopped at the shallow fishpond and smiled down at the rainbow-colored fish she had cooed over earlier. George came to a stop next to her, impatient but understanding. He couldn't keep from grinning when the huge fish turned on its side and seemed to wave one fin, glittering against the turquoise bottom of the pool.

Kathy sighed deeply. 'It's so peaceful, George.' she said softly.

He nodded and let her look a moment longer. He hated to end this – he hated to drag her back to the pain that was waiting in Arizona.

As if I had a choice, he thought bitterly. He put an arm around her waist. 'We have to go, Kath,' he said.

'I know,' she said sadly.

They started to walk towards the rock garden in front of an arched and intricate bridge. 'Maybe we'll come back someday,' he said.

'I hope so. I really hope so.' She sighed again and straightened, hefting the carry-bag on her shoulder with new resolve. 'Okay,' she said. 'Let's go.'

They turned the blind corner that led to the central bridge –

– and stopped, and looked around in confusion.

'That's strange,' Kathy said, frowning as she looked down at the path. 'I was positive this was the way to the lobby.'

George felt a shiver down his spine. 'So was I,' he said. 'I . . . guess we're both confused.' He moved forward cautiously. 'Come on. We probably just forgot this bend. It can't be too far now.'

He led the way. Kathy shrugged and followed him around the corner as it jagged sharply to the left –

– and they were in the Garden of Lights, the exquisite tangle of plants and trees strung with tiny lights of every color. Even in the fading light of day, it was a stunningly beautiful display, as if the stars had been snagged in the treetops.

But this is at the far side of the grounds, George thought with growing alarm. This is twenty minutes away from where we're supposed to be.

'George . . . ?' Kathy said unsteadily. She realized the same thing. 'George, how did we . . . ?'

'Must have come out a different entrance,' he said, not believing it for an instant. 'Must have taken a wrong turn.' He turned away from the glittering garden and saw a sign on a post at a nearby junction.

RECEPTION, it read, with an arrow pointing off to the right. The Japanese characters were printed underneath.

'This way.' He stalked off, following the sign, swallowing the fear that was rising in his throat.

I'll be glad to get out of here, he thought bitterly. *I'll be glad to be on that plane, going home*. The path widened ahead of them. They picked up their pace.

There it was. The bridge they remembered, or at least one of them. They had stood in its center their first night in Japan and admired the graceful lines, the intricate workmanship, the beauty of the stream that gurgled beneath it.

But it's the wrong bridge, he realized as he climbed to the crest. It had taken them half an hour of walking to get

233

this far from the complex. And it wasn't on the way to the Reception, not by a long shot.

He came to a stop at the top of the arch. Kathy was close behind him.

'What's going *on?*' she said. He could hear the tears of frustration in her voice, and he didn't blame her a bit.

'I don't know,' he said through clenched teeth. 'I wish to hell – '

She grabbed at his arm and pointed. A middle-aged Japanese couple were strolling arm-in-arm through a nearby garden, among the carefully cultivated flowers and shrubs. They were coming towards the Lutzes in a casual, aimless manner.

George realized suddenly they were the first people he and Kathy had seen since leaving the complex. He grinned with relief and said, 'I'll ask for help.'

He raised an arm in greeting. He opened his mouth to call –

– and a gray mist closed them off from the world. It fell down from above and rose up from the water like two ghostly hands coming together. In an instant, there was no water, no garden, no middle-aged Japanese couple. The Lutzes were standing on a carved-wood bridge in the middle of a gray and seamless bubble – a featureless egg of fog.

'Oh, *God* . . . ' Kathy gave a hopeless sigh. They both knew what was happening now. They knew it was nothing natural or random.

'Come on,' George said. He gripped her by the arm and pulled her forward, leaving the bridge in three long steps that hammered against the wood. 'Come on. We've got a plane to catch.'

He moved quickly and steadily down the pathways, moving from gravel to flagstones to grass and back again, intent on moving, just *moving*, until the lights of the lobby appeared through the mist.

A left turn. A right turn. A hairpin curve, past an eight-foot hedge he had never seen before –

– and they were back at the foot of the bridge. *The same bridge.*

George stopped and spat out a curse. Kathy panted heavily and leaned against his side. She said his name, but he ignored her. He was angry now, very angry.

He stomped to the crest of the bridge again, hoping without hope that he could see through some break in the mist that enclosed them. His boots made a hollow knocking sound against the wooden slats, oddly muffled by the fog.

Nothing. There was nothing but thick grey drizzle, wet enough to soak through their clothes. Kathy's hair hung in limp strands around her face. George had to brush his own hair away from his eyes, and his hand came away clammy and dripping.

Her hand on his arm tightened suddenly. 'George!' Kathy whispered. 'Look!'

The mist was changing color. There were streaks of deep red in the grayness now – flickering lines of scarlet that danced back and forth, up and down, in an endless and complex network of color.

'What is it?' she whispered.

George thought of a model he'd seen in a museum, many years ago – an artist's rendition of the human brain's electrical activity, as energy bounced and flashed across the cortex. He shook the image away. 'It's a wall,' he said grimly. 'Between us and the kids.'

He pounded down from the bridge as the red electricity danced around him. Kathy had to run to keep up. He was a receding black shadow, as big as a bear, moving swiftly through the mist.

She called to him, but her voice sounded strange – distant and muffled, as if she was shouting into a blanket. Over her own breath, lost in the fog, she heard a distant, sibilant buzz. *George*, she realized. *Talking to me*. But the fog wouldn't let the sound reach her.

She ran forward, suddenly terrified of losing him forever. She planted a hand at the back of his pants and snagged a beltloop, like a frightened child almost lost in a crowd.

He was nearly jogging through the grayness now. He took different turns than the last time, intent on keeping his bearings. A right. A left. A long, straight path downhill and forward, past statues and bamboo and a delicate waterfall.

Light broke through the mist. George grinned and laughed. He started into a run, to run to the light –

– and tripped as his foot snagged the bottom of the bridge. The same, damn, stupid, bridge.

He caught himself on the thick wooden railing before he went all the way down. Air rasped through his lungs. Water dripped into his eyes, equal parts sweat and dewfall, and he wiped it away with one hand.

The mist was moving towards them. The colors were changing again.

George straightened and leaned against the bridge, Kathy tight against his side. The crimson discharge was faster and brighter than ever, building with frantic speed. He saw the mist ripple, and sudden bursts of orange sent veins of color coursing in every direction. Electronic blue fluorescent bolts sparkled and were gone. A wide, wavering aurora, every color he could imagine, welled up from the bottom of their misty sphere and penetrated everything: the fog, the bridge, their own flesh.

Beams. Sheets. Candlelight. Beacons. They were standing in the center of a sea of luminescence. Streaks of sudden brilliance scored the light like meteors. Many-fingered explosions, almost dim against the background's brightness, expanded and shrank without sound.

The light was congealing into a physical mass – intensifying as it thickened, growing darker and more solid. The yellows turned to browns. The reds became purple, and finally shifted to a scarlet so deep it looked like drying blood.

George realized he wasn't really seeing it at all anymore. He was feeling it, feeling it *inside*. He was experiencing the essence of the light and the mist, and the essence was . . .

. . . *evil*. He had felt that sensation too often before.

His fists clenched. He pulled Kathy tightly against him and shouted into the light. 'I want off this bridge!' he bellowed. '*I want off this –*'

It shimmered very slightly – a light different than the others – and George felt the ground beneath his feet soften and shift. He stumbled and reached for the railing, but it was no longer there. The lights were still all around them. Kathy was still at his side. But . . .

. . . they were standing beneath the trees in the Garden of Light. The twinkle of its lamps were drab against the swelling, exploding, impossible color still swirling around them.

Back where we started, he realized. *Even farther away*.

The red luminescence behind it all began to pulse – a steady, heartbeat throbbing that slowly grew faster and faster.

Whatever it was, it was growing more active. Whatever it was, it was starting to wake.

George dragged at Kathy's arm and ran from the colors. But she didn't move with him. She was dead weight at his side.

He turned and looked at her, ready to shout. But Kathy was staring into the light, her eyes wide and unblinking, her mouth slack and wet. He watched in shock as a thin line of drool appeared at the corner.

'Kathy! Kathy, *come on!*'

She didn't respond. She could only stare.

George bent and put one arm behind her knees. The other went across her back. He straightened, lifting her, frowning with the effort, and turned once again to run.

The pulsing was coming faster. It was hot and bright at his back.

Kathy moved in his arms. 'It's beautiful,' she whispered, still staring at the light. 'We can't go. It's too beautiful.'

He staggered away, putting one heavy foot in front of the other. *Don't think about the light*, he thought. *Don't think about the beauty . . . the peace . . . the . . .*

237

Kathy shoved sharply at his chest and tried to jump from his arms.

'Don't!' she cried. 'I don't want to go!'

One foot in front on the other, he thought. One. Two. One. Two.

Kathy was wriggling wildly now, fighting and clawing to climb over his shoulder. She was hungry for the light. She was mad to return to it.

'Don't! *DON'T LEAVE*!'

The blood pounded in his head. His arms throbbed as he held her more tightly than ever.

One. Two. One. Two. One. Two.

His feet thumped on the flagstones like lead weights as he entered the blinding gray fog.

One. Two. Faster. Faster. One-two-one-two-one-two-one-two-one –

Long black arms thrust out of the mist and grabbed him around the shoulders. George shouted and shut his eyes, almost dropping his wife on the hard flint stones.

Get away get away GET AWAY –

'Mr. Lutz! Are you all right?'

Kathy stopped struggling. George caught his breath. Slowly, very slowly, he opened his eyes and lowered his wife to her feet.

Mr. Matsumi released the American and took two nervous steps back. He looked surprised and confused and even a little hurt.

Kathy's legs buckled under her, and George caught her moments before she crashed to her knees. 'Mr. Matsumi?' he said, helping her stand again.

The fog was lifting. The only lights he saw was the glow of the lobby behind their Oriental guide, and the distant illumination of the city.

He looked down at his clothes, and saw the smears of dirt, the crumbling remains of plants and shrubs clinging to the grimy cloth. He turned and looked back into the garden. The last wisps of the mist were trailing away, but the landscape itself was broken and twisted.

He could see a torn trail of footprints – *his* footprints –
winding through the garden. Arrangements of stones and
pebbles had been kicked into chaos. Bonsai trees, ancient
before George's birth, were crushed and broken. Flower
buds and shrubbery had been smashed beneath his boots.

'God,' he said, swaying. 'I didn't mean to. I'm sorry, I – '

Tamuro Matsumi took him firmly by the shoulder, and
turned him around. He looked deeply into the American's
eyes. 'Mr. Lutz! *Are you all right?*'

George stared at him for a long time, then nodded.

Kathy suddenly stiffened. 'George! The plane!'

Mr. Matsumi looked slightly embarrassed. 'The hotel
manager called me when you did not arrive here at Reception,' he said apologetically, glancing back into the lobby,
then out into the shattered garden. 'I searched the grounds
and the buildings for you *three* times.' .

George looked up and squinted at the light. It was
nighttime, he realized. It had been late afternoon when
they'd entered the garden, and now it was dark.

'So we waited,' Mr. Matsumi said. 'In hopes you had
just taken a short walk and perhaps lost your way – '

George seized him by the arm, and Mr. Matsumi's eyes
grew wide.

'The time?' he asked. 'The flight to America? What – ?'

'It left three hours ago,' Tamuro Matsumi said, swallowing hard. 'I am very, very sorry.'

CHAPTER TWENTY-SIX

HARRY WAS turning in circles and whimpering. He would scratch at the floor, then turn abruptly to bark at the empty air.

'It's okay, Harry,' Terri said, kneeling to hold him close. He struggled out of her arms and bolted across the room to sniff at an empty spot in the air. Then he was back at her side, trying to burying his head in her lap.

'Really,' she said. 'Take it easy, take it easy.'

She remembered with chilling clarity how the dog had acted at La Costa. And the metal pin in her leg, the space between the muscles in her arm, the permanent twinge in her back, all sang with the memory of what had happened next.

Get home fast, you guys. Fast.

Harry pulled away again and ran in a small tight circle, yapping in a strange, high voice.

'What is it, boy?' she said, dreading the answer. 'What *is* it?'

He stopped in the middle of the room. His ears lifted up. The fur on his back rose and stiffened.

Terri strained to hear what the dog could hear. For a moment, she thought she had found it: a deep, grumbling snarl that seemed to come from all around her.

Then she realized the sound was coming from Harry.

The dog lunged forward one pace and froze. The growl rose in his throat. He bared his teeth.

'Harry,' she said, thinking of the stories she had read about the dog's attacks. 'Harry, calm d – '

He leaped forward. She screamed and jumped out of

the way, and Harry kept moving, through the space she had occupied an instant earlier, then out of the room, across the hall.

The children's rooms! she realized, and ran after the dog, almost tripping as she went.

She found him standing in the corridor in front of Amy's door, barking like a wild animal. 'Harry!' she said, and reached out to calm him.

He turned for an instant and snapped at her hand. Terri reared back with a squeak, but she called his name again.

Harry backed up three steps. He hunched down on his hind legs, then sprang forward, howling madly, and slammed against the wood a full three feet above the floor.

His body hit it solidly and bounced away. The sound of flesh against wood was thick and sickening, and Terri couldn't keep from moving forward again.

'Harry, *don't!* You'll hurt yourself!'

The animal's eyes were glowing like embers. He backed to the far wall and jumped a second time – higher, harder, with a howl that cut through the house.

But he twisted as he slammed against the wood and fell like a bag of bones, flat against the carpet. Terri cried out at the impact, whispering his name.

He was only half-conscious now. He backed up again. He braced his feet. There was blood dripping from his muzzle as he howled and leaped a final time.

Terri jumped forward to stop him. The door swung open. In an instant the dog was blown back by a wind as cold as death. And Terri saw the creature that had killed her once before.

It rushed out, screaming in pain and brushed her aside with the sweep of one talon. Terri was lifted up, off the carpet. Her back, her legs and her skull, hit the wall more than ten feet away with one simultaneous, terrifying *crack*.

As she slowly slid down the wall, she could feel the creature fading – at least for the moment. And consciousness – life – was slipping away.

The last thing she heard was a tiny voice – a girl's voice. 'Jodie,' it said.

Then she fell into darkness.

'He's very persistent, isn't he?' Mr. Matsumi said softly. Kathy couldn't tell if it was admiration or surprise in the dapper Oriental's tone. Maybe equal parts of both, she decided.

George came stalking down the major thoroughfare at Tokyo International, fists clenched. He had visited every airline with a flight to the United States. He was right back where he started.

'George . . .' Kathy tried to stop him as he passed them. He waved vaguely in her direction and went back to the ticket counter where their original flight had been booked – the one they had missed six hours earlier.

'Any cancellations?' he said shortly.

The young Oriental woman looked up from her computer and sighed. Kathy and Mr. Matsumi had watched her pass through politeness to thinly veiled hostility. Now she simply looked sorry for George. 'Nothing, sir,' she said. 'Seats on the next available flight are Tuesday after –'

'That's *forty-eight hours*!' he said, slamming a fist on the counter for emphasis: *forty; eight; hours*. 'Isn't there anything, *any*thing you can do – '

Kathy moved forward and put a hand on his shoulder. 'George,' she said, 'she's doing the best – '

He shrugged off her hand and turned on her. For one instant she thought he was going to shout at her or worse. She could see the frustration and pain and guilt in his eyes.

But in the next instant he deflated. His shoulders slumped. His head dropped. He seemed to shrink six inches in height. 'Sorry,' he said, passing a hand over his face. Then to the ticket agent: 'Sorry, I just – *we have to get back*, that's all. We have . . .'

He walked quickly to the bathroom, mumbling something about splashing water on his face. She knew as soon as he returned he would make the rounds again: any cancellations? he would ask. Any additional seats? When's the next flight, where are the connections?

She couldn't take it any more. She just couldn't take it.

Kathy forced herself to turn back to the quiet, strong Oriental who had given them so much already. 'Thank you, Mr. Matsumi,' she said. 'We couldn't have gotten out of the hotel without your help – especially after the – the trouble.'

He bowed very slightly, looking painfully sad. 'You are kind,' he said. 'Too much so when I have failed so completely.'

'Oh, you haven't failed,' she said quickly. 'It was beyond your control – it's beyond *anyone's* control, I –'

She realized she was saying too much. She stopped herself and looked away. Then she shrugged.

'It's just hard,' she said quietly. 'So *hard*.'

Mr. Matsumi frowned deeply, thinking seriously before he spoke again. 'Mrs. Lutz,' he finally said, choosing his words with care. 'I understand, it is not my place to ask you of things personal to your family. But I have read your books.' There was a brief, proud smile. 'Even the new one, I received on a recent trip to your country.' Then the smile faded again. 'I understand what has happened with you. I can only assume that it is happening again.'

He dared to reach forward and touch her arm lightly. He leaned to her and spoke with a quiet intensity. 'There is danger if you do not join your family soon?' he whispered. 'You must get home for this reason? Yes?'

Kathy couldn't bear it. The concern in the man's voice – his understanding in the face of it all. He hadn't even asked where they had been during their 'disappearance'. He had just accepted it all, patched it up with the hotel, and raced them to the airport at top speed.

Kathy covered her face with both hands and sobbed. Mr. Matsumi pulled a handkerchief from his pocket and offered it to her, eyes averted.

'We have to get home,' she said. 'We *have to*.' She tried

to straighten up, sniffling bravely. 'God, I'm making a fool of myself,' she said.

Mr. Matsumi shook his head.

'We'll get out of here, Kath.' George had returned from the bathroom. 'Don't you worry.' He put a hand on his wife's shoulder, and she started to cry again.

George opened his arms and she hid inside them, hunching herself up, ignoring the curious stares of passersby. 'Oh, *George*,' she said, letting it go. 'The *kids* . . .'

'I know,' he said softly, stroking her hair. 'I know.'

He was angry – as angry as he'd ever been. He wanted to scream at people, to hit them. He wanted to steal a plane and fly back to Arizona himself.

Then he felt Kathy's tears through the rough cloth of his shirt. *Stay calm*, he told himself. *You have to stay calm*.

Neither of them noticed Mr. Matsumi as he stepped away, moving with new purpose to the main doors of the airport.

He was waiting when Amy Lutz woke up. Hovering there at the end of the bed, just like always.

A cloud thing, kind of. A presence in the air. She smiled when she saw it. She called it by name.

'Jodie?' she whispered.

Yes, Amy, it said in her head. *It's me*.

Amy was happy to know he was back. She had missed her friend very much. But she frowned when she remembered the promise she'd made. 'You're not supposed to be here,' she said severely. 'My daddy made me *promise* we wouldn't play any more. And *you* promised not to come back. You did that. I remember. You *promised*.'

I missed you, Jodie told her.

'Well – well, yeah, I missed you, too. But you shouldn't be here. Daddy said. 'N I don't want Daddy mad at me, okay?'

For a long moment, the presence simply hovered at the end of the bed. After a while, Amy wondered if Jodie understood. Sometimes, in the old days, her friend didn't do what she wanted, didn't answer her questions. But finally he spoke, and she could see that something was *different* about Jodie this time.

She couldn't see through him like she always did before. And he didn't bubble and boil like he used to.

Amy, Jodie said. *How would you like me to do a trick?*

Her eyes narrowed. 'What kinda trick?' she said.

A very special trick.

'I don't know . . .' She still remembered the promise. She knew he wasn't s'pozed to be here.

How would you like it if I was a real person?

'. . . Real?' She didn't quite understand.

Flesh and blood, Jodie said. *Just like you.*

'But nobody else can see you but *me*!' Amy protested. 'You told me that.'

I know, Jodie said. The voice was very soothing inside her skull. *But now I can be different . . . if you want.*

'I don't know,' the little girl said. There were things around Jodie she didn't remember before. He looked all different now, even though he was the same. She didn't like it. It wasn't *right*. 'I don't *know* . . .'

You have to want me, Jodie said. *You have to ask me. But if you ask me, I'll stay with you forever.*

She could hear her dog, Harry, barking 'way far away. The voice in her head was confusing her. She didn't know what to do.

Amy started to climb out of bed. 'Come meet my friend Terri,' she said. 'I bet she'll know what – '

NO! Jodie shoved Amy back into bed. The voice inside her skull got big – *too* big.

'But she's my other best friend,' Amy pleaded. 'I only want to ask – '

NO!

Amy clamped her blonde head between two tiny hands. 'You're hurting me!' she said. 'Don't hurt me!'

Harry was barking outside her door. Amy was getting scared.

Just ask me, Jodie chanted. *Just ask me to stay here, ask me to join you, that's all. That's all.*

'You're not acting right! You feel funny in my head!'

Amy . . .

She heard something thump against her bedroom door. It just made her madder and more frightened.

'I don't want you to be here! You better leave like my Daddy said! And never come back! *Never come back*!'

DON'T SAY THAT!

The pain was the worst she had ever felt. Something slammed against her door again.

'*Go away*!' she shrieked. '*Go away, go away*!'

AMY! AMMMMYYYY!

It rushed from the room with a blast of cold air. Amy's bedclothes were ripped from the mattress. Her door exploded open, and she screamed as she saw poor Harry fly like a bird and go *splat* against the wall.

There was someone else out there, too. Someone that Jodie hurt bad when he flew away.

Amy ran into the hall and found Terri in a heap at the far end of the corridor. She shook her by the shoulder and called her name.

'Terri? You all right! *Terri*?'

Her friend didn't move. She just slumped over on her side when Amy touched her.

Amy started to run for the phone to call the police, just like Mommy had taught her. Then Matt and Greg came home from their game, and together they carried the twenty-year-old to the bed, in Amy's room.

Amy went to the kitchen, to get some ice for her head.

Be all right, she prayed. *Please, please, be all right.*

'Jodie,' she said to herself, with all the hate a little girl can muster. 'I'm *glad* you're gone! I'm *glad*!'

Jack and Elaine Meyerson were from Eugene, Oregon. They were finishing up one great ten days in Japan, but they were ready for the trip home.

Lionel and Sonny would be waiting at the airport. They would stop by Al's on Sixth and have a big, thick steak that didn't cost 'em a damn arm and a leg. Sure, Japan was terrific, but *Oregon*, now *there* was God's country for you.

They were killing time before take-off in the airport bar when the clean-cut, serious Japanese in the dark suit came up and introduced himself. 'My name is Tamuro Matsumi,' he said, bowing and offering his hand. 'You are on your way home to the United States, I believe?'

They were kind of suspicious – you got like that when you did a lot of traveling overseas. But Mr. Matsumi seemed straight enough. Even showed them his I. D. from a big Japanese corporation.

'I would like to offer you a special deal,' he said. 'I have two associates who must get back to the United States. So, I will pay you twice the value of the plane tickets you hold, if you leave for your country two days from now. *And* provide you with rooms at a fine hotel in Tokyo for your extended time.'

Jack Meyerson looked at him closely. 'What hotel?' he said.

Elaine slapped him on the arm. 'Jack! Are you *crazy*?'

Mr. Matsumi named one of the better luxury hotels in the city. Even Jack Meyerson had heard the name before.

He thought about Lionel and Sonny. He thought about one pound of medium rare at Al's. And he thought about the price of two coach return tickets, Tokyo to San Francisco International, with connections to Portland.

He grinned. 'Pull up a stool, Mr. – ah – Matsumi,' he said, referring to the card. 'You and me got some talking to do.'

The bags were safely on the plane. Mr. Matsumi had seen personally to that. Now they were standing at the end of the causeway, about to board the 747. And they couldn't bear to say goodbye.

'I still don't know how you did it,' George said, waving the boarding passes. 'But I guess it doesn't matter.' He shook the Oriental's hand in both of his own. 'Thank you, Tamuro. Sorry if I came a little bit unglued there, but . . . *thank you*.'

Mr. Matsumi was beaming again. 'You are kind,' he said. 'Very kind. But it is my job, you see.'

George grinned. 'Sure it is,' he said. 'Just a job.'

Kathy swept forward and hugged the precise little man as tightly as she could. Her shoulder bag slipped from her arm, but she didn't let go until the steward cleared his throat.

It was time to board.

'If you don't call us the next time you're in the United States,' she said as she wiped the tears from her eyes. 'We'll never forgive you.'

'I shall,' he promised. 'Oh, yes, I shall.'

He looked away, embarrassed and touched. He was not accustomed to Americans like these.

They stepped into the fuselage of the plane. The door was sealed shut. Mr. Matsumi stepped back, behind the crew, and thanked them again for their special permission to see his charges off.

He walked from the terminal as the jet taxi'd for take-off, quietly wishing them a speedy and safe trip home. *I hope it is in time*, he thought.

He smiled as he met the Meyersons at the taxi stand and held open the door to the cab as they climbed in, chattering wildly.

Exactly how, he wondered, will I explain this to my superiors? And will they believe me in any event?

And really, he wondered, does it matter at all? As long as the children are safe.

Greg Lutz was stroking her forehead, over and over. 'You okay?' he kept saying. 'You *okay*?'

Terri tried to open her eyes. It was hard, the hardest

thing she'd ever done. ''M . . . 'M okay,' she said, slurring her words badly.

She was stretched out on Amy's bed. Her feet dangled over the end; the top of her head touched the wall.

'Maybe we should've called the doctor,' Matt said quickly. 'I said we oughta, but Greg said no.'

'She doesn't need no doctor,' Greg snapped. 'She's just, whaddyacallit, she's just *dazed*.'

Matt was getting angry. 'Then why's she been sleeping for so long?' he demanded.

Amy slid onto the bed next to Terri and put one arm across her shoulders. 'Please be all right,' she whispered. '*Please* be all right.'

''M fine, guys. R'lly, fine . . .' She couldn't wake up. She couldn't focus at all. There was something wrong with her eyes. With her brain . . .

'Are you *sure*?' Greg said.

'Shurr . . .' she mumbled. 'Juss . . . gotta sleep . . .'

She was drifting away again.

'Parens . . . coming?' she slurred.

Matt nodded solemnly. 'They called from the airport in San Francisco. They said they'd be home in a couple of hours.'

'Good,' she groaned softly. 'Home . . .'

She couldn't stay awake any longer. But in the last precious seconds of awareness, Terri Sullivan somehow knew the truth.

She could still feel the blast of the creature's passing, colder than an arctic wind. She could still feel the sweep of its ghostly arm, cutting through her like lightning. It was a vicious, ripping, tearing sound of separation.

She knew as she faded that the creature had escaped with a part of her.

It had stolen most of Terri Sullivan's soul.

CHAPTER TWENTY-SEVEN

GEORGE BURST through the front door of the Tucson home and shouted their names. 'Greg! Matt! *Amy!*'

They rushed in from the other room, shouting with joy, and he scooped all three of them up in one massive bear hug. *Together*, he thought. *At last*, we're together.

He glanced over their shoulders at the house around him. It looked as it always had – cool and serene in the warm desert light. Quiet and undisturbed.

What did I expect? he asked himself. *Fountains of fire? Gremlins crouching in the corners?* It had never been like that before. It probably wouldn't be like that now. He realized he couldn't imagine what it *would* be like, when it came.

But it was coming, he was sure of that.

'Where's Terri?' he said as he let them go, and Kathy knelt to embrace her children.

'She's sick,' Amy said quickly. 'You better go see her. She was talking to us, and then she kinda – ' the little girl swallowed. ' – she just kinda *stopped*.'

George glanced at his wife. Her eyes were wide. 'Where is she?' he said.

'In your bedroom,' Matt told him. 'We moved her – '

He was out of the hall in an instant.

Kathy looked down at her children, and held all their hands at once. 'You're all all right?' she said, still scarcely believing they were home.

'We're okay,' the boys said together. She nodded and sent them out to retrieve their luggage from the curb, where the taxi had left it.

The she knelt again to talk to her daughter. 'Amy,' she said quietly, sensing the worst, 'are *you* all right?'

'Well,' her daughter said, looking away. 'Yeah.' She swung her small hands back and forth in a restless, guilty gesture Kathy had come to know very well.

'What is it?' she said, brushing the hair from Amy's eyes. 'Come on, honey, you can tell me. I won't get mad.'

'Promise?' Amy demanded.

'Double promise.'

Amy told her mother about Jodie coming to visit. She told her what had happened. How Terri and Harry had gotten hurt.

'Harry's okay now,' she said. 'But he keeps snuffling a lot, like he hurt his nose. He's out in the backyard . . .'

Kathy felt cold all over. She was remembering a story the Hardings had told her long ago – a story about a young girl in the Midwest who had contacted something – some *thing* – through a ouija board. It had made the same request that Jodie had made of her daughter— *invite me in. Ask me to stay.* And the young girl had done as she was asked.

The haunting that resulted, the Hardings had said, lasted many months. Someone was hurt. Someone else was killed. And even after the Hardings had cleared the house and helped the family . . . the girl was never the same again.

'Are you sure you said no, Amy?' Kathy said. She took her daughter too tightly by the arms. 'Are you *sure* Jodie went away?'

'Yes, Mommy,' Amy said, squirming in her mother's grip. 'I'm sure.' She flinched again. 'You're *hurting* me, Mommy!'

Kathy let her go. She stared at her own hands for an instant, then gathered Amy up in a close, warm embrace. 'I'm sorry, honey,' she whispered. 'I was just worried about you, that's all.'

'Jodie was crying Mommy,' Amy whispered in her mother's ear. 'But I said go away, I said *go away*!'

'I know you did, love. It was the right thing to do, too. And I'm very proud of you.'

'I didn't ask Jodie to come, Mommy. *Honest!*'

'I know. I *know*.' Kathy kissed her daughter on the cheek, and they held on to each other for a long time.

Finally Amy stirred and pulled herself away.

'Did you bring me anything?' she asked brightly.

George sat on the bed next to Terri Sullivan. There was something strange about her – something *wrong*. She was pasty white and slightly swollen – *bloated*, he thought. But there was something even *more*. Something he couldn't quite put his finger on. Something . . . *dark*.

'Terri?' he said, shaking her gently. 'Terri, it's George.'

Her eyes fluttered slightly. One hand twitched.

'Shorzh . . .?' she said, and licked her lips.

'I'm here,' he said.

Her hands waved at her waist for a moment, then dropped again. *She's sick*, he realized. *Really sick*.

'Terri?' he said, starting to stand. 'We better get you to a doctor. I'll take you to the hospital myself, right now.'

A swollen hand reached out with amazing speed and caught him by the arm. George froze for a moment, then sat down again.

Terri's blue eyes fluttered open. The pupils were huge. They nearly covered the cornflower irises, one slightly larger than the other.

'Zhodee . . .' she said, her tongue thick in her mouth. 'It was . . . Zhodie, th' creature.'

'I know,' he said, not knowing at all – not yet.

'Not sick,' she said, coughing shallowly. 'S . . . stolen.' The hand tightened on his wrist. George could feel her ring cutting into his skin.

'Terri . . .'

'Kill it, George,' she said, gasping. 'Kill it or . . . or I . . . or I'll . . .'

252

Kathy came into the room and stood silhouetted in the doorway. 'George . . .' she said.

He turned to her, tears in his eyes.

'. . . die,' Terri Sullivan said. And her eyes closed again.

Kathy found it when she was looking through the accumulated mail, between the bills and the circulars and stop-payment notices. It was a heavy package in brown wrapping paper, with Father Mancusso's return address.

She called George away from Terri's side to open it. They had already talked about Jodie and what had happened. They decided to keep Terri close by – at least for the moment.

He opened the package with uncharacteristic delicacy, as if jewels or Steuben glass was hidden inside.

It was a book – a worn Bible with gold stamp letters on its black leather binding. And there was a note from Father Mancusso attached:

Dear George and Kathy,

I have struggled much with the implications of my absence at this crucial time. But now I wage my war on a different battlefield, though the war itself is the same, and you more than any others on earth know the price I pay for the fight. It is the price we all pay. The wounds that this evil inflicted on me – within me – still exist. I cannot confront it again on those terms. But I am with you. I will always be with you.

Here is the Bible – a possession of priests for more than five hundred years, witness to power beyond all understanding. Hold it dear.

The blessing I have written inside it is my own. I invest it with all that I know of the evil, all the damage it can do and all that can be done to it.

The vial of holy water is the product of my faith. It holds the product of all my love, for you and for God, and my fear and loathing of the evil you face. But remember, as always, my family: it is your own faith, your own love, that will sustain you, as it has for so long. That, and God, are your only salvation.

We shall speak again soon. To celebrate.

'There is a destiny that shapes our ends, rough-hewn though it may be.'

Mancusso

George clutched the Bible. His knuckles were white with the pressure. Kathy laid the vial of water, a cylinder no larger than a plastic bottle of pills, in the palm of her hand. She looked at it for a very long time.

'I love you,' she whispered to her husband.

'I love you, too,' George told her.

CHAPTER TWENTY-EIGHT

THE FINAL confrontation came that night. It began with the shaking and the noise.

George had checked on Terri an hour earlier. She was in something like a coma, her body more swollen than ever. Her breathing was shallow; her skin like wax.

After reluctantly leaving Terri, he had walked Harry outside and fixed his rope to the metal post in the far corner of the yard.

Now he was dozing in the armchair. Kathy was with him, her head in his lap. The children had fallen asleep in front of the T. V. while a ten-year-old Japanese monster movie flickered on the screen.

A neat stack of artifacts lay waiting at his right hand: Mancusso's Bible, the vial of water; the letters with scriptures and prayers for safe conduct. On the top was a photograph of a man named Padre Pio.

George was dreaming about Padre Pio. He had heard the stories about him – about his power over evil, and the artifacts he blessed that had changed the lives of thousands.

He was dreaming of a figure of light. An old, old man with a beatific smile, and hands like the welcoming desert. He smelled of life. He spoke of hope. He drifted like luminous cloudwork above their Tucson house . . .

The room began to shake and outside, Harry was suddenly barking out a warning.

George snapped awake, lunging forward in his chair. Kathy started and straightened at his side.

It was a subtle, growing vibration. The glass coffee table began to hum and jitter. The pencils and mugs on the tray began to dance. Even the light from the hanging lamps seemed to jiggle and sputter, alive with the new vibration as Harry let loose a mournful howl.

The children scrambled to their feet. 'Daddy . . .?' Amy called, her blue eyes rimmed in white.

'It's happening,' George said, scooping up the artifacts. He could feel it in his soul.

He parceled out the objects to each member of the family. Kathy held tight to Mancusso's Bible. He split the stack of letters between Amy and Matt – and imagined a warmth, a tingling sensation as they passed from his hands. He gave Greg the picture of Padre Pio, remembering his dream as he did so. And he slipped the vial of holy water into the pocket of his shirt. *Like party favors*, he thought. *What did you bring me, Daddy?*

'Stay close to me,' he said as the vibration grew worse. 'Don't – '

A babble of voice arose from nowhere. It started as a whickering hum, a knot of unraveling sound, and it grew, drowning Harry's baying, to fill the room in an awful crescendo.

Amy put her hands over her ears and screamed. It was far too small a sound to survive, and as Kathy called to her, equally mute, the little girl backed away from her family – away from the quaking and shrieking of voices.

She stood with her back against the long, blank wall of the living room squeezing her eyes tightly shut. Her mouth was an 'O', screaming and screaming –

– two huge, bluish-green arms of putrifying flesh punched out of the wall, one on each side of the little girl's shoulders, then wrapped her in a tight embrace.

Kathy screamed as shards of plaster and paper flaked from the wall in fragments as big as books and heavy as pewter plates.

Amy was frozen in the monstrous arms. Her mouth was still open, but no sound could be heard: the babbling, screeching sounds of the voices effectively blotted out all earthly sounds.

256

The wall was dissolving now – melting away. But the scene behind it was not the star-filled night sky of the Arizona desert. It wasn't the city of Tucson, or the vacant lot . . .

It wasn't Earth at all.

The Lutz family looked in horror at a landscape in Hell: The wall was a window that led into Purgatory.

It was as George always imagined it: scarlet fountains of flame; sulfurous billowing clouds of smoke; and far in the distance, impossibly far, the almost shapeless shadows of '*The Damned*', groaning and shrieking in pain and despair.

The thing has drawn it from my subconscious, George realized. From what I believed as a child. From what I *prayed* it would never be. *It's making it all I'm afraid of*.

He wondered what the others were seeing. For him it was a nightmare coming to life.

And, from somewhere deep inside this infernal nightmare, stretched the arms of rotting flesh that encircled Amy: that rubbed against her soft, blond hair; that touched the pure white innocence of her skin; caressed her tiny body. Long bony limbs that shed skin in oozing sheets. With stringy muscles that flapped and glittered in the fiery light.

Then, suddenly, the shapeless mass of tissue that had spawned these hideous appendages floated forward, through the flames of Hell, towards the living room.

Features – whole faces – bubbled up from this mount of roiling, gelatinous liquid flesh, then disappeared. Hands thrust forward; eyes opened and blinked, then closed and were gone. It was the thing from Amityville trying on shapes, reaching for images that would strike terror and loathing into the hearts of its victims. Only the arms that held Amy remained solid and constant – the arms and a thousand writhing tentacles at the bottom of the mass, that tried incessantly to drag it back, slowly back into the landscape of Hell.

The mound of putrescence moved out of its fiery domain,

slithering forward to sit, pulsing, expanding and shrinking on the carpet near the center of the living room, while its two mercenary arms pulled Amy slowly to it.

AT LAST! said the beast. The voice was so deep, so loud, so strong, that crystal and shelves on a glass-and-steel bookcase shattered at the syllables. AT LAST WE MEET!

George gave no attention to its words. All he could see, all he could think of, was Amy. The *thing* was pulling her towards it. Was trying to take her from them.

'Daddy!' the little girl screamed, dragging at the immovable arms.

The wailing babble of the other voices receded a fraction. George could hear Amy screaming – he could hear his daughter dying as her fragile body began sinking into the pulsing mass. She was standing upright, but she began sinking into it. Like slipping under a filthy wave.

'Hold onto the letters, honey! Don't let them – '

A gust of wind gushed from the black and red world, flickering where the wall once stood. The letters were torn from Amy's fingers and fluttered like confetti back into the world, bursting into flames as they flew.

George moved forward and the stench slammed into him. It invaded his nose, his eyes, like a poison gas. He choked and doubled over. He could barely breathe or see.

Amy began slowly disappearing into the rotting flesh –

George clamped one hand over nose and mouth. 'No!' he bellowed between his fingers. 'No, *NO*!'

He lunged forward and threw his arms around his little girl's waist; pulling her body to him, as his arms sunk into the mound of living tissue. It hissed and bubbled beneath him; but he had her – had her tightly locked in his arms.

He heard the creature laughing – a thick, choking, evil sound that thundered through his soul.

SHE'S MINE, GEORGE LUTZ! MINE!

It began sliding away from his world, back towards the Hellish nightmare. It had them both. Was taking them both. George tried desperately to break free.

But he wasn't strong enough. He couldn't do it alone.

'Kathy!' he shouted over his shoulder. 'Kids! *Help me*!'

The boys pulled at his back, adding their weight. Kathy grabbed his belt and heaved backward with all her might.

The little girl screamed. The mouthless, eyeless, bubbling tissue laughed even louder at the sight.

NOW I HAVE YOU ALL!

Kathy reared back and slashed at the arms with the Bible – and fire exploded where she touched it. The creature shrieked in surprise, and for an instant the arms came loose, flailing in pain and rage.

George tightened and pulled for all he was worth. Amy slid out of the creature, falling over his shoulder, limp and unconscious.

He staggered back. The others scrambled to their feet.

The wind was rising and growing hotter. Sweat blossomed on his body, but he didn't care. He laid the tiny girl on the living room couch, and turned the light to fall on her face.

Dark blotches, grayish-green and the size of silver dollars, spread across her soft white skin. They were on her face, her neck, her arms. Kathy gasped when she saw them and clutched at George's arm. He touched one blemish lightly – it was gooey and scaly at once – and as he watched they began to grow. To spread.

He turned back to the writhing mountain of flesh that hovered now between the living room and the vision of Hell beyond. 'What have you done to her? *What have you done*?'

MY MARK, the creature said. I HAVE MADE HER MY OWN. LIKE THE COW IN THE OTHER ROOM — THE OLDER ONE. SHE IS NEARLY MINE ALREADY.

'Not a chance,' George said, shaking his head. 'Not a *chance*.'

MY PRIZE, the creature chuckled. I WIN.

George turned back to his daughter and tried to wake her. 'Amy?' he said, patting her lightly on her sickening, scaly cheeks. 'Pumpkin? Wake up. Come back to us.'

She was limp as a rag doll, barely breathing. 'Baby? Please, *please*,' Kathy sobbed. 'Come back.'

George straightened and turned to face the hideous mound. 'Why are you hiding?' he bellowed. 'Why do you use little children as shields? Come out and fight me! *Show yourself!*'

DO YOU CALL? the creature said – too quick, too eager. DO YOU WISH ME TO VISIT YOU? TO SHOW MYSELF TO YOU?

Something, some inner sense, made George pause to think. The voices babbled madly. The light pulsed and roared. The wind tore at his face and beard.

And then he remembered Father Mancusso's words: '*What it does, what it tries, the horrors it brings will be your fault because you asked it to come.*'

'No!' George shouted. '*NO*! I want you out of our lives forever! I want you gone from this moment forward!'

NEVER, the abomination bellowed. NEVER!

The wall of flesh exploded. Gobbets of tissue and blood-colored light burst forth from the mass, with a scream from the distant collection of souls that tore at George's brain as well as his body.

Kathy was hurled back by the impact, turning in the air like a twig in the wind. The boys threw themselves over Amy and shrieked, and the couch that shielded all of them flew from the ground and rammed head-on into the far wall.

The roaring voice reached an ear-splitting resonance and the entire room frantically oscillated. The glass patio doors and all but one window in the room shattered instantly.

George was thrown flat on his back, slammed against the carpet spread-eagle. The wind screamed over him; the stench penetrated every pore. For a long moment, no one moved. In the bubbling, whistling aftermath of the detonation, the wind subsided and the smell fell back. Even the window to the other world seemed to shrink, if only by millimeters.

Kathy finally found her feet. There was a long red welt of raw flesh down one side of her body. Her left eye was swollen shut, and something was wrong with her knee – she could feel it pound with the slightest exertion, and the cap felt pulpy and out of place. But she pulled herself upright and hobbled to her motionless husband as the children stirred on the couch.

She cradled his head in her arms and called his name. George was limp and unresponsive. His eyelids didn't even twitch. 'Wake up,' she whispered. 'God, George, *wake up*.'

There was a plaintive cry from the overturned couch. 'Mom?' Greg wailed. 'Mooooom?'

She looked up, weeping. 'Matt! Greg! Are you all right?'

The boys lashed out in unison, kicking the couch over. Both looked bruised and terrified, but still in one piece. 'We're okay,' Greg said.

'Amy?'

Matt looked down. 'Okay, I guess. But she's still got those ugly black things all over her.'

Kathy hugged her husband. She whispered in his ear. 'Oh, God, George, please, *please*. We need you, *we need you*.'

She bent over double and laid her ear against his chest. Searching . . . searching . . . *yes*. A heartbeat. Thank God, he was still alive.

'Mom!' It was Matt again, screaming like never before. '*Mom, look!*'

She snapped around to look through the torn hole where the wall had been. The vision of Hades was back and she gasped at the form that was rising from it, straight up, towards them.

The head was distorted, a puffy gray blob. Rows of brown and dripping teeth lined its lipless maw. Yellow liquid oozed from the holes where the eyes should have been, and its short, snuffling breath burst out of a nose shaped like a twisted boar's . . . a snout like the one in Amy's crude drawing of Jodie, Kathy thought.

The arms were far longer than physically possible, with joint after knobby and sinewy joint. *Another form*, Kathy realized. *Another attempt to scare us to death*. She realized then that its versions were endless. They were merely expressions of different styles, different tactics. It could change its form at will.

And it only wanted one thing.

Its arms reached out from the dark-red vision. They snaked across the room, dripping ooze and stink, reaching towards the couch and the dying girl.

It wants Amy, Kathy knew. And when it had her little girl, it would come for each of the rest of them. Terri. The boys. Her.

And George.

'Get away from my sister!' Greg shouted, and threw himself at the beast. He passed through one arm like a stone through fog, falling heavily on elbows and knees.

It hadn't resorted to physical mass. Not now, she somehow knew. Not now that it was reaching directly for the soul.

'George? George, come *on*!'

He was still unconscious. He could be for hours. Kathy laid him back against the filthy carpet, knowing it was her turn, knowing what she had to do. She snatched up Father Mancusso's Bible from where it had fallen moments before, and scrabbled frantically through the opening pages.

Where is it? He wrote it in the front, right near the title page, WHERE IS IT?

The arms were coming closer. Amy was whimpering softly as they approached.

There! On the flyleaf!

The glistening fingers were inches from Amy.

'L-Lord of Lords!' Kathy shouted. 'Protect us, your helpless children, in this our hour of need!'

The stretching arms stopped. The fingers trembled.

SAVE YOUR BREATH, the voice said in her mind. It was that same deep and hideous voice. IT CAN DO YOU NO GOOD.

She struggled to her feet and took a step forward. 'Protect us, Oh Lord, we beseech thee . . . '

I SAID STOP IT, BITCH!

The arms swept towards her, and she steeled herself. *Not there*, she told herself –

– and the arms passed harmlessly through her with only an arctic chill.

'We, your children, who are too weak – '

STOP IT!

The wind rose again – cold this time, impossibly cold. It tore at her dress. It plucked at the book she held tight in her hands.

'We give ourselves into the hands of the Lord God Almighty! We abide by His Will in all things!'

The arms were flailing madly about the room, dancing and shivering – and *steaming*, she realized. Gouts of vapor streamed off as she read.

'Save us, O Lord, if such be Your Will! Save us, Lord! *Save us!*'

The vibration started again. The window to Hell burst into flame. Successive waves of heat, then cold, then heat again gushed from the opening as the beast came forward.

Into the room. Into their world. Straight for Amy.

Kathy stood in its way. She faced it full on. She slammed the Bible shut and held it above her head, shrieking the final words: '*In the name of the Father*! And Son! And the Holy Spirit, Amen! *AMEN*! *AMEN*!!'

She threw the Bible straight into the wheezing, gaping face of the thing. A brilliant flash erupted as it touched. A noise like no other tore at her head.

Kathy fell to the carpet, blinded.

The shrieking and tearing wind was gone.

The red light was fading. The wall had returned. Whole. Untouched.

And George was sitting up, groggy but awake.

'A-Amy?' he said. He passed a hand over his eyes.

Kathy struggled to her feet. 'Amy? *Boys*?'

They went to Amy's side together and all looked down as her eyes fluttered and opened.

The black blotches were gone. Her skin was clear. She focused on her mother's face and smiled a gap-toothed smile. 'Oh, Mommy,' she said, full of sleep and wonder. 'I had a horrible dream.'

Kathy gathered her daughter in her arms. Tears squeezed from under her lids.

Out in the yard, Harry barked sharply, calling to be set free.

'Can I let Harry in now,' Greg asked.

'Sure, why not,' George said tiredly –

'Hey,' came a weak, but cheerful voice from the doorway. 'Is there anything to eat around here! I'm *starving*.'

George turned from Greg to find Terri standing in the doorway. She leaned heavily on the frame. But she was *standing*, smiling weakly, somewhat herself again.

He went to her side and embraced her. The boys gathered round and did the same. 'Welcome back,' he said.

'My pleasure,' she told him. 'To tell you the truth, I thought I was – '

In the yard, Harry's playful bark changed suddenly to a funereal warning howl.

A section of the wall exploded again. And another. And another. Terri screamed and backed away. The boys dived for the carpet.

A huge gray fist came through the wall. Taloned fingers tore more of it away, and thick feet kicked out even larger holes. Both arms smashed the board. An entrance was formed.

The creature was returning, its maw open wide. Coming through the wall itself, this time.

WORDS WILL NEVER STOP ME! it bellowed. WORDS, WORDS, WORDS! I'LL NEVER LEAVE YOU, MY PRIZES! NEVER! NEVER!

George leaped forward and herded the children behind him. Kathy stood on one side; Terri on the other.

ADMIRABLE, the creature chuckled as it approached.

BUT POINTLESS. One flickering hand reached out for them. COME TO ME. COME TO ME.

George backed away. He was out of ideas. The prayers were used up. The artifacts gone. The Bible, even the Bible, had exploded in all of its power, and nothing, *nothing* –

Wait.

He groped at the pocket of his shirt, searching for the final weapon. Still he backed away from the approaching creature and the family retreated, hiding behind him.

'It's not there,' he said, searching frantically. '*It's not there!*'

'George, what is it? What – '

'The holy water! *The holy* – 'Here it is, Daddy!'

Amy had found it in the corner of the room. She held it high, like a trophy – and George saw it throb with a light of its own, pulsing in her hand.

A chair launched itself at the little girl. She ducked under it and ran to Matt.

The creature bellowed and pointed its arms, and the half-shattered couch rose from its resting place and flew at the family. They hurled themselves every which way, dodging the missile as it exploded in a thousand sharpened splinters against the wall behind them.

Amy passed the vial to Matt's hands – and the light grew stronger as he touched it.

The last remaining window exploded inward, a sea of glittering knives. Matt dived and rolled, shielding the vial with his body – and passed it expertly to Greg's waiting fingers.

Brighter, George saw. *It's gathering power as it comes.*

The creature's bellow grew louder and longer. It dragged its massive talons down the side of the wall, gouging plaster and lath in huge fistfuls. It flung the detritus at the oldest boy as he ducked behind the coffee table and tossed the vial, blazing with light, into Terri's outstretched hand.

She paused for an instant, in the midst of the chaos. The

wind rose up in hurricane gusts. The light, like fire, roared and bolted around her.

Terri Sullivan raised the vial to her lips and kissed it. It coruscated, silver and gold, shimmering with heat and light.

She turned and put it in Kathy's palm. And Kathy, smiling, gave it to George.

The creature stood nine feet tall before him. Its mouth yawned open. The teeth dripped bile. Its blood-red eyes shot flames and steam, and its claws reached out to crush his life away.

And the vial, invested with Mancusso's blessing, enriched and alive with the love of his family, burned like a torch in George Lutz' hand.

He tore off the cap and swept the open vial across the creature's massive shoulder, right to left. The abomination squealed. Every droplet burst to liquid flame as it contacted the skin, biting into the flesh like acid. He swept the vial a second time, top to bottom, to form a cross. Deep crevices opened in the abomination's body. Yellowish ooze spurted out, the hideous blood of evil made solid.

George splashed the contents of the half-empty vial into his hands. The water mixed with his own blood – red, healthy, *human* blood. And he lunged to meet the creature.

He wrapped his hands around the abomination's throat, and *squeezed*.

DON'T DO IT. DON'T DO IT. LISTEN TO ME.

George dug his fingers into the flesh. Rivulets of ooze welled up around his nails, and he squeezed. He *squeezed*.

I CAN MAKE YOU RICH BEYOND YOUR WILDEST DREAMS. I CAN MAKE YOU POWERFUL. ALL POWERFUL. YOU CAN HAVE ANYTHING YOU WANT. ANYTHING.

'Don't listen to it!' George shouted over his shoulder to his family. 'Help me, *help me*!'

Kathy seized her daughter's hand. Terri took the other

one and put her hand in Greg's. 'Quick!' Kathy said. 'Hold on! Make a chain!'

LISTEN TO ME! *ANYTHING! EVERYTHING!* LISTEN TO ME!

Kathy threw her arm around George's chest. She squeezed as hard as she could. Power – raw, pure *power* – coursed through the family and flowed into George.

He squeezed the flailing creature's throat. It bent backwards beneath him, legs snapping like matchstick. He glowed with the power, in bright blue flames, and he squeezed, *he squeezed!*

The creature tried one last ditched effort to stop George: Blood-red flames roared in his head. Liquid rose in his throat. Waves of helplessness washed over him.

But the power exploded in bolts and auroras, crackling around George. He squeezed. And squeezed. And *squeezed*.

The creature fell beneath him. It twitched on the ground, oozing puss from its wounds.

DON'T DON'T DOE-DOE-DOE . . . The pleas melted into a guttural groan that grew weaker . . . and weaker . . . and . . .

. . . died. The thing from Amityville died in his hands.

The bright blue-white power faded from his body. Kathy and Terri and the children fell back, shaking and exhausted.

George held tight for another long moment, and one more for good measure. Then he released the dripping corpse and straightened very tall and gulped in air.

Suddenly Harry was there in the room, trailing part of the rope George had tied him with. The dog growled and stood poised . . . over the remains of the *thing*.

George kicked it. Without thinking, without knowing exactly why, he raised a booted foot and drove the toe into part of the gray, suppurating carcass.

A large piece of the creature's body broke away in a spray of wet powder – *like fine sand*, he realized. Gritty pieces of ash that soon were crushed to dust.

He kicked it again. Greg came forward, swinging his legs and drove them deep into the evil carcass.

Another piece broke off and was soon dust – soggy, stinking dust and nothing more.

Part of the creature moved a fraction. The tiniest gabble, a fragment of life, still whimpered and flickered in the beast.

Harry snarled and seized one of the limbs in his strong jaws. It fell to dust.

Terri slammed both her feet into the stomach area of the creature. Then Kathy swung out with all her might. Matt and Amy came forward and jumped on the remains, slamming and grinding the dust deep into the already ruined carpet. And they shouted with joy at this release of pain.

Suddenly the entire group locked arms and bore down, stomping harder and harder. In a craze now. Caught up in it, like the dancers in some frenzied African tribal ritual.

George was dizzy with the heat, mad with the stink, and joyous in the relief.

It was dying beneath their feet. The last spark of its hideous life was extinguished, destroyed. They were killing it completely with a madness of their own.

The ashes flew in every direction. They disappeared into the carpet. They smeared on the walls. They were kicked into corners, rose into the air and drifted out the open, shattered windows.

Finally, the desert wind, clear and healing as it had always been, whispered up with the sunrise and carried away the last remains of the abomination's final form.

The Lutzes and Terri held each other in a single, communal embrace, and each bent and hugged Harry. Then they helped each other from the devastated room, to the relative calm of the adjacent den, and slept in a huddle, too drained to move apart, too full of warmth to let the contact pass.

George was the last to let sleep claim him. He let his

eyes close as the sun's shining disc appeared on the eastern horizon.

It was dawn.

The Amityville Horror was over.

EPILOGUE

FOUR WEEKS later, the Lutzes were still waiting for the wall to be repaired. Late one evening, George was sitting at his makeshift desk, held together with masking tape and propped up on books, going over the newest collection of bills and overdue statements that had come in that day's mail.

They couldn't find a carpenter who would do the work on credit. And without an adequate explanation, the insurance company was holding up their claim. George tried to find that funny, but he was in no mood. *Not covered for demonic attacks, I guess.*

Kathy came into the living room, her bare feet slapping softly on the concrete floor. They had pulled up the ruined and filthy carpet the day after The Night.

That was what they had come to call it: simply 'The Night.' And though they had intended to replace the carpet immediately, there wasn't enough money to buy and install new material. Not yet, anyway.

George sighed deeply as Kathy put a fresh cup of coffee at his elbow. Her arm was still in a sling, and she walked with a small and temporary limp. The last bit of scabbing and new skin was about to disappear from the children. Even the bald patches of burnt and torn hair in George's beard were all but invisible now.

'I kept one piece of mail,' she said, kissing him on the ear.

'Oh, great,' he groaned. 'What is it, another reminder of an unpaid bill?'

She grinned. 'Almost as good.' She showed him the

postcard from Terri in San Diego. *Going great*, it read. *No ill effects. And wait 'till I tell you about this guy from Point Loma . . .*

George couldn't help but grin. 'She sounds terrific.'

'She is,' Kathy said. 'I can tell.'

He put the card aside and looked at the stack of bills again. The smiled faded. 'I wish we were the same,' he said glumly.

'It's okay, babe,' she said, and stroked the back of his head.

He scowled. 'How are we going to tell the kids? "Well, guys, we survived seven years of pain and destruction, but Daddy can't pay the bills and keep the house so we're moving again, okay? We're filing for bankruptcy. Hello, Chapter 13." '

'It'll be okay,' she said. 'We can do it. I mean, we may not live happily ever after, but at least we'll *live*. That's what everybody else does babe.'

He snorted out a laugh. 'Well, that's what we always wanted, wasn't it? To be like everybody else?'

They laughed together. 'I guess we got our wish,' she said. 'I suppose we deserve it.'

George's laughter faded, but the smile didn't. He put the bills away for the night, and put the depression away with it. Tomorrow was another day. He'd worry about it then.

'Well, we can always look on the bright side,' he said, rubbing his face with one hand, and drawing his wife close with the other. 'If we could survive Amityville and all that came after, we can survive just about anything.'

'*Absolutely*!' she said, and kissed him. 'We're a family. *We'll make it*.'

NEL BESTSELLERS

ORBIT	*Thomas Block*	£1.95
FOREFATHERS	*Nancy Cato*	£2.50
THE CITADEL	*A. J. Cronin*	£2.50
SCHISM	*Bill Granger*	£1.75
MAURA'S DREAM	*Joel Gross*	£2.25
FRIDAY	*Robert Heinlein*	£2.50
THE WHITE PLAGUE	*Frank Herbert*	£2.50
SHRINE	*James Herbert*	£2.25
CHRISTINE	*Stephen King*	£2.50
SPELLBINDER	*Harold Robbins*	£2.50
THE CASE OF LUCY B.	*Lawrence Sanders*	£2.50
ACCEPTABLE LOSSES	*Irwin Shaw*	£1.95

All these books are available at your local bookshop or newsagent, or can be ordered direct from the publisher. Just tick the titles you want and fill in the form below.

NEL P.O. BOX 11, FALMOUTH TR10 9EN, CORNWALL

Postage Charge:

U.K. Customers 50p for the first book plus 20p for the second book and 14p for each additional book ordered to a maximum charge of £1.63.

B.F.P.O. & EIRE Customers 50p for the first book plus 20p for the second book and 14p for the next 7 books; thereafter 8p per book.

Overseas Customers 75p for the first book and 21p per copy for each additional book.

Please send cheque or postal order (no currency).

Name ....

Address ....

....

Title ....

While every effort is made to keep prices steady, it is sometimes necessary to increase prices at short notice. New English Library reserve the right to show on covers and charge new retail prices which may differ from those advertised in the text or elsewhere. (A)